BURIED SECRETS

MIKE MARTIN

OTTAWA PRESS
AND PUBLISHING
MYSTERY

**Also by Mike Martin
in the Sgt. Windflower Mystery Series**

The Walker on the Cape
The Body on the T
Beneath the Surface
A Twist of Fortune
A Long Ways from Home
A Tangled Web
Darkest Before the Dawn
Fire, Fog and Water
A Perfect Storm
Safe Harbour

Christmas in Newfoundland: Mysteries and Memories

ottawapress and publishing.com
Copyright © Mike Martin 2021
ISBN 978-1-988437-78-1 (Pbk.)
ISBN 978-1-988437-774 (EPUB)
Printed and bound in Canada
Design and composition: Writers First
Cover art by Hunter Martin

Library and Archives Canada Cataloguing in Publication
Title: Buried Secrets / Mike Martin. Names: Martin, Mike, 1954- author. Description: Series statement: A Sgt. Windflower mystery
Identifiers: Canadiana (print) 20210218916
Canadiana (ebook) 20210218959
ISBN 9781988437781 (softcover)
ISBN 9781988437774 (EPUB) |
Classification: LCC PS8626.A77255 S24 2021
| DDC C813/.6—dc23

This is a work of fiction. All of the characters, names, incidents, organizations, and dialogue in this novel are either products of the author's imagination or are used fictitiously.

DEDICATION

To Joan. Thank you for helping bring Sgt. Windflower to life. I am so happy you are on this adventure with me.

ACKNOWLEDGMENTS

I would like to thank a number of people for their help in getting this book out of my head and onto these pages. That includes beta readers and advisers: Mike MacDonald, Barb Stewart, Robert Way, Lynne Tyler, Denise Zendel and Karen Nortman. Allister Thompson for his excellent copy editing and Alex Zych for final proofreading

ONE

Sergeant Winston Windflower was hot, thirsty, and tired. It had been a long day. He and his team at the communications section of the Royal Canadian Mounted Police had just spent the day touring several high schools in St. John's, Newfoundland, doing marijuana safety checks. Even though cannabis was legal in Canada, there were still many concerns about teenagers misusing drugs and the increased potential for impaired driving.

It was easy work, if long, and a pleasant day. One of the last warm and humid days of the year. Soon, this early September weather would move into a more familiar pattern of cooling days and even colder nights. Perfect sleeping weather thought Windflower. He also thought about his family, who had just returned to Grand Bank, a small community on the island's southeast coast.

His wife, Sheila Hillier, was from Grand Bank, and that was where Windflower met and fell in love with her and the community. Now they had two kids, Amelia Louise, who was two and a half, and five-year-old Stella, who they were in the final stages of adopting and had fully accepted as their own. Sheila had gone back home because her university courses were complete for the year, while Windflower continued his year-long assignment in the big city.

But this was not the year they had planned. Like most of the world, St. John's went into an almost complete lockdown that started in March and only started to be partially lifted in June. That meant schools and daycares and the university were closed, and Sheila was stuck at home as a full-time parent, caregiver, teacher and housekeeper. Not how she had envisioned her year in St. John's. Windflower, as a Mountie, was an essential worker, and he had been redeployed to a special safety and security unit that was set up to deal with the crisis.

The crisis was the coronavirus pandemic. It had started in China and spread rapidly throughout Europe and then North America, leaving a trail of disease and death wherever it went. Some parts of the world were still battling the first phases of this virus that was both invisible and prolific. In Canada, most of the initial cases had been resolved, but at a very high cost among the most vulnerable in society. On the island of Newfoundland, with the protective barrier of the Atlantic Ocean, there had been no new cases for weeks. Authorities were confident in reopening many parts of the economy, although social distancing and handwashing were still the predominant themes.

Windflower would get to go back to Grand Bank himself this weekend to join his family and hopefully see old friends for the first time in what seemed like forever. That cheered him, despite his tiredness as he pulled into the driveway of his rented house on Forest Road. He had a long, cool shower and put on his shorts and tee-shirt to enjoy a beer and the last of this fine summer day.

He sat on the back deck and popped the top off his Quidi Vidi Honey Brown Ale, one of his local favourites. He called Sheila to see how she was faring in Grand Bank.

"Hi, Winston. I'm doing grand, thank you. Although the fog is rolling in from Saint-Pierre. That'll cool things down pretty good. Uncle Frank is coming over for supper."

"How's he doing?" said Windflower. "He must be bored out of his mind with the B&B shut down."

"You know Frank," said Sheila. "He's always got something to do. As far as the B&B goes, I guess it's a write-off this year. Levi is okay. He's getting the employment benefits, but even if they say we can open, there are no tourists anyway."

"I guess it's hard on anybody that depends on tourism," said Windflower.

"But everybody here is safe and well. That's what really counts," said Sheila. "When are you coming down?"

"I thought I'd leave first thing Friday morning," said Windflower. "I'll be there by lunchtime, and I'm going to take Monday, too."

"Excellent," said Sheila. "The girls miss you terribly. Me, too."

"I miss you guys a lot," said Windflower. "I'll call later to say goodnight."

Windflower hung up and drained his beer. He thought about another but didn't want to get into another bad habit. One he was already trying to break was eating take-out. When you were by yourself, it wasn't as much fun to cook alone. He wasn't walking as much either. Sheila had taken his collie, Lady, with her to Grand Bank. But he missed her companionship, and she was always ready for a walk. Come to think of it, he even missed Molly, the cat.

He and Molly had a love-hate relationship. She demanded love and she hated him. Well, hate was a strong word. But she didn't like him, and if he was really honest, he was afraid of her. Despite all of that, he missed them all. Sheila, the kids, the animals and the eternal chaos that surrounded all of them. It was his life, and he really missed them.

To cheer himself up, he made a plan to have a steak for supper. And so he wouldn't be too lonely, he called his neighbour and new friend, Wilf Pittman. Wilf was a widower who had helped Windflower with numerous projects around the house and had become a surrogate grandfather to his girls, both of whom adored him. That was especially true of Stella, who'd had a hard life so far and who clung to Wilf Pittman as one of her anchors. He was happy to love them both in return and to be part of the extended Windflower family.

Wilf had already eaten, but he was happy to come over for a visit. He was there in a couple of minutes.

"You get used to eating early when you're by yourself," said Wilf. "But I love the smell of barbeque."

Wilf and Windflower chatted while he cooked his steak and continued while Windflower ate his dinner. Windflower made a pot of tea and cut the last of a cherry pie into two pieces as they went back out on the deck to enjoy the evening.

Later, Windflower walked Wilf home and continued his walk alongside Quidi Vidi Lake, walking to the bottom of the lake and circling back. He watched TV for a little while when he got home and read until bedtime. He called Sheila to say goodnight and drifted off to sleep.

His peaceful repose was disturbed when he woke up in a dream. Windflower knew it was a dream because when he felt himself stir, he looked down at his hands. That was one trick his Auntie Marie and Uncle Frank, master dream weavers, had taught him. "Look for your hands," Uncle Frank had said. "Then you'll know you're in the dreamworld and you will be able to understand more of what's going on."

Auntie Marie, his most dear and cherished family member, had passed not long ago, but before she left, she had taught Windflower many things about dreaming and how to interpret his own dreams and those of others. Windflower was a Cree from Northern Alberta, and while his family was known for its dream-weaving abilities, it was not a common thing among his people. Most knew and believed in a spirit world, but few had mastered the art of dream weaving.

Uncle Frank had tutored Windflower, along with his wife, and while Auntie Marie was the true master, his uncle had a lot of skills in this area that Windflower took advantage of too. After Auntie Marie's death, Uncle Frank had decided to move to Newfoundland and stay in Grand Bank. He would look after the beautifully restored B&B that Sheila and Windflower had brought back to life. Unfortunately, the pandemic put a cold, wet blanket on those plans.

As he thought about his uncle and aunt with fond memories, Windflower's dream became more vivid. He found himself in a small boat, a fishing dory, at sea. He could see nothing but water in all directions. Then he felt the boat being lifted into the air. At first, he thought the boat would rise and lift off into the sky. But just as quickly as it rose, the boat fell down again. Then it was lifted up again. Then lay gently down on the water.

When Windflower looked around and underneath his boat, all he could see was a mass of black in the water. Then a giant eye appeared. Windflower realized it was a whale. The whale blinked. Did that whale just wink at me? Windflower didn't have much more time to think because he could feel the whale diving below the boat, and he and the vessel were being sucked underneath with it. Just as he thought he would surely drown, he woke up.

He shook himself awake and went to the bathroom. That was strange, he thought. I wonder what that was all about. Because dreams were always about something. Maybe he could talk to Uncle Frank about it when he saw him on the weekend. That was as much as he could do for the night, so he turned off the lights and went back to sleep. He must have been tired, because he didn't wake until his alarm went off in the morning.

TWO

Mornings were much quieter without the girls around. That was good and bad. Good, because there was no fighting or delaying or squabbling over breakfast. Bad, because it was lonely without their little faces staring at him while he shaved or making him laugh when they smeared jam or peanut butter or pancake syrup all over their faces. He missed them.

Their absence gave him more time, though, and after a cup of coffee on the deck he got out his smudging kit. Windflower wasn't a big religion guy, but he did practice a few things from his Indigenous culture. One of those was smudging. In his smudging kit was an abalone shell, a small box of wooden matches and an eagle feather fan that had been gifted to him by his grandfather many years ago. There were also small packets of his four sacred medicines: cedar, sage, sweetgrass and tobacco.

He had been taught that smudging was a way to cleanse his body, mind and spirit. He put a pinch of each medicine in the bowl and lit it with a match. Then, as the smoke rose, he used the fan to pass it over himself, pausing at his heart, his head and his mouth to keep him pure of thought and mind and body. He even passed the smoke under his feet to remind him to stay on a good path throughout the day.

He allowed the smoke to linger around him as long as he could this morning. It reminded him of who he was in the world and to remember to be kind and thoughtful as he went about his work. Then he laid the ashes from his bowl on the ground so that all negative thoughts and feelings would be absorbed by Mother Earth. Before he left his place this morning, he would also pray.

He prayed for his immediate family, all of whom, including Uncle Frank, were in Grand Bank today. He was grateful to be seeing them soon. His partner, wife, and still the love of his life, Sheila, and his two beautiful girls. He said a special prayer for his ancestors, especially Auntie Marie, who he missed dearly. But he remembered as he prayed to miss her well.

That was a lesson he had learned from an Ojibwe author, Richard Wagamese, who had written a book of meditations that Windflower read from time to time. Wagamese had been sad about the early death of his mother, and he was really missing her. He went to an old woman, an elder in his community to ask for help in dealing with his great loss.

The old woman suggested that he learn to miss his mother well. When Wagamese asked how he could do that, she suggested that he look for the beauty and the wonder in the world. She told him his mother lived in that beautiful sunset or the sky full of stars at night. This morning when Windflower looked out into his backyard, he could see the dogberry tree drooping with berries and the last of Sheila's asters reaching for the sky. He saw Auntie Marie in those beautiful growing parts of creation and missed his aunt well.

He put away all his smudging stuff, grabbed his briefcase and drove the short distance to work. His vehicle was, as always, the Public Outreach van. When he first got assigned this van, he was told he couldn't miss it in the parking lot. They were right. It was a white panel van with the RCMP stripes and logos prominently displayed all over it. Plus foot high lettering that said "RCMP Public Outreach: Helping Your Community."

As he had found driving around St. John's, it was a mobile ad for the RCMP, and he was playing the starring role. At first, it felt uncomfortable because everywhere you went people would wave. If you stopped, people came up to the van and asked to take a picture with a Mountie. But over time, Windflower had learned to embrace this role as roving ambassador, and most days he loved it. This morning was like that, as he waved and mouthed good mornings all his way to work.

When he got there, he picked up a muffin and a coffee and was on his way to his office when his supervisor stopped him.

Sergeant Terry Robbins was the relatively new head of the Royal Canadian Mounted Police Communications Section at the St. John's headquarters. Public Outreach came under him. He and Windflower had an affable relationship, and Windflower was helping guide Robbins, who knew all about communications, into the wider and often complex world of RCMP politics.

"Come with me," said Robbins.

Windflower followed behind with his coffee and muffin. He said good morning to Muriel, Robbins's executive assistant, and went into the office. Robbins closed the door.

"I've got some bad news," he said. "Morecombe is dead."

"What?" asked Windflower. "What happened?"

"We're still trying to figure that out," said Robbins. "I got the call late last night. The locals are investigating. I guess there was a break-in, and the place was ransacked. Morecombe was found dead. Foul play is definitely suspected."

"That's too bad," said Windflower. "I was hoping she would get some peace and quiet after her husband's death."

"Yeah, after watching him die of cancer, everybody was hoping for better for her," said Robbins. "I was hoping she was going to retire and enjoy herself. I didn't want to get this job by default."

"Well, it's yours now," said Windflower. "Anyway, thanks for telling me. And let me know about the wake and funeral arrangements." Windflower stood to leave. Robbins stopped him.

"We need your help," he said. "Because Morecombe was technically still on staff, we need someone to serve as liaison with the locals. That would be you."

"Okay," said Windflower. "What do you want me to do, and who is my contact?"

"The brass wants us, and that means you, to monitor the investigation and provide us with an independent report," said Robbins.

"Spy on the Royal Newfoundland Constabulary?" asked Windflower.

"Basically, yes," said Robbins. "Without getting them mad with us. Your contact is Detective Carl Langmead. You remember him? He's expecting your call."

"Sure, I remember Langmead," said Windflower. "I'll give him a call. Oh, and I'm going to Grand Bank tomorrow and not coming back until Tuesday."

"That should be fine," said Robbins. "Maybe you can get a look at the scene and get a preliminary report from Langmead. Unless they know who did it, the investigation will likely take some time. Any questions?"

"Can I eat my muffin now?" asked Windflower.

Robbins laughed. "Yes, you can have your breakfast."

"And I'm still getting a pool car for my trip to Grand Bank?" asked Windflower.

"Muriel has the keys," said Robbins. "I'm surprised you didn't want to show off your van to your friends in Grand Bank."

Windflower laughed and left Robbins's office. He chatted with Muriel for a moment and exchanged keys.

"It's the unmarked white Crown Victoria," said Muriel. "The license plate is on the key chain. If I don't see you before you go, have a great time in Grand Bank. Say hello to Betsy if you see her." Betsy Molloy was Windflower's executive assistant and office manager in Grand Bank. She and Muriel were old friends and had taken training together over the years.

"I will absolutely do that," said Windflower, happily clutching the keys to his car. He went back to his office and had a few moments of relative peace to eat his muffin before his phone rang.

THREE

Windflower answered the phone. It was Detective Carl Langmead from the Royal Newfoundland Constabulary. The cops called it the RNC, but most locals called it the Constabulary.

"Good morning, Winston, how are you?" asked Langmead.

"Good morning, Carl," said Windflower. He'd worked with Langmead a few times now, including helping to break a human trafficking ring operating out of the province a few months ago. "I'm doing well. I hear we're going to be working together."

"That's what I heard, too," said Langmead. "Some people said you were going to be my RCMP minder."

Windflower laughed. "I'm just following orders. I promise to stay out of your way if you promise to make me look good."

"I like the first part," said Langmead, laughing too. The two men got along, and even more importantly, neither of them had a big ego or a desire for the spotlight. "I'm not sure what I can do about the other part. Listen, I'm over at the house this morning. Do you want to come have a look?"

"Sure," said Windflower. "Something in particular you're looking for?"

"Here's the address. Why don't you meet me over there and we'll talk?" said Langmead.

"Okay," said Windflower. He wrote down the address. It wasn't too far away, off MacDonald Drive. "I can be there in twenty minutes."

"See you there," said Langmead.

Something was up, thought Windflower. Normally when he was working on a case with someone, they would talk about it and go over what they knew first. Langmead was keeping his cards close to his chest. That was okay, thought Windflower as he walked out to the parking lot, it wasn't his case.

He found his Crown Vic in a line of cars, all white Crown Victorias. He pressed on his key fob, and one of them blinked. He checked the license plate and hopped in. It was nice to be in a normal car and anonymous. But when he pulled up at the first stoplight, an elderly man in the next lane looked over, smiled and waved. Windflower smiled and waved back. I guess I'm on permanent community relations, he thought.

He didn't have much more time to think as he turned onto MacDonald Drive and found his street. The good thing about St. John's was that it took you no time to get anywhere. Not as fast as Grand Bank, maybe, but still pretty fast. It was easy to find the house. Two RNC vehicles were outside and yellow police tape all around the perimeter. He parked in front of the ranch-style bungalow and walked up the driveway. He admired the well-tended lawn and the array of perennial flowering bushes along the pathway.

He didn't know Morecombe was a gardener. But then again, there was lots he didn't know about her.

A rather large Constabulary officer greeted him at the door and offered him a pair of gloves. Langmead came to the door while he was putting them on.

"Morning," said Langmead. "Thanks for coming."

"Good morning," said Windflower as he stepped inside the house. "Nice place," he added, noting the artwork on the walls, some of which looked original.

"Not so nice in here," said Langmead as he led Windflower through the house. In the back part of the house was an office with an adjacent sunroom overlooking a spacious backyard. It was a beautiful area.

But Windflower could see that beauty had been disturbed when he got closer. File cabinets were overturned, and desk drawers emptied on the floor. Papers were everywhere. "Looking for something?"

"We thought break-and-enter, robbery, at first, but there appears to be little missing," said Langmead. "Come inside the bedroom."

This was clearly where Morecombe had been killed. A lampshade lay on the floor. Windflower looked but didn't see the base. He looked back at Langmead, who seemed to be reading his mind.

"We have the base in evidence, some kind of metal," he said. "The murder weapon, we believe. She was found with her hands tied behind her back. Right over there." He pointed to a spot between the bed and the door.

Windflower looked around the room again. All the dressers had been emptied, and there were clothes, knick-knacks and jewellery, some of which looked like gold, strewn over the floor.

"We also found her wallet," said Langmead and held it up in a plastic pouch so Windflower could see it.

"Anything unusual?" asked Windflower.

"Driver's license, credit cards, hand cream and sanitizer and about three hundred dollars cash. And of course, her RCMP ID card, which is why you're here." He pulled out the RCMP card. "Staff Sergeant Alison Morecombe, Comms, St. John's, NL. What do you know about her?"

"I hardly knew her," said Windflower. "She left shortly after I got to St. John's. I don't even know how long she'd been there, only that she was close to retirement. Her husband was dying of cancer, and that was taking a toll on her. As he moved into palliative care, she left the job to be with him temporarily. She was technically still on leave, but nobody expected her back. Nobody expected this either."

"What was the husband's name?" asked Langmead.

"Jerome Morecombe," said Windflower. "He was some kind of scientist. A big deal at one time, it seems. There were a lot of people from the university and some people from the National Research Council in Ottawa who came for the funeral. That was the last time I saw her."

"Maybe they were looking for something from him," said Langmead. "Can you get me her RCMP file?" asked Langmead.

"Sure," said Windflower. "I'll see what we have on the husband, too. Anything from the neighbours?"

"Still working through that," said Langmead. "But it looks like there was a struggle, and somebody must have seen or heard something in this quiet neighbourhood."

"One would hope so," said Windflower.

"The only thing we really know is how she was killed," said Langmead. "That's usually the easiest part. We have no idea who had the opportunity and even less about a motive."

"It's clear that whoever came in here was looking for something," said Windflower. "But what?" asked Langmead.

FOUR

Windflower was thinking about that question all the way back to work. He was so busy thinking that he almost hit a pedestrian crossing at the light near the Holiday Inn. He didn't get any wave back this time when he tried to apologize, just the universal finger sign for not being grateful.

Back at the office, he talked to Muriel and got her to pull Morecombe's service records. He also got her to do a check on the husband.

"What are you looking for?" asked Muriel.

"I'm not sure," said Windflower. "Anything that we might have. Do a media scan on him to see what shows up, too. Thanks."

Windflower got himself another cup of coffee while he was waiting, and by the time he got back to his office, there was a message from Muriel and several email notifications.

He opened the first one marked S.S. Morecombe, A. It was Morecombe's RCMP file and service record. She was born in Baker Lake, Northwest Territories, the daughter of Reverend G. Morecombe and R. Morecombe. She had an older brother who had died in a floatplane crash many years ago. She did her training in Regina, like all RCMP recruits, and was first assigned to Winnipeg, then to the remote Saskatchewan community of La Ronge. Almost twenty years ago, she went to Headquarters to do her Comms training. Then, stints in Communications across the country, and finally, nine years ago, she came to St. John's.

There were no blemishes on her record and a few service commendations for her work in La Ronge, where she helped develop a suicide awareness program with the community and another for designing the new Comms training program. So that's why she was so keen on it, thought Windflower. Morecombe had pushed him hard to do a series of online training modules that Windflower initially resisted, but once he got into it, he it found extremely helpful to his work in Public Outreach.

Not much here that's helpful, he thought as he closed that file. The next was the media scan on Jerome Morecombe. This was much more interesting. Windflower went back to the earliest dates in the file clippings. The first showed a very young Jerome wearing a tweed jacket and holding up a large silver plate that the caption showed was the Special Medal of Achievement from the University of Edinburgh. There were many other award stories and pictures over the years.

Then, near the end of the file, was a story about a scientist being escorted out of the National Research Council building in Ottawa. There had been a controversy at the institution about pure and commercial research, and it looked like the main proponent of pure scientific research, Jerome Morecombe, was on the losing side. There were also a couple of other stories about him in private companies, but Windflower didn't see much of interest in those.

Then he opened the RCMP file on Jerome Morecombe. It had one large word printed across it in large black letters: CLASSIFIED. There was some smaller lettering underneath it. Windflower squinted to read it and then made it larger. "By orders of NSCI," he read. What was that? He googled NSCI. It came back as the RCMP National Security Criminal Investigations program.

"You look puzzled," said Robbins, who had shown up unannounced in Windflower's doorway. "I was going for coffee, but I see you already have one."

"Do you know anything about the NSCI?" asked Windflower.

"I used to work there," said Robbins. "But if I tell you anything, I'd have to kill you."

"Spy stuff?" asked Windflower. "I thought the Force was out of that business."

"It had to be dismantled after a series of unfortunate incidents, like burning somebody's barn down in the sixties," said Robbins. "But it got a new lease on life in this format after 9/11."

"What does it do, in general terms?" asked Windflower. "I don't want to get shot."

"Mostly commercial crime, intellectual property and patent thefts," said Robbins. "The section developed a capacity in detecting cybercrime. That came out of our work on child porn. So when the Chinese and other bad international actors started snooping around corporations, the NSCI got called in."

"Interesting," said Windflower. "Do you know anything about Jerome Morecombe?"

"Only that he was Morecombe's husband and that at one time he was a big-shot scientist," said Robbins. "Is he involved with NSCI?"

"There's a file on him," said Windflower. "Do you still have connections? Can we get access to the file, or someone to talk to?"

"Maybe," said Robbins. "I'll make a few calls. I'm assuming you have talked to Langmead."

"I was just over at the house," said Windflower. "Looks like a break-in, but nothing stolen."

"You're thinking that it might involve the husband?" asked Robbins.

"I don't know anything yet," said Windflower. "That's the problem. And neither do Langmead and the RNC."

"Okay," said Robbins. "Let me see what I can find out. Can you do me a favour, too?"

"Sure," said Windflower.

"Can you get me Morecombe's ID and service weapon?" asked Robbins. "I need it to forward with the preliminary report on her death. They've already asked for it."

"I'll talk to Langmead," said Windflower.

After Robbins left, Windflower went through the rest of the files that Muriel had sent, but nothing drew his attention. He called Langmead and left a message.

He got a call back soon after from the RNC. But it wasn't Langmead. It was Constable Anne Marie Foote. Foote and Windflower had developed a good relationship last year as the primes on the human trafficking case that had involved gangs recruiting local girls to work in the sex trade.

"Good morning, Anne Marie, how are you?" asked Windflower.

"I'm well," said Foote. "I was calling to see if you are still interested in being part of our training program. We have eight girls registered, and we'd like you to be part of the session around getting help from the police."

Foote was working with a number of girls and young women who had been rescued from dangerous situations, come into contact with the police or volunteered for a program to get out of the sex trade and back into a more normal lifestyle. Foote and the RNC had a grant for a pilot project that was working with a sex trade workers' organization to help them make this transition. The idea was that if they could make a clean break, they could not only create better lives for themselves, but also encourage others. A key step in this process was that the girls had to ask for help, and their first point of contact was often the police.

"Sure, I'd love to do it," said Windflower. "If we can get them to open up to the police, we can start helping them."

"Exactly," said Foote. "Although right now they don't trust us very much. That's where you come in. Friendly Sergeant Windflower."

Windflower laughed. "What's the schedule?"

"Looks like we will start next week," said Foote. "We're running the workshops in the evening because the girls are at school or working during the day. I could slot you for Thursday, if that works."

"Sounds good," said Windflower.

"I'll send you an email to confirm. Thank you, Sergeant," said Foote.

"You're welcome," said Windflower. "It's my pleasure." It really was, thought Windflower after he hung up with Foote. What a gift to be part of something that gave these girls a second chance. Feeling both grateful and now a little hungry, he walked down to the cafeteria to get a bowl of soup for lunch.

FIVE

After lunch, Windflower called Sheila in Grand Bank.

"Everybody here is pretty excited," said Sheila. "The girls are making a list of things they want to do with you. Or maybe it's to you."

"What exactly do they have in mind?" asked Windflower.

"Making a fort in the living room, sleeping out in the backyard, playing dollies and a tea party, to start," said Sheila.

"All of that sounds like fun," said Windflower. "Now here's my most important question. How did you make out with fish?"

"Herb got me cod fillets and a large piece of halibut," said Sheila. "And I got fresh shrimp and scallops from the guy with the red truck in Marystown."

"Excellent," said Windflower. "Any other news?"

"Carrie was over with the baby. He's such a sweetheart. Three months old and starting to gurgle. I love that time," said Sheila.

"They're so helpless at that stage," said Windflower. "How is Eddie doing with fatherhood?"

"Carrie said he's loving it," said Sheila. "He takes little Hughie Richard with him in his snugly wherever he goes. But I hear Eddie's dad is the one who's really gone for the baby."

"Richard is such a nice man," said Windflower. "Between him and Eddie, that baby will be spoiled for sure."

"Well, you'll get to see them all on Saturday night," said Sheila. "I've invited them over for supper. I'll make something with the shrimps and scallops if you'll do the halibut."

"Absolutely," said Windflower. "I'll call you tonight."

"I love you," said Sheila.

"Love you, too," said Windflower.

When he hung up with Sheila, he allowed himself a few minutes to think about all that seafood and how he might cook the halibut. He also thought about Eddie Tizzard and Carrie Evanchuk. They were RCMP constables that had been under his direction in

Grand Bank, but the pair had grown to be good friends of both Sheila and Windflower.

Eddie Tizzard had been Windflower's 2IC before he had a run-in with one of the high-ups. He had even left the Mounties for a little while to pursue a career as a private investigator, but that hadn't worked out, and he was drawn back into the RCMP. He was a native Newfoundlander, born in the small, isolated community of Ramea, who moved to Grand Bank when his father, Richard, got swept out of the fishing industry when the inshore cod fishery collapsed.

Carrie Evanchuk was a prairie girl, born and raised in Estevan, Saskatchewan. Her whole family were police officers, and she followed her older brothers into the RCMP. She had been transferred to Grand Bank a couple of years ago, and she and Tizzard soon developed a relationship that led to their engagement and now little Hughie Richard Tizzard. She was currently off on maternity leave, but knowing her, Windflower expected that she would try to get back on the job as soon as she could.

Those were all pleasant thoughts and memories, but Windflower was jolted out of his reverie by the ringing of his cell phone. It was Langmead from the RNC.

"We didn't find a gun," said Langmead.

"That's not good," said Windflower.

"Nope," said Langmead. "I've got my guys going through again to see if they can find anything."

"She might have a safe," said Windflower. "Many of us do, now. Especially if you have kids."

"I keep mine locked in the trunk of my car," said Langmead. "My wife doesn't even want it in the house. Did you get any more info on the deceased or her husband?"

"Not much in Morecombe's file," said Windflower. "I'm still looking into the husband. I'm working on getting some more info from HQ. I'll let you know."

"Okay," said Langmead. "Talk soon."

Windflower stood and stretched. That wasn't enough, so he walked out of the building and around the perimeter. Another gorgeous day, he thought, but then he felt a cool breeze. When he looked up, he could see fog creeping in from the Atlantic and starting to envelope the White Hills above him like a damp blanket. By the time he got back around, the fog was growing closer, and when he got to his office to look out, everything had disappeared into the mist.

That was fast, he thought. But that was the way the weather was around here, so near to the water. It changed with the wind, which was ever-present, and Windflower had indeed experienced the four-season effect. That was when you had some combination of warmth, cool, damp and colder all in one day. Like sun in the morning shifting to rain by noon, sleet by suppertime and snow before you went to bed. The good news about the weather on the island was that if you didn't like it, no need to worry, it would soon change.

The afternoon flew by as Windflower did his paperwork and filled out all his requisite reports and time sheets. He even had a few moments to go through all the info and notices in his email. Feeling like he accomplished something, he turned off his computer and left for the day.

SIX

He had just arrived home and changed into his sweatpants when his cell phone rang. It was a private number. Usually, that meant another police officer, thought Windflower. He was right.

"Sergeant Windflower?" the voice on the other end asked.

"That's me," said Windflower.

"Albertson, NCSI," said the other man. "Everything I tell you is off the record and not to be divulged under any circumstances. Is that clear?"

"Clear," said Windflower.

"I'm only doing this as a favour to Robbins," said Albertson. "And I'll deny everything if you tell anyone else."

"Okay," said Windflower. "I am an RCMP officer, you know."

"We operate under the *Security Act*," said Albertson. "Not the *RCMP Act*."

"Okay," said Windflower again. "But we are dealing with a dead man."

"Doesn't matter," said Albertson. "Do you agree with my conditions?"

"Yes," said Windflower. "What can you tell me about Jerome Morecombe?"

"Morecombe was approached by the Iranians, who were acting as proxies for the Chinese," said Albertson. "They made him an offer he couldn't refuse."

"So he was working with the Iranians?" asked Windflower.

"He started to and then realized that it was actually the Chinese," said Albertson. "That's when he came to us."

"What was he working on?" asked Windflower. "Or can you tell me that?"

"Morecombe claimed to have designed a lithium-ion battery that could go for a thousand kilometres before it needed to be charged. That's public knowledge," said Albertson.

"That's like five times more than the current batteries in electric cars, isn't it?" asked Windflower.

"Not only that, but he said that he could make it less than a hundred kilos," said Albertson.

"Wow, that's half the weight of the current ones," said Windflower.

"Morecombe tried to get the National Research Council to patent and develop it for free, but there's a lot of money in automobiles," said Albertson. "They wanted to sell the idea to the highest bidder, and Morecombe got the boot over it all. He set up his own company and got backers from outside to start it up. That's when the Chinese through the Iranians came in as investors. But of course, they wanted everything for themselves. That's how they work."

"So what happened when he reported all this to you people?" asked Windflower.

"I wasn't here back then, but it looks like we chased the Chinese away, but after that Morecombe got sick and his project was never realized," said Albertson. "Our last contact with him was over two years ago. The file is still open, but dormant, and I guess dead like him now."

"Interesting," said Windflower. "Can I call you back if I have any more questions?"

"Give a message to Robbins, and I'll try to call," said Albertson.

Windflower hung up and pondered what he'd just learned. It would take some time to process all of that. In the meantime, he was hungry.

Tonight's supper was quick and easy. He barbequed a hamburger and even managed to make a salad without adult supervision. He enjoyed his meal tremendously, if a little too quickly, and watched the TV news to let it digest.

Not much on the news tonight. But near the end, in one of those feel-good stories they often utilize to block all the death and destruction of the first twenty-eight minutes, he saw Foote and a young woman at a podium making an announcement. Windflower recognized the girl. It was Cassie Fudge. She had been working on the street when she approached Windflower one night in his RCMP van, asking for help. He got her safely to the RNC building, where Foote took over.

Foote was an officer on a mission to rescue as many street girls or girls who had gotten themselves into unsafe or dangerous situations as possible. And she was very good at it. Cassie was one of her prized projects. She had not only gotten off the street herself, but she was also back in school and helping the police to bring in other girls when they were ready. That was what the new program was all about. It was the one Windflower would be part of next week.

He felt a great satisfaction in seeing Cassie and Foote at the podium together. That was what interested him in the Public Outreach program in the first place. After the news, he forced himself off the couch and found his running shoes. He was putting them on when he looked out the window. By some miracle, the fog had cleared, and the evening was bright and sunny. No reason not to go for a run now.

He'd gotten back into running recently. He hadn't completely left it behind. He still tried to do a Sunday morning run with Amelia Louise on his back or in the carrier. But the long winter and wet spring limited many more opportunities and dampened his enthusiasm. He'd started up again on an almost daily basis once Sheila and the girls were gone to Grand Bank, and it kept him sane and healthy.

He was even beginning to manage the many steep hills in the lower part of St. John's and recently added a trip up Signal Hill every so often to his repertoire. Tonight, as he rounded the corner and looked up, he thought he'd give it a shot. But his ambition was stronger than his legs or his lungs. He made it to the Interpretation Centre and paused, pretending like his lungs weren't going to explode. Several other runners on their way down looked at him with a small sense of pity and a large dose of superiority, while those passing him on the way up smiled knowingly.

As he sat on a large rock off the side of the road, Windflower could see St. John's spread out below him. Pleasantville and the RCMP HQ were to his right, while to his left was the magnificent St. John's harbour. There was a pilot boat bringing a coast guard vessel in through the slit between the rocks called the Narrows, and a scattering of supply boats on the docks being refilled and refuelled for their trip out to the offshore oil rigs. No cruise ships this year, thought Windflower. Another victim of the ongoing crisis that was still causing havoc all over the world.

But not here in Newfoundland. They were on an island, protected on all sides by the Atlantic Ocean. That was part of what gave this place its unique character and identity. For hundreds of years, people from all over Europe had been coming to these waters to fish for cod, the king of the sea. For most of that time, until the 1700s, nobody was even allowed to live here year-round. You could come and fish, but then you had to go back at the end of the fishing season.

But people wanted to stay, and every year a few more hardy souls would try to cling to this rock in the middle of the ocean through long and bleak winters until spring came and fishing began again. Over time, they branched out from St. John's to surrounding areas and then all over the island in every small cove and inlet where they could shelter from the storms and make a life and a living from the sea. It was a hard life, but at least they were free.

Windflower also thought about his own life and why he loved living in Newfoundland. It had been more than ten years since he first showed up in Grand Bank. At that time, he had no idea what to expect. He'd been a Mountie all his working life, starting with a couple of years in British Columbia on the highway traffic patrol after his training. Then, two more years in Halifax, where he worked at the airport and earned his sergeant's stripes after a major drug bust. But Grand Bank was completely different than anything he'd ever known.

It was certainly different than growing up on the reserve in Pink Lake, although he somehow felt a kindred spirit with these Newfoundlanders who connected so much to the land and the water. The water was the Atlantic Ocean, and Windflower grew to love that incessant pull that it had on all life in this small community. Even though only a handful of them earned a living from the sea, they all were strongly bonded to its whims and tides.

Windflower also learned to love the pace of life in this part of the world. Very little was done in a hurry. Why bother? But most of all, Windflower had fallen head over heels in love with Sheila, who had been the owner of the Mug-Up café, the only café in Grand Bank. Over many cups of coffee and his favourite chocolate peanut butter cheesecake, she had fallen for him, too. He was still madly in love with Sheila and with Grand Bank. The only questions were how long he would be able to stay there, and even if he wanted to continue to be a Mountie.

SEVEN

Those were bigger questions than could be answered tonight, and Windflower took one more long look around at the view before beginning his descent. It was much easier on the way down, and he was hardly breathing fast by the time he got to the bottom and his cell phone rang. Windflower took a peek at the number. Carl Langmead.

"Did you know that Jerome Morecombe worked at the university?" asked Langmead.

"I did not," said Windflower. "I thought he was retired."

"So did I, but I went back to look for the gun and found some papers from the university in his desk. No gun, by the way, sorry about that. But he was on a contract with the Physics department," said Langmead.

Windflower thought about how he was going to respond. The NCSI guy had been pretty clear about the confidentiality of the information he'd provided. He decided to play it safe.

"He was a scientist," said Windflower. "Maybe he was helping them out with a project. Did you find the safe?"

"I did," said Langmead.

"It was in the bedroom closet behind all the clothes. Open, but no gun. Lots of papers, though."

"Can I have a look at those papers?" asked Windflower. "Might be something about who he might have been working with and stuff."

"I'll get my assistant to make you copies and leave them at the desk for you," said Langmead. "Although it was all a bit of mumble-jumble to me."

"Probably will be for me, too," said Windflower. "Thanks for the info."

Windflower put his phone back in his pocket and jogged back home. He had a quick shower and called Sheila.

"Are the girls down yet?" he asked.

"Like clockwork," said Sheila. "Feed 'em, bathe 'em, read them a story. Then, unless they're sick, they're gone until the morning."

"That's great, at least you get a little break," said Windflower.

"It's so much better here in Grand Bank," said Sheila. "Amelia Louise is back in daycare a couple of days a week, and Stella loves senior kindergarten. I can get my studying done, and if I need another break, Moira and Herb are more than happy to help out. They've appointed themselves acting grandparents over both girls."

Moira and Herb Stoodley were the proprietors of the Mug-Up Café. Moira had bought it when Sheila had a serious accident a few years back, and Herb was her able assistant. Windflower and Herb had become close over the years. Herb shared with Windflower his love of both classical music and any kind of sport fishing. He was also a retired crown attorney who Windflower often turned to for advice about cases, and sometimes life in general.

"I can't wait to see Herb again," said Windflower.

"He was asking about you the other day. He was pleased when I told him you were coming for a visit," said Sheila.

"We'll go over for por' cakes and pea soup on Saturday morning," said Windflower. "I love that tradition."

"For sure," said Sheila. "Every Saturday without fail we'd have por' cakes and pea soup when we were growing up. Now almost nobody makes them at home; everybody goes to the Mug-Up."

"And we'll be with them this week," said Windflower. "I'm going to have an early night. Is there anything you need me to bring?"

"Not at the house," said Sheila. "But pick up a couple of loaves of that molasses raisin bread at Goobies, if they have any."

"I will," said Windflower. "Okay, goodnight, and I'll call you in the morning when I'm on the road."

After hanging up with Sheila, Windflower packed an overnight bag and premade a pot of coffee that would be ready to take with him in the morning. He went upstairs and started reading his book. It was one of Wayne Johnston's books, *First Snow, Last Light*, the last of a trilogy of books that featured some of the same characters with differing story lines. This one had a new character, a fourteen-year-old boy who returned home from school to find his parents gone. Windflower was engrossed in the story, but that still could not keep him from falling asleep. He laid down his book and didn't see or hear anything until the birds woke him in the early morning.

Windflower got up and turned his coffee on. He wiped his eyes and went out to the backyard. He was not surprised to see the fog back, thicker than ever. To be surprised at the weather was more than foolish; it bordered on the insane around here. He did notice, however, that the wind had died down. He wasn't sure if that was a good omen or a curse that something worse was on the way. He searched his brain for a quote from the Bard, but all he could come up with was 'many can brook the weather, that love not the wind.' Most days here had both, so he'd take just the fog this morning.

He thought about smudging again but decided to get his pipe instead. He'd been bequeathed the pipe by his Auntie Marie, who had told Windflower that she used it to connect to Creator and the spirit world. He'd used it a few times now and each time had received information or a revelation about himself and his world. This would be a good morning to try it again.

He took the pipe out of the blanket it had been wrapped in and admired its long hand-carved wooden handle and bowl.

He put a pinch of his sacred tobacco in the bowl and lit with a wooden match. He puffed on it to get it going and then watched as the smoke encircled his head and stayed around him. Slowly, the smoke lifted, and as it did, it seemed to take away the morning fog as well.

He waited in the stillness and closed his eyes. When he opened them, his auntie was sitting on a blanket on the ground in front of him.

"Good morning, Winston. You look surprised to see me," said his aunt. "Although you know it is not really me, just a vision."

"I know," said Windflower. "But I like to imagine sometimes that you're with me, so this is pretty nice. How are you, Auntie?"

"Like I've told you before, if I knew how good it was over here, I'd have died years ago," said Auntie Marie, and she started to laugh and laugh.

"I see you still have your sense of humour," said Windflower. "Do you have a message for me?"

"Very good," said Auntie Marie. "You have learned to ask questions. You had a visitor, I believe, a very large visitor. Did you know that some of your ancestors hunted whales? Some of our people still do. Not your family, but your eastern cousins. In James Bay. There is a place called Great Whale River where the belugas came and both your brother Cree and the northern peoples would chase them in small boats and hunt them down."

"I did not know that," said Windflower. "It must have been very dangerous and hurtful to the whales."

"Every living thing serves a purpose to everything else," said his aunt. "We are all one family on this planet. Every animal, every plant, every rock. We all serve each other. Humans think because we walk upright and speak that we are special. But birds can fly and trees can grow fruit. They don't need us. They tolerate us because we serve them, too."

"So I should seek to serve others?" asked Windflower.

"Serve and be served," said his aunt. "But don't jump to conclusions so quickly. That's been your problem in life. Big-time policeman." Then she started laughing again. "Sorry, I couldn't resist. You were sitting there so serious and all."

Windflower smiled at his aunt. "What is the meaning of the whale's visit?"

"The whale is coming to bring healing. Even after he and his family have been hurt so badly, they want to help us and Mother Earth heal. But the whale is also the wisdom holder for this world. If you are lucky enough to see one again, ask them any question you want. They have the answers," said Auntie Marie.

"What kind of questions?" asked Windflower.

"They are also the keepers of history," said Auntie Marie. "Ask them about your past, your history."

Windflower had many more questions to ask his aunt, but as he started to speak, he could feel the fog coming back, and almost as fast as she had come, Auntie Marie disappeared into the fog. Windflower shouted, but she was gone, and he was left sitting on his back steps with his pipe in his hands.

EIGHT

Windflower went back inside and put his pipe away. He sat and drank a cup of coffee and thought about what he'd just experienced. He didn't try to figure it all out right away. That wasn't how these things worked. They were messages, information that he had to use his intuition to interpret. And that took time and patience, he had learned. The good news was that he would have lots of time on the drive to Grand Bank. Maybe an hour and forty-five minutes to Goobies, the turnoff to the southeast coast. Then a short stop for breakfast and another two hours down the other highway to Grand Bank.

He ate an apple and a banana and filled his thermos with coffee for the road. Then he threw his bag in the backseat and his briefcase and laptop in the front and headed out. He had left a note for himself to pick up the file from Langmead on the way, so he drove across town to pick it up. Ten minutes later, he had his file and was on the ramp to take the arterial highway out of town.

This route took him high above the harbour on the south side of St. John's and then up near Kilbride and the route to the Southern Shore. He wasn't taking that turnoff today and continued through Mount Pearl until it connected up to the Trans-Canada Highway. The TCH was the main route across Canada and the only way across the island of Newfoundland. It had finally been paved all the way in 1966 to help Newfoundlanders celebrate one of their very first Come Home Years.

Now every community, large and small, in Newfoundland held a Come Home event every few years, and the novelty of a paved highway had long since evaporated into the fog. Now it was just another road, one that was very busy this morning with commuters travelling in to work in St. John's. Not as much traffic going out, for which Windflower was eternally grateful. It meant that he arrived at

Goobies in great time to have a little break and enjoy a hearty breakfast.

Not only that, but the fog had lifted along the way, and when he pulled up to the restaurant the sun was shining, making his mood even brighter. He had the breakfast special. Actually, it was the Trucker's Special. But he was hungry. Three eggs, bacon and fried bologna along with beans and home fries. And homemade toast. The toast reminded him to look for bread on the way out. The lady was just bringing it out from the back. He grabbed two loaves of molasses raisin bread off her cart, filled his coffee cup, and headed back to his car.

He rifled through his briefcase and found the couple of CDs he had selected for his trip. Since being introduced to classical music by Herb Stoodley, he tried to listen to some as often as possible. Today, he picked Dvořák's Symphony No. 8. Windflower loved this piece for travelling along the road down toward Grand Bank. It was light and cheery and a bit whimsical.

The first part featured cellos, horns, clarinets and bassoon with trombones, violas and double basses joining in. It reminded Windflower of birds singing and suited the winding tree-lined road as he came into Swift Current, the first and last major community until he hit Marystown an hour or so later. The music grew louder and more excitable as it moved along, turning into what almost felt like a thunderstorm, which lent itself well to the barren lands that he was approaching.

He felt himself lost in the music as it went into something like a Bohemian folk dance that had of course heavily inspired the composer. Then, finally as the symphony reached its conclusion, there was a cascade of instruments playing slowly, and then faster and faster.

Windflower had read that for some people it felt like a call to battle, but when he listened, he heard what one reviewer had named as 'a call to dance.'

When the music was over, he called Sheila, but there was no answer, so he left a message. When the phone in his car rang a little while later, he thought it was her.

"Good morning, Sheila," he said.

"Good morning, Sergeant," said Inspector Ron Quigley. "It's easy to get us mixed up, though. We sound and look much the same."

"An honest mistake," said Windflower. "I was expecting a call from Sheila, but happy to talk to you, Inspector."

"'Laughing at your own mistakes can lengthen your life,' you know," said Quigley.

Windflower laughed. "And 'laughing at your wife's mistakes can shorten it.' I know."

Ron Quigley was a long-time friend and his boss when he worked in Grand Bank. They had been friends ever since they both worked in Halifax. Quigley was already moving up the ranks then, and about four years ago he took over as the RCMP Inspector for the southeast region. He and Windflower worked well together and were more like brothers or cousins than employee and supervisor.

"I hear you're coming back this way for a visit," said Quigley.

"I'm on my way now," said Windflower. "It's nice to hear from you, but I have a feeling this is not a social call."

"'Our doubts are traitors,'" said Quigley. "'And make us lose the good we oft might win.'"

One of the things that both men specialized in was quoting Shakespeare. It was a trick that both of them picked up at the training academy in Regina, where one of the teachers was a former Shakespearean scholar. They tried to outdo each other with quotes whenever they came into contact.

"I may be gullible, but not naïve," said Windflower. "'A fool thinks himself to be wise, but a wise man knows himself to be a fool.'"

"Okay," said Quigley. "Can you stop into the office on your way down? I'm here all morning."

"Any hints?" asked Windflower.

"Ignorance is the curse of God; knowledge is the wing wherewith we fly to heaven.' We'll talk when you get here. It's a sensitive situation," said Quigley. And then he hung up.

NINE

Windflower didn't have time to really think about that, because his phone rang again. This time it was Sheila. For real.

"I just spoke to Ron Quigley," said Windflower. "I have to stop in and see him on the way."

"No worries," said Sheila. "How far along are you?"

"About a half hour from Marystown," said Windflower. "So I'll be in Grand Bank in a couple of hours."

"That's great," said Sheila.

"And I got your bread," said Windflower.

"Even better," said Sheila. "We'll see you when you get here."

Windflower hung up and half an hour later was pulling up at the RCMP regional HQ in Marystown. He knew his way around this place, so he walked right up to Inspector Ron Quigley's office. His admin assistant wasn't around, but a friendly face greeted him outside Quigley's door.

"Bill Ford," said Windflower. "How are you doing?"

"I'm okay," said Ford. "I've been working a couple of days a week helping out the inspector."

"That is great," said Windflower. "The last time I saw you was when you were leaving the Miller Centre in St. John's. How's your rehab going?" Ford had been shot a while back during a prisoner transfer that ended very badly. He and Windflower had known each other and worked together for years and had developed a friendship that extended well beyond work.

"I'm a bit slow, but all the parts still work," said Ford. "I thought about retiring, but I figured I'd be bored out of my mind sitting around. Especially when the pandemic hit and everything shut down. This keeps my hand in, and I think it's helpful to the boss."

Ron Quigley came out of his office just in time to hear that last remark. "I'm glad someone is thinking about the boss. Bill, can you see if you can find out what's going with this file?" He handed Ford a manila folder and gestured to Windflower to come into his office.

"Nice to see you, Winston," said Quigley. "Looks like bachelor living suits you. Put on a few pounds?"

"Thanks for noticing, Ron," said Windflower. "How's Bill doing?"

"It's great to have him," said Quigley. "Especially since I had to send Smithson back to Grand Bank." Rick Smithson was another of Windflower's former staff who had been seconded to work as Quigley's assistant in Marystown.

"Oh yeah, you needed someone to fill in while Evanchuk is on mat leave," said Windflower.

"Exactly," said Quigley. "None of this is ideal, but we do what we can. And it seems like my transfer to HQ in Ottawa is not going to happen quickly either. Pandemic."

"Sorry about that," said Windflower. "I know you were looking forward to it."

"Plans change," said Quigley. "Which is why I wanted to talk with you. I need you to come back here. To Grand Bank."

"I have some responsibilities in St. John's, you know," said Windflower. "I'm part of an investigation to look into the death of my former boss, Morecombe. And I have training with the RNC."

"All looked after, my friend," said Quigley. "You can continue that investigation remotely and go back and forth for the training if you want. I talked to Robbins."

"Okay," said Windflower. "But what's the rush? I'm supposed to come back in a few months anyway."

"Two things," said Quigley. "One is Lundquist. He needs to go back to Grand Falls. Personal issues. But even more than that, we have a death that I need you to investigate. Quietly."

Windflower nodded.

"Do you remember Reverend Prowse?" asked Quigley.

"I do. He was retired and lived at the old manse," said Windflower. "Nice man."

"He died recently," said Quigley. "He was in his seventies, so not totally a surprise. But how he died was."

"How did he die?" asked Windflower.

"He drowned in his bathtub," said Quigley. "It was assumed that it was accidental. But now we have the toxicology report back. He may have been poisoned."

"Wow," said Windflower.

"Indeed," said Quigley. "I have talked to Reverend Elijah Woods here. He is the kind of the head of the church council in this region. He agrees with keeping this quiet for now. But eventually it will get out. And before it does, he and I agree that we need a quick investigation. That's where you come in. Here's the file, and you can start with Doc Sanjay."

Windflower took the file. "Who else knows?"

"You and me and Reverend Woods," said Quigley. "And Doc Sanjay. Talk to him first. I'll tell Woods you'll be in touch. And welcome back."

"Thanks, I think," said Windflower. "I mean, I'm glad to come back, just seems a little quick. But I guess 'all the world's a stage and we are just players.'"

"'And one man in his time plays many parts,'" said Quigley. "Thanks for doing this."

"And Lundquist?" asked Windflower.

"I hear he got himself into some personal difficulties. He requested a compassionate return to Grand Falls, and I approved it.

You'll probably get more details from the rumour mill," said Quigley. "Enjoy your weekend off. Then on this case on Monday, okay?"

"Got it," said Windflower.

"Say hello to Sheila and the girls," said Quigley. "Tell her I'll be over for a visit soon."

"I will," said Windflower, and he left Quigley's office and walked to his car. There was a lot to process. He drove out of Marystown in his own kind of fog and headed for Grand Bank. He stopped just before there at a place where he knew he could think clearly.

He turned down the road to the T at L'Anse au Loup. The T was a special place for Windflower. The narrow strip of land crossed by a little peninsula formed the distinct shape that gave the place its name. It was quiet and more than a little magical. Even better, it was often deserted. That made it a perfect place for walking and thinking.

Windflower used this place for his own form of walking meditation. He parked and began. First, he gazed around and admired the natural beauty of the wild and wilderness. The sea and the birds and the beautiful flowers that sprang up and held on against the pushing and punishing wind off the water. Then he started walking, trying to push out all his thoughts and fears until his mind and his heart felt clear.

He stopped and sat by the beach and allowed the universe back in. It was interesting to see what came first. It was always his doubts and fears and anxieties. But as he separated them out, he realized that right at this moment, sitting on the rocks and watching the eternal ocean, that none of them were real. His world at this moment was perfect. He could feel all those negative emotions lifting.

Then he thought about the issues in his life, his life situations. Yes, there were things to work through and problems to solve, but nothing that he couldn't do with the help of his family, his friends and allies, and the support he could feel from Creator. A thought came to him, an inspiration really.

It was that maybe he was resisting the changes in his life and trying to hold on to things the way they were. When, in fact, they had already changed.

He remembered something that Richard Wagamese had written in his book of meditations. That was nothing ever stays the same. Even stationary objects are moving, though we often can't see that. Like a tall building is swaying in the wind. If we accept that, then there's no point in trying to stand still or stop change from happening. We have to accept reality as it is. If we really want to do something, we simply have to change trajectory or direction that can move us towards peace.

Windflower chose to accept the recent changes in his life and his work and let Creator, or maybe even Inspector Ron Quigley, look after things. He breathed out a great sigh of relief and walked happily back to his car for the short trip to Grand Bank.

He made the turn past the Welcome to Grand Bank sign and the replica lighthouse and drove down by the wharf and then back up the main road where all the shops used to be.

TEN

When he got near their house, he could see some kind of commotion outside. As he got closer, he saw balloons and a big sign on the lawn with 'Welcome Home Daddy' written in crayons. Sheila and Amelia Louise and Stella were all standing on the lawn, waving. He even saw Uncle Frank standing on the porch with a big smile. He got out of the car and started laughing and kept laughing until he and both kids were rolling around on the ground together.

They were soon joined by Lady, who came bounding across the lawn once Uncle Frank opened the door and let her out.

"She was whining so bad, I had to let her go," said Uncle Frank.

"No worries," said Windflower as he stood and shook the dog and children off so he could hug Sheila and say hello to his uncle.

"Welcome home, Nephew," said his uncle as the men embraced in a long hug as well.

"It's good to be home. Crazy as usual, but great to be home," said Windflower.

"Let's go inside," said Sheila. "We've got some soup and sandwiches."

"Great," said Windflower. "Do you want some soup?" he asked Stella and Amelia Louise.

"Yes, please," said Stella.

"She's talking more?" asked Windflower.

"Nonstop," said Sheila.

"How about you?" he asked Amelia Louise.

"No," said Amelia Louise, almost defiantly.

"That's her new word," said Sheila. "For everything. It's the beginning of her independence. Wait until you see her tantrums."

"Uh-oh," said Windflower. "Terrible twos?"

"Let's have lunch," said Sheila. "You'll see soon enough."

Nothing unusual happened at lunch, and the girls were excused after they'd eaten a bit. That gave Windflower a chance to get caught up on all the local news. And to reveal his big news as well.

"Ron Quigley has asked me to come back to Grand Bank early," he said. "He wants me to work on a case."

"That's great news," said Sheila.

"I may have to go back and forth a bit, though," said Windflower. "Still a few loose ends in St. John's."

"That is good news," said Uncle Frank. "Maybe we can go blueberry picking. They're almost perfect now."

"That would be fun," said Windflower.

"What about that young feller that's over at the cop shop now?" asked his uncle.

"I don't know," said Windflower. "I just got here. I heard he has to go back to Grand Falls."

"We'll talk later," said Sheila. "Help me clean up. It'll be good to have someone help out around here."

"What about me?" asked Uncle Frank.

Both Sheila and Windflower laughed. Uncle Frank was a great companion and an even better storyteller but helping out around the house was definitely not his forte.

Meanwhile, it didn't take long for Amelia Louise's new behaviours to come out in open display out in the living room. She was in full-throttle screaming mode by the time Windflower got there.

"Just let her go," said Sheila. "She'll work herself out of it."

"I didn't do nothing," said Stella. "Mila grabbed my dollie and took it."

"It's okay," said Sheila. "Why don't you take Stella upstairs and read her a story?" she said to Windflower. "Better yet, get her to read you one."

"I can read now," said Stella with a big grin. "Well, some books anyway."

Windflower left as Amelia Louise had shrunk herself into a tight ball on the floor. She'd stopped screaming and was now sobbing quietly. Sheila sat beside her and rubbed her back.

"Does that happen much?" he asked Stella.

"Sometimes, but Mom says it's only a phase or something," said Stella. "I don't even know what that means."

"It means that it won't last forever, maybe just a little bit longer," said Windflower. "So, what book are you going to read me today?"

Stella went to the bookshelf and took out a book titled *Big Cat*. "I can read this one. And a few more, too," she announced proudly.

She sat on Windflower's lap and got him to turn the pages. While they were reading the story, or while Stella was reading the story, Windflower heard Sheila come upstairs. She went into Amelia Louise's room, and he could hear her talking quietly to her. She was putting her down for a nap.

When the story was finished, Windflower pronounced the reading absolutely perfect. In return, he got another big grin from Stella. They went downstairs, and Sheila took Stella with her to pick up some groceries at Foodland.

That left Windflower and Uncle Frank alone to sit on the back porch and chat.

"Those are two great kids you have," said Uncle Frank. "Stella seems to really like me."

"We think it's a grandfather thing," said Windflower. "Not that you aren't wonderfully loveable on your own. She had a special relationship with her grandfather that still continues today."

"That's a good thing," said his uncle. "She's had a hard life and needs some elders to love her right now. She is also a great teacher."

"I know," said Windflower. "I've already learned so much from her. Like how to learn to trust other people and how to adapt to completely new situations. But I can't do it as fast as her."

"That's a gift of youth," said Uncle Frank. "They don't think about things as much as we do. They trust their instincts much more."

"How are things going for you here in Grand Bank?" asked Windflower. "You must have been disappointed about the B&B closing down."

"I was looking forward to it, but that can come later," said his uncle. "The whole world has been slowed or shut down completely. It's as if Mother Earth told us all to take a break. I'm listening to that advice."

"It must have been hard during the shutdown," said Windflower.

"No, it wasn't too bad," said Uncle Frank. "After a couple of weeks, the danger subsided around here, and once the Mug-Up opened for take-out, I was fine. I'd get my coffee and we'd stand around on the wharf having a yarn each morning. Social-distanced, of course. Didn't really matter anyhow since nobody listened, but just yakked."

"That's good," said Windflower. "So, are you going to stick around or go back home to Pink Lake?"

"I don't know," said his uncle. "I'll probably stay until Christmas, but we'll see how it goes. I have to admit, I'm a little homesick."

"You're welcome to stay as long as you want," said Windflower. "I think I hear Amelia Louise inside. Excuse me for a minute."

ELEVEN

A few minutes later, Windflower came back down with a much happier Amelia Louise. She found her bubble mower in the yard, and Windflower filled it up. Soon, the backyard was filled with bubbles and Amelia Louise's laughter. She even gave Stella a turn with the mower when she came back from grocery shopping with Sheila.

"I've got a roast chicken for supper," said Sheila. "Are you staying, Frank?"

"No, I'm going over to Jarge's," said Uncle Frank. "He said he's got some frozen seal that he's going to thaw. We're having flippers. I think I'll walk over now and see how he's making out."

"See you later," said Windflower.

After Frank left, Windflower and Sheila took the girls down to the beach. It wasn't your traditional sandy beach in Grand Bank. In fact, sand beaches were rare in Newfoundland. The beach in Grand Bank was composed of millions of beach rocks in every size and colour imaginable. It was a little difficult to walk across, but everybody, including Lady, managed to tiptoe their way over and around any obstacles. The reward was to be next to the ocean that today rolled in relatively calmly and to pick your choice of rocks from the vast array before you.

The girls especially loved that, and their parents loved watching them do it.

"Amelia Louise really calmed down after her nap," said Windflower.

"That's usually the way," said Sheila. "It's like she has all that emotion inside of her that has to get out somehow. The first tantrum she had shocked me. I didn't know what to do. Now, unless we're somewhere public, I let her work it out on her own."

"Stella seems happy," said Windflower. "Uncle Frank said they get along well."

"Stella loves Frank and Herb Stoodley, too," said Sheila. "Her grandfather is coming next weekend, by the way. Just for the day on Saturday."

"That'll be nice," said Windflower. "Did we get anything else on the adoption?"

"Still in the process," said Sheila. "But it looks like it's in the final review stage. That's what the social worker said when I called. "

"I'd like to have that over with," said Windflower. "I heard her call you Mom. That was nice."

"It's nice for me, too," said Sheila. "Now that you're back, don't be surprised if she calls you Daddy."

But someone else was calling Daddy when he looked up.

Amelia Louise was running up the rocks towards them with a very large brown rock that she was determined to show him. "For you, Daddy," she said when she finally got there.

"Thank you, Amelia Louise, I really like it," said Windflower.

It was a great day, and Sheila and Windflower let the girls stay as long they wanted. When they got bored, they all walked home, although Amelia Louise insisted on being carried at least part of the way.

Stella was happy to walk alongside, holding Lady by the leash and skipping as much as she could. Windflower was very happy to be home in Grand Bank and enjoyed the walk back home as much as anything else.

Sheila started getting supper ready while Windflower got working on the girls' to-do list. Number one was to build a fort in the living room. He got the blankets and cushions together, and soon all three were inside with their flashlights. Windflower left the girls to play together and went to help Sheila.

He spooned potato salad out of a tub onto everybody's plates while Sheila put cut-up chicken beside it along with a helping of green salad. Amelia Louise would simply not eat salad, so she put a couple of extra carrots on her plate, too.

"Supper's ready," called Sheila, and the girls came running. Windflower had a chicken breast and salad and then took another chunk of chicken to go along with his potato salad. Dessert was strawberries and ice cream, and that too was delicious.

After dinner, the girls watched *Finding Nemo* while Windflower helped Sheila clean up. When they were done, they had a cup of tea and watched the last of the movie. Sheila took them up for bath time, and Windflower took Lady out for her evening stroll. He didn't start out with a jacket, but once he felt the cool breeze and the fog it was carrying into Grand Bank, he went back and grabbed his fleece.

The night was pleasant, despite the fog and the wind. Windflower loved walking around Grand Bank. At nighttime in the fog, it was like a mysterious ghost town, with flickering lights and sometimes things moving in the shadows. They walked down by the wharf, which used to be the hot spot in Grand Bank, where all the action happened. But that was a long time ago. Now the area was pretty quiet, most of the time, and the few old buildings that remained were sagging and fading faster than ever.

But he and Lady liked walking alongside the ocean. Windflower loved staring out at the lighthouse blinking in the fog. That lighthouse had been a beacon to weary sailors and fishermen who had been journeying on the sea for weeks and sometimes months. A sign that they were close to home again. That must have been a tremendous feeling, thought Windflower. To know that you were coming home.

As they turned their corner to their house, Windflower saw the lights on in his house, in his home, and felt the same thing. He left Lady in the kitchen with a treat. Gave one to Molly, too when she came to demand it. And walked upstairs where Sheila handed him a cleanly bathed Amelia Louise and then took Stella for her story.

Windflower managed to get Amelia Louise to stay still long enough to get her pajamas on, but they had some difficulty selecting a book. Windflower tried about nine but each was greeted with a defiant no. It was getting dire, so Windflower did what he should have done all along: he let her pick.

"Why don't you pick a story for tonight?" he asked.

Amelia Louise strode confidently to the bookcase and came back with three books.

"No," said Windflower. "One book tonight."

His daughter put one book back and looked at him triumphantly. He gave in.

The first book was *Grumpy Monkey*. It had a picture of a very unhappy chimpanzee on the cover. "Are you sure?" he asked Amelia Louise. She vigorously nodded her head. "Okay," said Windflower.

The story turned out to be about helping kids deal with unexplained or uncomfortable feelings. And what could happen when they keep them to themselves. The bottom line was that sometimes kids and all people have a bad day, and that's okay, too. Windflower enjoyed that story much more than he thought he would.

The second book was *The Snail and the Whale*, about a snail who hitches a ride with his friend, the whale, to go all over the world. It was very exciting, and Amelia Louise was rapt as the pair went past icebergs and volcanoes. The best part was when the little snail was able to save his huge friend at the end. Interesting that she picked a story about a whale, thought Windflower, but he said nothing and kissed her goodnight.

He didn't say anything to Sheila about it either when he sat with her on the couch to watch their own movie.

Tonight, it was *Once Upon a Time in Hollywood*. Sheila had made popcorn, and both of them really enjoyed the movie and just hanging out together. The movie featured a great dynamic between Brad Pitt and Leonardo DiCaprio and an ensemble cast that followed multiple storylines in what people called the golden age of Hollywood.

TWELVE

After the movie, Windflower put away the popcorn bowl and made a fresh pot of tea.

"It seems like nothing ever changes around here, but then you see that everything is changing all the time," he said. "Like the waterfront. Even if all the buildings were gone, it would still be the wharf and people would go down for a walk to see the water."

"I know," said Sheila. "I miss all the buildings that have gone, but I still love going down there."

"What else has changed around here that I don't know about?" asked Windflower. "What's going on with Lundquist?"

"I don't know everything, or even if it's true," said Sheila. "But the story was that he was having an affair and the husband wasn't very happy about it."

"Who was the woman?" asked Windflower.

"Nobody knows. That's what makes it so juicy," said Sheila.

"Your source for all this gossip?" asked Windflower.

"I won't be interrogated in my own home," said Sheila with a laugh. "My sources are confidential. What's going on in Marystown?"

"Well, Bill Ford is working part time with Quigley in Marystown," said Windflower. "A couple of days a week. He looks great."

"That's good news," said Sheila. "I see Rick Smithson is back here."

"Yeah, Smithson is back to fill in for Carrie while she's on maternity leave," said Windflower. "I like him. Did you know he studied music at university? Gave it up to go into law enforcement. When I asked him about it, he quoted Plato. 'Music is a moral law. It gives soul to the universe, wings to the mind, flight to the imagination and charm and gaiety to life and to everything.'"

"Wow, that's beautiful," said Sheila. "He sounds interesting. And what case are you going to be working on here?"

"What makes you think I have a case?" asked Windflower. "Maybe they just needed me. Badly."

"I need you badly, but that's not why you're here, is it?" said Sheila.

"Now who's being interrogated?" he protested mildly.

"Come on, Sergeant. I can keep a secret," said Sheila.

"I've been asked to take a look at the death of Reverend Prowse," said Windflower. "Nobody knows about this except for Doc Sanjay, Quigley and Minister Woods in Marystown. And now you."

"Oh my God," said Sheila. "The rumours are true."

"What rumours?" asked Windflower.

"Lots of people were talking about how healthy Reverend Bob looked, and then he suddenly died. Some said it was a heart attack. But he was always out walking. He looked fine and was in great spirits. There were lots of whispers," said Sheila.

"Whispers? About what?" asked Windflower.

"That the new minister wanted him out," said Sheila. "She'd pushed him aside and wouldn't even give him the job when she was out of town or on holidays. Always brought in another minister from Marystown. Last year she had someone from St. John's."

"But she had the job. What else would she want?" asked Windflower. "Plus, she's a very nice person. She's always been nice to me."

"She was nice to me when I was mayor," said Sheila. "Now she hardly talks to me. People say she's mean, and they don't like how she treated Reverend Bob."

"I'll treat you nicely," said Windflower.

"Okay, I'll give you a second chance," said Sheila. "You close up, and I'll meet you upstairs."

Windflower did not have to be asked twice.

That night he had one of his best sleeps in a long, long time and didn't stir until he heard Sheila get up to go check on Amelia Louise. He lay there for a moment, grateful just to be alive.

When he got downstairs, Sheila and the girls were making pancakes. He kissed them all on the top of their heads.

"No Uncle Frank this morning?" asked Windflower.

"Frank is a night owl," said Sheila. "He's out half the night with his buddies. Some days he doesn't get up until noon."

"I was hoping to go berry picking today," said Windflower. "He said he wanted to go, too."

"Let's all go," said Sheila. "Go wake him up, and we'll go this morning."

Windflower went to Uncle Frank's room and knocked on the door several times. No response. Finally, he just yelled that they were going picking berries and left. He went back downstairs, grabbed a cup of coffee and his smudging kit, and went outside. Lady, of course, was close behind.

Somehow, the fog had blown out again overnight, but Windflower could tell by the nip in the air that it wasn't far away. It was still nice to just be outside this morning, and he enjoyed the sun and Lady's company after he smudged.

His heart was overflowing with gratitude, so he started thanking Creator for his many gifts. It was a long list and ended with being grateful for Lady, who looked at him with pure love in her eyes, and even Molly. At least she tolerated him, he thought, even if she didn't really like him. Maybe that was all we could ask for in another creature. "Now then, Lady, it's time for breakfast."

Uncle Frank was sitting at the kitchen table in his long johns. "Why didn't you tell me there was food?" he asked Windflower.

Windflower just laughed and sat at the table. The girls were already eating the first batch, and Uncle Frank and Windflower got the second.

"Pancakes with syrup and berries," said Windflower. "Perfect. Thank you, ladies."

"You're welcome," said Stella.

"Purrfect," said Amelia Louise.

"They are good," said Uncle Frank. "Did I hear you say something about going berry picking?"

"After breakfast," said Sheila. "We've got to get organized and cleaned up, but let's go right after. The girls have a birthday party this afternoon. And I took the halibut steaks out of the freezer."

"Thanks," said Windflower. "I think I might marinade them and put them on the barbeque."

"That sounds good," said Uncle Frank. "I'll be here for supper."

"Do you ever miss a meal?" asked Windflower.

"Not unless I have a better one lined up," said his uncle. "But I try to eat my share."

"You sound like Eddie Tizzard," said Windflower.

"They're all coming tonight," said Sheila. "Eddie and Carrie and the baby and Richard Tizzard."

"Oh, good," said Uncle Frank. "That'll give me a chance to beat Richard at crib again."

THIRTEEN

After breakfast, Windflower and Sheila packed his car with picking containers and drinks and snacks in a cooler, and her car with Stella and Amelia Louise. They drove both cars to the parking lot beside the clinic and walked down along the brook. They took the trail up the hill, and while the girls stopped along the way to pick some berries by the side of the track, Windflower and Uncle Frank headed for the better berry-picking areas higher up on Farmers Hill.

Uncle Frank was right. The blueberries were fat and plentiful. He and Windflower found a patch that hadn't been picked over yet. By the time Sheila and the girls reached them, they had both filled half their containers. Windflower took a break to play with Stella and Amelia Louise while Sheila and Uncle Frank continued picking. He took them to the top of the hill, where they looked out over the town of Grand Bank on one side and Fortune on the other.

Windflower had to carry Amelia Louise down, but Stella trooped on in front of them. When they reached Sheila and Uncle Frank, they were all ready for a drink and a snack.

"I think we did pretty good for a short period of time," said Uncle Frank.

"Enough for a pie and some muffins," said Sheila.

They all walked together to the other lookout on the top of the trail.

Sheila poured everyone a glass of lemonade from her thermos and passed around a container of apples and mini carrots to munch on. It was still a gorgeous day, but Windflower's premonition about the fog was coming true. A large bank was parked just offshore and creeping towards them. By the time they finished their snack, it was right overhead, and at the car, the fog had completely taken over.

When they got home, Sheila dumped the girls in the bathtub while Windflower and Uncle Frank cleaned the blueberries.

"I'll go back up a few times this week and get a couple of gallons," said Uncle Frank.

"If I have time, I might go with you," said Windflower. "I find it very relaxing."

"It's like meditation," said his uncle. "Being so close to the ground, you can hear Mother Earth breathing. Anyway, I'm going over to the Mug-Up to see if they've got any of those por' cakes left."

That got Windflower's attention. "I almost forgot about por' cakes." He ran upstairs to see Sheila.

"Yes, I thought we could go after I drop off the girls," said Sheila. "If you want to go over with Frank, I'll meet you there."

Windflower was back downstairs in a flash to offer Uncle Frank a ride to the Mug-Up, which he gladly accepted.

The café was hot and crowded, but most had finished their lunch, and after checking with Marie, the long-time waitress, that there were in fact por' cakes left, they managed to grab a table as people were leaving.

"I'll be back to clean that off for you in a minute, ducky," said Marie as the men both ordered a coffee to start. Sheila came in a few minutes later to join them, and together they put their orders in with Marie.

"You know, I love those por' cakes, but I have no idea what's in them," said Uncle Frank.

"Just minced pork, pork back fat and potatoes, along with some baking powder and flour to bind everything together," said Sheila. "My family used to make them at home for years. Now everybody comes to the café instead."

Their order came, and all three of them happily dug into their pea soup and por' cakes, which they dipped into little pools of molasses.

"I don't care how they make 'em," said Uncle Frank, the first to finish. "They're sum good, b'y."

Sheila left to stop at Warren's on the way home for the last few things she needed for supper and the liquor outlet for a bottle of wine. Uncle Frank wandered down by the wharf to see if any of his buddies were around. Windflower sat sipping his coffee when he was joined by a familiar face, Herb Stoodley.

"Winston, I heard you might be in town," said Stoodley. "Nice to see you."

"You might see more of me," said Windflower. "I've been called back early."

"That's great news," said Herb. "Unless it isn't what you want."

"No, I want to be here," said Windflower. "A few loose ends in St. John's, but that will all work out."

"So, why the early return?" asked Stoodley. "Or are you at liberty to say?"

"I'll be over to see you again real soon," said Windflower. He went to the cash to pay while Herb cleaned up the tables behind him. He waved goodbye to Herb and drove home. Sheila was sitting on the couch reading a magazine when he got back.

"That looks relaxing," he said.

"Take your breaks when you can get them," she replied.

"Great idea," said Windflower, and he went upstairs and lay on his bed. Five minutes later, he was out cold.

But that state of peaceful sleep didn't last long. Soon after falling asleep, Windflower found himself again in the dream world. At least he hoped he was having a dream. Otherwise, he was in big, big trouble.

He was in a boat again, out on the ocean, with no land or anything or anyone else in sight. The difference this time was that it was stormy, and he was in the same little boat. The waves were picking him and his boat up in the air, maybe ten or twelve feet, and then slamming him back down on the water with a thud and a great splash. It must be a dream, he thought, and if it was, his second thought was that he had nothing to worry about.

That was good until he saw the giant eye looking at him from below the boat. The whale was back. This time he tried a different tack. "Hey, whale, how's it going today?" But no response. "How's the water?"

"Wet," came the reply from the whale in a low, guttural tone that echoed off the boat. "What did you expect?"

Windflower had forgotten how sarcastic some creatures could be in dreams. But he persisted. "I hear you are the keeper of great wisdom and that you know the history of the world. And my family," he added.

The whale looked at him and blew a giant spout of water high into the air next to the boat. Most of it came down on top of Windflower, completely drenching him.

"I'll take that as a yes," he said. "Tell me where my parents are and if they are okay?"

The whale spouted another stream and then started talking. "They are well and waiting for the next journey," said the whale. "They watch you. Sometimes they are proud of you."

"That's a little harsh," said Windflower. "Aren't they supposed to love me unconditionally?"

"Who said anything about love?" asked the whale. "Of course they love you. It's not the job of our elders just to love us, but to teach us so that we don't make the same mistakes they have made."

"What mistakes?" asked Windflower.

But the water underneath the boat was churning now, and almost like a volcano erupting, he and the boat were sent flying high into the air and then came crashing down. Just before he landed and the boat burst into a thousand pieces, he woke up.

More to talk to Uncle Frank about, thought Windflower. But he didn't have much more time to think right now because he had to get his fish ready.

FOURTEEN

Windflower got up and went downstairs. The house was empty and quiet, but there was a note from Sheila that she was gone to pick up the girls. He noticed the bags of shrimp and scallops in the sink as he took the halibut out of the fridge.

He mixed up his marinade. A little white wine, lemon juice, olive oil and rosemary for now, salt and pepper for later. He put the halibut in a small shallow baking dish and poured the marinade over it. Then he turned it over to coat both sides and put the baking dish in the fridge. All set for now, he thought, and just in time as he heard Sheila and the girls come into the house.

"Somebody's a little grumpy," said Sheila.

"Mila didn't get her nap," said Stella, still wearing her party hat and clutching her loot bag.

Amelia Louise was holding her loot bag, too, but she clearly wasn't as excited as her sister.

"Is everything okay?" asked Windflower. "Did you have a nice time at the party?" Amelia Louise stomped off by herself to the living room. That didn't stop Stella from answering on her behalf.

"We had cake and ice cream and there was a clown and balloons and everything. I want a party just like that.

Can I have a party just like that, Mommy?" asked Stella.

Windflower didn't hear Sheila's reply because he had gone to the living room to check on Amelia Louise. She was curled up in a ball and had her loot bag in her fist. Windflower gingerly went closer and put his arm around her. She kind of fell into him, and before he knew it, she was asleep. Sheila took a quick peek at Windflower holding Amelia Louise and smiled at him. He nodded back and mouthed, "She probably needed a nap."

Sheila went back to the kitchen and got Stella to help her make the shrimp and scallop dish. After a few more minutes, Windflower laid Amelia Louise on the couch and covered her with a blanket. He went to check out the delicious smells coming from the kitchen.

"That smells fabulous," he said. "What is it?"

"Creamy shrimp and scallops," said Sheila as she added some broth, cream, sun-dried tomatoes, Parmesan cheese and Italian seasoning to the shrimp and scallop mixture. "I'll just boil this and add some spinach right before we're ready to eat. Pour it over a little rice and it'll go great with the halibut. Help me make the salad before our guests arrive."

Sheila and Stella and Windflower got everything ready and had just finished setting the table when the Tizzards arrived, with Uncle Frank in tow. That woke Amelia Louise from her slumber, and she came running out to greet everybody.

"Unca Eddie, Unca Eddie," she cried.

Eddie Tizzard had little Hughie in a snugly but still managed to pick Amelia Louise up and swing her around.

"How's my special little girl?" he asked. Then, putting her down, he held out his arms to Stella. "How's my other special girl?" Stella came for a hug, too, but she was more interested in her real friends, Uncle Frank and Richard Tizzard.

Windflower got everybody a drink and the two older men, with Stella tagging behind, went out on the back deck to talk.

Eddie took the baby out of the snugly, and everyone else gathered round to see their little miracle. The baby was quite pleasant and looked like he laughed when Eddie tickled him. Everyone else laughed, too. But it wasn't too long before Baby Hughie wanted a snack and Carrie went to the kitchen with Sheila and Amelia Louise to look after his needs.

"Welcome back," said Eddie. "We got the word yesterday afternoon."

"How are things around here?" asked Windflower.

"Me and Smithson get along great, and Lundquist turned out to be not a bad guy after all. Too bad he couldn't stay the full assignment," said Tizzard.

"What's going on there?" asked Windflower. "Quigley wouldn't tell me, and Sheila's got some crazy rumour about him being involved with a married woman."

"More than a rumour," said Tizzard. "Not many people know, but Carrie saw him coming out of the minister's house late one night. When her husband was away."

"Maybe he's religious," said Windflower.

"He is religious," said Tizzard. "Went to church every Sunday. Helped out with some stuff around there, too. But he might have been a bit too devoted."

Their conversation was interrupted by the return of Carrie and the baby entourage.

"Time to get the barbeque going," said Windflower.

He walked out on the deck, where Uncle Frank and Richard Tizzard were engaged in a vigorous conversation. "Great, you're here. You can settle this for us," said Uncle Frank. "I said that—" he started.

"Nope," said Windflower, interrupting. "I'm not getting in the middle between you two. Sort it out yourselves or find another sucker."

The two older men started laughing. "You're too smart for us, Winston," said Richard Tizzard. "Usually we can reel 'em in like fish on the line. Must be all that time you spent in Sin Jawns."

Windflower cleaned the grill and brushed it lightly with olive oil before starting it up and closing the cover. "There's some nice people in St. John's," he said.

"And crazy drivers," said Uncle Frank. "Half of them drive like madmen, and the other half drive so slow, they're a menace on the roads." His uncle was well into another rant about the time he went to St. John's with his friend Jarge when Windflower went back in to get the halibut.

When he came back, they'd moved on to one of their favourite topics. Who was better? The Leafs or the Habs? Richard was arguing for the Canadians and talking about Jean Béliveau. Uncle Frank was going on about Darryl Sittler. Windflower didn't have the heart to point out that their teams were not going to repeat their past glory any time soon. Instead, he listened to their passionate banter as he cooked the halibut on one side and then another.

When he announced that the fish was ready, they paused the conversation and followed Windflower inside.

Sheila served up a little of her shrimp and scallop dish over rice, along with some buttered green beans and broccoli. There was a large green salad on the table with a fresh raspberry vinaigrette on the side. Windflower gave every adult a large piece of halibut and cut a piece in two for the girls.

Sheila opened the wine and passed glasses around. Little Hughie was asleep in a snugly on Eddie, but that didn't stop him from digging in and announcing his love for the halibut and Sheila's shrimps and scallops.

The conversation was limited while people ate, but Windflower asked Carrie how she was doing being a full-time mother.

"You know, it's easier being at home than it was trying to work while pregnant," said Evanchuk. "I enjoy it, a lot. But I also miss the job. It's all I've ever done as an adult. I can't wait to get back."

"My sister Margaret is looking after a couple of kids, so she'll be happy to take Hughie," said Eddie.

"And I'll take him from time to time when he gets a little bigger," said Richard. "It's fun being a grandfather."

"I have five grandfathers," announced Stella. "My Grandpa Peter, Grandpa Richard, Grandpa Herb, Grandpa Wilf in St. John's and Grandpa Frank, even if he's my uncle, too."

"Mila have grandpa, too," shouted Amelia Louise. She pointed to both the older men.

"You do indeed have a lot of grandpas," said Uncle Frank. "That means you'll get lots of presents for Christmas this year."

"It's a bit early for that, Frank," said Sheila. "Let's get through the fall first. Who wants dessert? Carrie and Eddie brought us something special."

FIFTEEN

Windflower took the large white cardboard box out of the fridge while Sheila and Carrie cleaned the table and loaded the dishwasher. He laid it on the table between the two girls and opened it so they could peek in.

"It's a pie," shouted Stella. "With cream on top."

"Pie, pie, pie," started Amelia Louise, and soon both of them were sing-songing the word. Eddie Tizzard might even have joined in.

"It's a lemon meringue pie," said Windflower. "Thank you, so much, Carrie and Eddie. It's one of my favourites."

"Right out of Beulah's kitchen," said Eddie.

"We love Beulah's baking," said Sheila. "It's too bad the B&B was shut down this summer. I used to love to go by there just for the aromas from her kitchen." She took the pie out of the box and cut a piece for everybody.

After dessert, Uncle Frank and Richard Tizzard had a game of cribbage in the living room while the rest of them looked on. Tonight, it was Uncle Frank's turn to win, and he was pretty happy about it.

"I'll never live this down," said Richard. "Not until I beat him again, anyway."

After the game and another cup of tea, the Tizzards headed for home with Uncle Frank as an escort. He was going to Jarge's house to see what he was up to. Windflower and Sheila tidied up and the girls ran around the living room, chasing Lady. Molly was having none of that. She sat on her top-of-the-couch perch and stared daggers at anyone who came near.

Windflower picked up the two girls under each arm and carried the squealing pair upstairs. He started their bath, and once he caught them again, he put them both in together. They each had their own toys and played until Sheila came up to wash their hair. When they were all clean, Windflower took Stella and Sheila took Amelia Louise for pajama and story time.

Stella picked *Ice Cream Soup*, a cute little story about someone who wanted to make an ice cream cake but added too many ingredients. They ended up with, of course, ice cream soup. Stella loved reading this story, and both she and Windflower were laughing when she finished.

One more cup of tea rounded out a very full day for Windflower and Sheila. He took Lady for a very quick walk around the block, and by the time he got back, Sheila was in bed. She had obviously been trying to read, but the opened book lay on her chest. He turned out her light, got in bed and turned out his. Not long after, he was asleep, too.

Windflower was the first to wake up in the morning. He got up and quietly slipped downstairs, put the coffee on to brew and put on his runners. He looked out the window. The fog was back, thicker than ever. He got Lady's leash. She was more than ready.

Windflower would run the highway this morning from Grand Bank for a couple of kilometres and then circle back. Lady was up to the task, and this was the perfect time of day to do it before the traffic picked up. He got a good speed going and was starting to feel the dopamines kick in.

That gave him another boost, and he decided to add another kilometre to his run. But as he turned the corner, he saw her. A very large moose walking across the highway. He and Lady paused, and the moose turned to look at them. Then she continued across the highway and disappeared into the bushes.

"Well, that was a blessing," said Windflower to Lady. "Something else to talk to Uncle Frank about. Not every day you have a moose cross your path." Lady just sat, awaiting further instructions. When he said, "Let's go, girl," she was off and running.

When they arrived at the house, there was still no one else stirring, so Windflower enjoyed a cup of coffee before jumping in the shower. When he got out, Stella was already in Amelia Louise's room, and it was like they were waiting for him.

"Are we having Pop Tarts for breakfast?" asked Stella.

"Pop Tarts, Pop Tarts," Amelia Louise started to shout.

"Shushhh," said Windflower. But it was too late.

"There's no Pop Tarts," said Sheila from the other room. "Maybe you can make waffles."

"I love waffles," said Stella.

"Mila loves waffles," said Amelia Louise.

Soon both girls were chanting, "Waffles, waffles, waffles."

"I guess we're having waffles," said Windflower as he took the girls downstairs. Rather than have them 'help,' he turned on the cartoon channel and gave them half an apple each to tide them over. He brought Sheila a cup of coffee.

"I'll make the waffles in a few minutes," he said.

"Great. It's time to get out of the Pop Tart for breakfast tradition," said Sheila, who was propped up in bed with her book. "I don't even think they're a food product."

"They are sum good, though," said Windflower. "I'll need a few minutes with Frank today," he added.

"Things moving around inside that crazy head of yours?" asked Sheila.

"Could be," said Windflower. "Maybe after lunch he and I can go for a walk."

"That sounds good," said Sheila. "Stella will come to church with me, and we'll have a light lunch. Amelia Louise will probably have a nap. That would be a good time. The church ladies have a cold plate today. I'm assuming you don't want that for supper."

"Two scoops of mystery salad with two slices of unidentifiable meat? No thanks," said Windflower. "I'll make us some hamburgers."

Sheila laughed. "Just asking," she said. "Call me when the waffles are ready."

Windflower went downstairs, mixed up the waffle batter and sliced up fruit to go along with them. When he announced the waffles were ready, the girls ran in from the living room and got the first large waffle between them. Windflower poured the syrup over them, putting a small pile of fruit on to ensure they might have something healthy with their breakfast.

Sheila came down shortly afterward, and they enjoyed the rest of the waffles together. Sheila and Stella got ready for church. Stella was the perfect daughter for church. She was able to sit still and look interested. Amelia Louise was on a temporary ban from church. Sheila had tried her again when she came back to Grand Bank, but she was not cooperative. The last time, Sheila had to carry a screaming girl out in the middle of the service while Stella walked placidly behind, looking aghast at the scene her sister had created.

Windflower put Amelia Louise in her stroller, and he and Lady accompanied Stella and Sheila to church. They were bundled up a little against the fog and coolness, but otherwise they were fine.

After stopping near the church to wave goodbye, Windflower and Amelia Louise walked down by the wharf and up past the old B&B.

It had been several years since he and Sheila had bought and painstakingly restored the old beauty that looked out over the Grand Bank harbour. It was usually open from June until October, but this year it was shuttered tight. Last year they had even opened it in the off-season for dinners on the weekend, but that was gone, too. Maybe next year, thought Windflower as he looked up at the balcony on the third floor. No guests to gaze out in the harbour today, and even if they could, little to see with the fog.

SIXTEEN

He was still thinking fondly about the good times at the B&B when he almost ran into Herb Stoodley on the front steps of the café.

"Grandpa H," said Amelia Louise.

"Good morning, my sweetie," said Herb. "Out for a walk with Daddy?"

"Sheila's gone to church," said Windflower.

"Moira's over there, too," said Herb. "Singing the praises and gathering up the dirt."

"That's a bit cynical," said Windflower. "Maybe they're saving our souls, too."

"Maybe," said Herb. "But still not for me. I tried going again after the old reverend died, but the new one leaves me cold."

"Interesting," said Windflower. "You've got an issue with the minister?"

"Not personally," said Herb. "But if the rumours are true, then she is spreading her blessing very liberally among the congregation."

"Let me ask this straight-out," said Windflower. "Was she involved with Lundquist?"

"I can't say that for sure, but he was enamoured.

That's a fact," said Herb. "He had coffee with her a few times in here and mooned over her the whole time. 'Love is a smoke and is made with the fume of sighs.' And there were lots of sighs."

"Doesn't prove anything," said Windflower.

Herb Stoodley rolled his eyes. "You are ever the innocent, Winston. In any case, he's gone and she's still here. Most suspect the husband found out and that was the end of that."

"What does her husband do?" asked Windflower. "I don't think I ever met him."

"Some kind of scientist," said Herb as a couple nodded to Windflower and walked into the café. "I gotta go. Bye, sweetie," he said to Amelia Louise.

"Bye, Herb," said Windflower, and he and Amelia Louise waved goodbye and made their way home.

Windflower and Amelia Louise made some sandwiches. Or rather, she ate most of what he put near her and sang him a song while he made lunch. He had just finished and was making tea when Sheila and Stella came back from church. As the sandwiches were being put out, Uncle Frank strolled downstairs.

"Right on time," said Windflower.

"I thought we'd have something special on Sunday. Like waffles or eggs and bacon," said Uncle Frank.

"That was breakfast," said Sheila. "Looks like you missed a meal."

"I'll just have another one later on," said Uncle Frank. "Last night around midnight we had some fish and brewis that Jarge cooked up. So, I'm not worried about getting enough to eat around here."

"Can we get together after lunch sometime?" asked Windflower. "Maybe go for a walk out on the T?"

"That would be grand," said his uncle. "I haven't been out there for a while."

Windflower played with Stella and Amelia Louise for a while after lunch until Amelia Louise started to get a bit cranky. He took her upstairs and held her for a few minutes in the rocking chair until she got drowsy. Then, he laid her down and went back downstairs. Sheila already had Stella helping her make up her casseroles. Every Sunday, she made two or three that would serve as fast and easy suppers throughout the week.

Windflower got the green light to leave and drove with Uncle Frank out to the L'Anse au Loup T. Along the highway there were thick patches of fog and some areas where it was much lighter. Luckily, the part around the T was almost fog-free. There was one other person on the T that day, a man with his dog far along the beach. Windflower was pleased. He and Uncle Frank would have all this space mostly to themselves.

"This is a magical place," said Uncle Frank as they walked along the path by the side of the ocean. "Having the ocean move in over the land at high tide and then wash out like it is now is a place of great power. It is an opening to the bigger universe."

Windflower didn't say anything at first. Instead, he allowed the wind to blow the ocean air through his hair and tried to feel each footfall he planted on the earth. As he felt more grounded, he started to speak.

"I've been having some dreams, and a moose walked across my path this morning," he said.

"Let's talk about the moose first," said Uncle Frank. "You have had moose in your dreams before. What do you think it means?"

"Well, I remember one time I followed the moose through the woods, and he brought me to a campfire near the river," said Windflower. "That was when Auntie Marie was making the transition to the other world."

"So, maybe someone is trying to guide you home?" asked Uncle Frank. "It could be a message to listen to your elders. Tell me about your dreams."

Windflower told Uncle Frank about his two whale dreams. Uncle Frank listened closely and nodded a lot.

"In the first dream you are clearly adrift from your life, maybe your traditions and spiritual practices," said Uncle Frank. "It's easy to do in the city. A spiritual guide once told me that men need nature or a woman to make their spiritual connections. In St. John's, you probably had access to very little of either. That's why you are being called back to Grand Bank. To rebalance and refocus."

"What about the second dream?" asked Windflower. "Asking for help from my family."

"Why do you think I'm here?" asked his uncle. Then he started laughing. "You are a very smart man, Winston, but wisdom seems to elude you. Focus on what is front of you, and when you get stuck, ask for help. The lesson is always the same. Think about others and forget about yourself. You already have everything you need. More than enough for a lifetime."

Windflower and his uncle continued walking, with Windflower thinking about what Uncle Frank had said. It was like he had to let his uncle's words sink in. After a while, he spoke again.

"You know what? I feel better already," said Windflower. "Like a burden has been lifted from me."

"That would be worry and anxiety and fear," said Uncle Frank. "The manifestations of ego. When you let go, all is released. Let's go see the seals. I like to watch them playing."

Windflower and his uncle walked to the end of the beach, where a small herd of harp seals hung out. When the sun was out, like today, they would play fight among themselves for the privilege of sitting on a large rock out in the water. Uncle Frank sat on a rock with Windflower beside him as one after another tried to topple the seated seal from their perch.

As they were sitting there, Windflower felt the peace of being at home, being with family, being one with the universe. Uncle Frank was right. He had nothing to worry about.

Except for the fog that was creeping back in over the horizon and the first few drops of rain that started to fall. They got back to the car just as the rain got really heavy and sat there listening to it fall on the metal roof for a moment.

"Thank you, Uncle," said Windflower. "I'm glad you're here."

Uncle Frank smiled. "It is my pleasure. Now, if you'll drop me at Jarge's on the way back, that would be great."

"Absolutely," said Windflower.

SEVENTEEN

When he got home, Amelia Louise and Stella were playing noisily in the living room. Sheila had finished her casseroles and was now doing laundry. Windflower helped her fold the last batch from the dryer while the girls got even louder. They both knew that the next phase would be a fight.

"I'll take them out for a walk," said Windflower.

"It's pouring rain," said Sheila.

"Exactly," said Windflower. "That's why it will be so much fun."

He gathered up the girls and got everybody's boots and raincoats. The girls loved this. Even Lady, who had a mild aversion to rain, seemed eager to try it out as well.

When they got outside, Stella and Amelia Louise looked immediately for the largest puddle. That wasn't hard. They were everywhere. Soon, they were happily engaged in a puddle-jumping contest that even Windflower was recruited for. Lady didn't quite get the joy of jumping in the standing water, but she was just as happy to run around Windflower and the girls to offer encouragement.

Windflower looked back at the house and waved to Sheila, who was standing in the window, laughing at their antics. He managed to get the girls moving, and they walked all the way down to the wharf and back. They got home thoroughly drenched but equally happy, and Windflower took them directly to the bathtub, where Sheila gave them an early bath while Windflower got supper ready.

Sheila had gotten some fresh lean ground beef from Warren's, and Windflower mixed that up with Worcestershire sauce, seasoning salt, garlic powder and black and cayenne pepper. And he added his second favourite spice these days, smoked paprika. He loved the little spicy and smoky bite it gave all meats, especially beef.

He made two large and four medium patties and laid them in the fridge while he got the corn and broccoli ready. When the corn was boiling, he cleaned the grill and got it nice and hot. He cooked the hamburgers until they were done all the way through and finished them off with a little cheese to melt on top. He went back inside, took off his raincoat and called out that supper was ready. By the time he came back in with the burgers, Sheila and the girls were setting the table.

He and Sheila got the girls their dinner and sat down to enjoy theirs. After supper, they all watched a movie together. The girls picked *Frozen*, again, and happily sang along whenever they could. Story time was short, and not long after that, Sheila and Windflower had a pot of tea and the rest of the evening to themselves. Sheila got her book and curled up on the couch while Windflower retrieved his briefcase and took out the file that Langmead had given him from Morecombe's house.

There were letters to and from Jerome Morecombe and various institutions and companies, even the electric car maker, Tesla. From Elon Musk, no less. Windflower was impressed. There was a lot of discussion about the merits of hydrogen versus lithium-ion batteries, but in the stack of notes and diagrams he didn't see much else he recognized. Near the bottom of the pile was a series of emails and other correspondence with Memorial University, mostly about support and funding for several projects by Morecombe.

One caught his attention. Not for the content; that was still pretty much scientific gibberish to Windflower. It was from the associate dean of engineering, Charles Morris Frankford.

Could that be the minister's husband? Easy enough to check that. He picked up his phone and Googled the professor. There it was, among his many degrees and honours. Married to Elizabeth Moreen Frankford, née Worthington. This was interesting, he thought. Something to check into further.

For now, he needed a plan for the week. He made a short list, knowing that things often changed rapidly in an investigation. And he had two. So he started a list. Top of his list was to see Doc Sanjay in Grand Bank.

Doctor Vijay Sanjay was a fixture in the little community. He'd been there for over thirty years now. He didn't have a practice anymore; he gave that up when he turned seventy. But he still served as the unofficial coroner for the area. He was a noted expert in forensic medicine, and he was the first one called to any suspicious death scene. The clinic allowed him to maintain his office and examination room, and he would provide preliminary examinations of any sudden or unexpected deaths in the community.

He had become one of Windflower's first friends in this part of the world. He was a diminutive Bengali with a wicked sense of humour, and he used to joke with Windflower that they had to stick together because they were the only two Indians in Grand Bank. Sanjay also loved two other things that were close to Windflower's heart. That would be chess and single-malt whiskey.

Sanjay had a great collection of the good stuff, as he called it, and would invite Windflower to come over and sample his latest. He and Windflower would taste the Scotch and then play a few games of chess while enjoying some of Repa Sanjay's famous Bengali cooking.

After he saw Sanjay, Windflower made a note to make an appointment to see Elijah Woods in Marystown. The minister would give the parameters of the case, including how far he wanted Windflower to dig, and who he should speak with. Windflower could do his job, but better to understand what the politics of this case were before he began. Somewhere along the way, he would talk to Elizabeth Frankford, but he had some background work to do before that.

That reminded him that he needed to check in with Langmead about the Morecombe case. He wondered if they had anything on Charles Frankford at the RNC. So Langmead went on his list, as well as Terry Robbins at the RCMP in St. John's. He needed to double-check to make sure he wasn't needed for anything at Public Outreach and to check the RCMP files on the professor as well. Finally, he made a note to call Anne Marie Foote to reschedule his session on Thursday. Looked like he was going to be in Grand Bank and that he would be busy for a while.

His list complete for now, he went out to see Sheila.

"What's your week like?" he asked.

"I've got two online classes, one on Tuesday and one on Friday. That works because Stella's back in school and Amelia Louise is at the daycare Tuesday, Wednesday, and Friday. And I have a meeting of the Development Corporation tomorrow morning."

"Busy week," said Windflower. "I should be around all week, but I have to work. I'm likely going to Marystown to see Elijah Woods, probably on Tuesday."

"If you can make it in the afternoon, I'll go with you," said Sheila. "I have to pick up a few things at Sobey's, and I'll see if the fish man is back."

"That should work, depending on Woods," said Windflower. "It'll be fun to go over together. Like a road trip."

"Life is an adventure with you, Sergeant Windflower," said Sheila.

"'To unpathed waters, undreamed shores,'" said Windflower.

"Let the dog out, and then come to bed," said Sheila.

Windflower did as he was told, and not long after, both of them were in bed, soon to be asleep.

EIGHTEEN

Windflower heard Sheila stir and rise beside him. She was rousing Stella when he got up, and he went to Amelia Louise, who was still sleeping. He left Sheila with Stella and went downstairs to put the coffee on. He let Lady out, and the wind almost blew the door off and let a sheet of water rush in. Windflower struggled to shut the door but finally managed to pull it tight. He started the coffee maker, and by the time he returned to the door, a shrivelled and very wet Lady was waiting to be let back in.

"Eggs this morning?" he called out to Sheila.

"That will be great," she called back.

He mixed up the eggs, started the toast, sliced up the rest of the melon, and put a large piece on everyone's plate. He stirred the eggs and turned them down on low while he went upstairs to get Amelia Louise, who was calling out for attention.

Breakfast was loud and a little fractious but perfect, thought Windflower as he smiled at his little family enjoying their eggs. Stella was all set for school. Sheila had made her lunch, and her knapsack was waiting by the door. She finished her breakfast and went upstairs to have Sheila put her hair in a braid. A few minutes later, the school bus pulled up out front. Stella walked with her mom holding an umbrella and stepped inside the bus.

Windflower could see her little face pressed up against the window as he and Amelia Louise waved her goodbye.

"She's pretty small for the school bus," said Windflower when Sheila came back in.

"I know," said Sheila. "I'm a bit worried about the bus driving back and forth to Fortune, especially in the winter. But since they closed our school a few years ago, that's what we have. I'm sure not doing home-schooling. Nobody would after the pandemic."

"But when they get bigger, they can go to high school in Grand Bank," said Windflower.

"That seems like a very long time away," said Sheila. "Who knows where we'll even be by then. But that was the trade-off. We kept the high school, and Fortune got the elementary school."

"Mila wants da bus," said Amelia Louise, breaking into the conversation about schools and their future.

"Well, this morning you're going to work with Mommy," said Sheila. "Wish me luck with that," she said to Windflower. He nodded his support and went upstairs to change for work. He came down and offered a kiss on the cheek to Sheila and another to Amelia Louise, and he was off to work in Grand Bank for the first time in what seemed forever.

Somebody who was very happy to see him was Betsy Molloy, the administrative assistant for the Grand Bank RCMP Detachment. That was her title, but Windflower had learned over the years that she was so much more than that. She kept the office organized and everyone on their toes when it came to rules and regulations, and she also knew how to get around them if you needed to.

She also knew every living soul in Grand Bank and many of those that had passed in the last twenty-five years. She made it her business to keep up to date on all the goings-on and was an expert trader in the latest rumours. Betsy maintained an excellent communications network, and if Windflower needed information sought or shared, Betsy was the first person he turned to.

When she saw him come into the office, she grabbed him in a fierce momma bear hug before he had a chance to get away. "Muriel called me on the weekend to tell me you were coming back. I'm so happy I could cry."

"Don't cry, Betsy," pleaded Windflower.

"Corporal Lundquist is a fine RCMP officer, but as I told Muriel, there's nobody like our Sergeant Windflower," said Betsy. "You get yourself a cup of coffee, and I'll bring you a home-made muffin."

Windflower walked to the back and poured himself a cup of coffee. True to her word, Betsy came into his office with two blueberry muffins. "My Bob picks the berries, and I make the muffins. I hope you like them."

Windflower took a bite of one. "Perfect," he said. "Thank you, Betsy."

Betsy went away pleased with herself, and Windflower had a few moments of quiet before the day really began. Everything was so familiar that it was almost like he hadn't left. This was a good life, he thought. But unfortunately, it couldn't last. He'd been in Grand Bank far beyond the usual assignment period and was already feeling some pressure to leave. As long as Ron Quigley was in Marystown, he had a chance to stay, but that wouldn't last either. And when Quigley left, Windflower would have to apply for the inspector job or accept any assignment, anywhere in Canada that he was needed. Or leave the RCMP.

He didn't really like any of those options. The good news was that he didn't have to choose any of them today. He could just enjoy it, like his muffin. In fact, he enjoyed it so much that he had the second muffin.

He was finishing that off when he saw Constable Rick Smithson's car pull up in the parking lot.

Smithson was on the overnight shift and was coming to fill out his reports and head home for a break. He was glad to see Windflower as well.

"Hey, Sarge, welcome back," said Smithson.

"Thanks," said Windflower. "Anything exciting happening out there?"

"Not really," said Smithson. "Once the kids get back in school, it goes pretty quiet around here. Just the way we like it. I did see a moose on the road to Fortune, though. Big female."

"I think I saw her on the weekend," said Windflower. "My Uncle Frank said that moose are guides and reminders to listen to our elders."

"Uncle Frank is a wise man," said Smithson. "He's been very helpful to me when we've had a chance to speak."

Windflower's conversation with Smithson was interrupted by Betsy's voice over the intercom. "Reverend Woods on Line 1."

"Thank you, Betsy," said Windflower, waving goodbye to Smithson.

"Good morning, Reverend," said Windflower.

"Good morning, Sergeant," said the minister. "I am calling you about the unfortunate situation regarding Reverend Prowse."

That was an interesting choice of words, thought Windflower. Was it unfortunate for Reverend Prowse or the church council? He kept that to himself.

"Yes, Inspector Quigley has informed me that you wish me to conduct a discreet inquiry into his passing," said Windflower.

"Discretion is a primary concern," said Woods. "Reverend Prowse was an admired and beloved pastor to the congregation in Grand Bank. We would not wish to have anything blemish his immaculate record."

Or embarrass the church, thought Windflower. But he held on to that, too.

"I thought I would start with talking to Doctor Sanjay today and then come and see you tomorrow, if you are free," said Windflower.

"I have some time in the afternoon," said the minister.

"Can I come at two o'clock?" asked Windflower.

"That would be perfect," said Woods, and he hung up.

Perfect for him and Sheila, too, thought Windflower, and he called Sheila to tell her the good news. He also called Betsy to see what hours Doc Sanjay was working these days. Betsy said she would check and get back to him.

NINETEEN

While he was waiting, Eddie Tizzard showed up for his day shift.

"Good morning, boss," said Tizzard.

"Good morning, Corporal," said Windflower. "Ready for another exciting day in the life of a Mountie?"

"I am excited," said Tizzard. "But first I need a little snack. Want something?"

"No, I'm good," said Windflower. Tizzard stayed where he was. "Do you want something?"

"Well, I was going to ask about Reverend Elijah Woods," Tizzard said.

"What about him?" asked Windflower.

"He had someone over here last week snooping around," said Tizzard.

"Who was it, and what were they doing?" asked Windflower.

"It was a guy said he was from the church in Creston. Gregory Dollimont," said Tizzard. "He was talking to Lars, I mean Corporal Lundquist. I'm not sure what they were talking about."

"Interesting," said Windflower. "Thanks for telling me that." Tizzard stayed again.

"What are you waiting for?" asked Windflower.

"Aren't you going to tell me what you're working on?" asked Tizzard. "Maybe I can help you."

Windflower smiled at Tizzard's enthusiasm. "All in good time, Corporal. 'Tis better to bear the ills we have than fly to others that we know not of.'"

"What does that even mean?" asked Tizzard.

Windflower didn't have to answer because the intercom went off again.

"Doctor Sanjay is in the clinic now and will wait to see you," said Betsy.

"Thank you, Betsy," said Windflower. "Have your snack, Eddie. I'm going to see Doc Sanjay."

Windflower drove to the Grand Bank Community Health Centre, which everybody called the clinic. It was the first place anybody with a problem headed for in the case of urgent or emergency care. For many of the older folks in town, and there were lots of those, it was their primary health care option. He walked in the emergency door and put on his mask. The mask restriction had been lifted just about everywhere, but not in the clinic. That was good, he thought as he noticed the waiting room half-filled with elderly people and their caregivers this morning. He nodded good morning to everyone and to the nurse at reception and walked down the corridor to Doc Sanjay's office.

He knocked and was welcomed in with a cheery hello, and when the doctor saw Windflower, he broke into a wide smile. "Winston, my friend, it's been far too long. How's she going, b'y?"

Windflower laughed at his doctor friend's joke and replied in turn. "She's going good, b'y."

"I've seen that little darling of yours and your new little girl with Sheila a few times. You really should come over for dinner soon," said Sanjay.

"We will try, but I only returned this weekend," said Windflower. "How are your lovely wife and the boys?"

"Repa is well but missing her grandchildren terribly. But until the travel restrictions are lifted, we are limited to FaceTime and Zoom," said Sanjay. "She wants to hold them and kiss them all over like a proper nani would do."

"I understand," said Windflower. "This situation is very hard for many people."

"And you simply have to come try my new Scotch," said Sanjay. "I have been saving it for a special occasion, and now you have arrived."

"I would love that as well," said Windflower. "But I was hoping to talk about the late Reverend Prowse."

"Oh yes, of course, you are a very busy man, Sergeant, and I am moving into my doddering ages."

"You have many great years ahead of you," said Windflower. "The community still needs you."

"As long as I stay quiet and out of sight. 'Grey hairs are signs of wisdom if you hold your tongue, speak and they are but hairs, as in the young.' Let me get the file."

The doctor went to the file cabinet and pulled out the file on Reverend Prowse.

"Was he poisoned?" asked Windflower.

"The toxicology report doesn't lie. The good reverend, and he was one of the few good reverends in my book, had more than enough insulin in his system to kill him when he died," said Sanjay. "And a large bump on the back of his head. That may or may not have been accidental. It's easy enough to slip in the bathtub."

"Could he have taken the insulin voluntarily?" asked Windflower.

"I guess he could have self-administered it," said Sanjay. "But why would he? He wasn't a diabetic, which was my first question."

"So how did it get into his blood system?" asked Windflower.

"Given the amount of excess insulin, it would have had to have been injected," said Sanjay.

"How and who injected him, I really don't know."

"He lived alone in the old manse, right?" asked Windflower.

"Yes, there was a housekeeper, but she didn't prepare the meals. You know her. It's Beulah Stokes. That's who found him, dead in the bathtub."

"She was our cook and housekeeper at the B&B," said Windflower. "But where did his meals come from?"

"I understand they were prepared by Reverend Frankford's housekeeper and brought over," said the doctor. "But any more than that, I do not know. Outside my area of expertise."

"Okay," said Windflower. "That's good for now. If I have any more questions, I'll call."

"Don't forget. My Old Pulteney is waiting for you. I have been reading up on it. It's known as the Maritime Malt."

"I'll call you," said Windflower, and he extricated himself as quickly and politely as possible from the doctor. Lots to think about there, he thought. He was driving back to the office, when his car almost involuntarily turned towards the Mug-Up café and stopped in front.

He walked inside and was immediately greeted by the wonderful aromas of fresh coffee and baking. The menu at the Mug-Up was pretty small, but everything was great. They served an early-morning breakfast and lunch, but their speciality was homemade cheesecake, which was famous among locals and tourists alike. Many people stopped there on their way to visit Saint- Pierre, the French territory island that was just a short ferry ride away, just for a slice of that cheesecake.

TWENTY

Windflower surveyed the board for today's varieties and was pleased to see his favourite, chocolate peanut butter cheesecake, right on top. It was too early for dessert, but he could certainly use another cup of coffee, and when offered, ordered a raisin tea biscuit to go along with it. Herb Stoodley was bringing in supplies from his van when he saw Windflower and came over to say hello.

"How are you, my friend?" asked Windflower when Herb sat down.

"I'm well," said Herb. "A little damp, but well. I have some music for you if you'd like something new. Let me unload my van, and I'll get it for you."

"I would indeed," said Windflower. Herb Stoodley had been and still was Windflower's tutor in classical music. Before coming to Grand Bank, he had heard a little of the more famous composers, but Herb gave him the basics and then started adding more complex and interesting pieces to Windflower's classical repertoire. It may have been a strange place to learn about classical music, but Windflower was ready when his teacher appeared.

He enjoyed his coffee and steaming hot tea biscuit slathered in butter while he waited for Herb to finish his tasks.

Herb came back with the coffee pot, which he used to refill Windflower's and pour one for himself. Marie, the waitress, picked it up, along with Windflower's empty tea biscuit plate, on her way past. He also had a plastic bag. "It's Mendelssohn," he said.

"I know Mendelssohn," said Windflower. "The Wedding March, right?"

"Fanny Mendelssohn," said Stoodley. "His sister. Many believe that she may have been the best composer and musician in the family. But she never received the accolades and recognition because of the times she lived in. A number of her works were even published under her brother's name. I think you'll like this one. It's called the String Quartet in E flat major."

"Thank you, Herb. I really appreciate it," said Windflower.

He stood and was getting ready to pay and leave when Eddie Tizzard came flying into the café.

"Good morning, Eddie," said Herb Stoodley. "In a hurry this morning?"

"I'm always in a hurry," said Tizzard.

"That would be true," said Windflower. "Wise and slow, they stumble that run fast."

"That might be true, but the early bird gets a cupcake," said Tizzard.

"It's not even lunchtime yet," said Windflower.

"My dad said to never miss a chance to eat unless it was absolutely necessary. I haven't found that occasion yet," said Tizzard as he sat down in Windflower's vacated chair with a chocolate-filled cupcake.

Windflower went to go to the cash, but Tizzard called him back after Herb Stoodley had left.

"I know what you're working on is top-secret, but I forgot to tell you that that guy from Marystown, Dollimont, he was here the day after they found old Reverend Prowse," said Tizzard.

"What was he doing?" asked Windflower.

"He told everybody, including Smithson, who went over to look things over for his report, that the manse was off-limits. No one allowed entry," said Tizzard.

"Back it up a bit," said Windflower. "Who discovered that Reverend Prowse was dead?"

"That was Beulah," said Tizzard. "She called over to the detachment, and Smithson called Doctor Sanjay and met him over there."

"Is there a report?" asked Windflower.

"For sure," said Tizzard. "It was Smithson. He always writes a report. Do you want me to get it out for you? What do you think?"

"I think you've wormed your way into my case," said Windflower. "This is hush-hush, Tizzard. Not a frickin' word to anybody. Not even Carrie until I tell you. Got it?"

"Got it," said Tizzard.

Windflower scowled at him and went to leave again. "See you back at the office."

Windflower drove back to the detachment and was greeted by Betsy, who had a number of messages for him and a question.

"Sergeant, it's been bothering me for a while, and I didn't want to ask Corporal Lundquist. He seemed to have a lot on his mind," said Betsy.

"Go ahead," said Windflower. "You know you can ask me anything."

"Thank you. I was hoping you'd say that," said Betsy. "It's about Reverend Bob."

"What about him?" asked Windflower.

"Well, many people around here are pretty upset about his dying so suddenly, including me. I know that some says it wasn't an accident," said Betsy. "There now, I've said it."

"What makes you say that?" asked Windflower.

"Beulah was so upset, she couldn't talk about it much, but I heard that he drowned in the bathtub. How does someone die in their own bathtub?" asked Betsy. "It doesn't make sense."

"Someone might have a heart attack or stroke. Or you could fall and hit your head," said Windflower.

"You could," said Betsy. "But that's not what happened with Reverend Bob, is it?"

"I guess we really don't know everything yet," said Windflower, pausing to think about how much he wanted to tell Betsy at this point. "But let me assure you that if anything was amiss with Reverend Prowse's death, it will all come out eventually."

"I hope so," said Betsy as she handed him his messages and left.

"I hope so, too," Windflower repeated quietly to himself.

He checked his messages. Ron Quigley in Marystown and Carl Langmead from the RNC in St. John's. He called Quigley, but no answer, so he left a message and told him he was going to see Elijah Woods tomorrow. And maybe he could have coffee with him and Sheila, who was tagging along.

Then he phoned Carl Langmead. Better luck with this call; Langmead answered on the first ring.

"I hear you're back in Grand Bank," said Langmead. "Does that mean you won't be peeking over my shoulder from now on?"

"Sorry," said Windflower. "I'm still on the Morecombe file. At least until you find her killer. Any luck on that end?"

"Not much," said Langmead. "I was going to ask you if there was anything interesting in the papers, I left for you."

"Mostly scientific stuff. Like a foreign language to me," said Windflower. "But he had some contacts at the university that might be worth following up on.

One was Charles Frankford. He's a big deal at MUN. Or was. Can you check him out? See if you have anything on him?"

"Writing it down now," said Langmead.

"Foote asked me to pass along a message, too. The session this week is postponed."

"Any particular reason?" asked Windflower.

"I guess her star pupil is gone missing," said Langmead.

"Cassie Fudge?" asked Windflower. "What happened to her?"

"That's what Foote is trying to find out," said Langmead. "She's pretty upset."

"I can imagine," said Windflower. "Tell her to call me if she wants."

"Will do," said Langmead.

TWENTY-ONE

That wasn't good, thought Windflower. Either Cassie was in big trouble with some of her ex-associates who didn't like her new lifestyle, or she'd gone back out. He was about to call Foote when Tizzard walked into his office and handed him the file on Reverend Bob Prowse.

"Thank you," said Windflower.

"Anything else?" asked Tizzard.

"I have a meeting tomorrow, and I should have something for you by then," said Windflower.

"With Elijah Woods?" asked Tizzard.

"What part of patience don't you understand?" said Windflower.

"I had my patience tested," said Tizzard with a straight face. "And I came back negative."

"Get out of here," said Windflower, trying not to laugh, but had to, despite himself.

Tizzard went off, and Windflower started to read the file when his phone rang.

"Inspector, how are you today?" asked Windflower.

"I am well," said Quigley. "I am just checking in to see how you're doing with the Prowse case. Thanks for your message about the meeting with Woods, and yes, it would be grand to see you and your lovely wife for coffee after your meeting."

"I'm still gathering information," said Windflower. "I saw Doc Sanjay, and he confirms that Prowse had high levels of insulin, but no idea how it got there. And I hear that Woods' guy, Dollimont, has been over here exerting his influence. I'm not even sure we've done a complete search of the scene."

"Why would we?" asked Quigley. "As far as we knew at the time, it was an accidental death."

"Not many people around here feel that way," said Windflower. "It's a small sample, but everybody I talk to has more questions than we have answers for."

"Okay, see you tomorrow," said Quigley. "'Things done well and with a care, exempt themselves from fear.'"

"My motto is 'be just, and fear not,'" said Windflower. But Quigley had already gone. "It's still my motto," said Windflower out loud and to no one in particular.

But Eddie Tizzard was hanging around outside his door and answered him. "I think it's a good motto." Before Windflower could get mad at him again, he offered to walk him through the file on Reverend Prowse.

"Go ahead," said Windflower. "You're only going to tell me anyway."

"Okay," said Tizzard. "So, Smithson and Doc Sanjay get there and Sanjay pronounces Prowse dead at the scene. Smithson has to help Beulah calm down and ends up driving her home. He didn't even have a chance to take a good look around the place that night, because he's the only one on duty, and he gets a call about an accident out near Molliers."

"Did he interview Beulah?"

"He said she was too upset that night," said Tizzard. "When he went over the next morning, that guy Dollimont and Minister Frankford were there. That's when Dollimont told everybody that the manse was off-limits. Smithson brought Beulah back here to talk to her."

"What did Beulah say?" asked Windflower.

"Beulah had been out that day, over visiting her sister in Rushoon. She got back late and brought over clean towels that had been drying on her line. When she got to the manse, she let herself in and called out to the minister. But nobody answered, so she went upstairs to put the towels in the bathroom. That's when she discovered him," said Tizzard.

"Was there anybody else around? Did Beulah notice or see anything unusual?" asked Windflower.

"Other than Reverend Bob being dead, nothing seemed strange," said Tizzard. "She did say that the lights were on across the way at Frankford's house. But she didn't see anybody moving around. That's why she called us. She said Minister Frankford wasn't often home in the evenings." Tizzard stopped and paused at this point.

Windflower looked at Tizzard. "What else?"

"Well, I don't like telling tales out of school," said Tizzard.

"Since when?" asked Windflower. "Spill it."

"Our Minister Frankford had a thing for guys in uniforms," he finally said.

"I know about Lundquist. You already told me," said Windflower.

"Not just Lundquist," said Tizzard.

"What?" exclaimed Windflower.

"She had a thing for Smithson, too," said Tizzard. "It wasn't reciprocated by him. That's what he told me. But she had the hots for him. I've seen it. Carrie, too."

This time it was Windflower who stayed silent. He didn't quite know what to say about that revelation. Finally, he came to. "I want you to go over to the manse and do a complete tour," he said.

"What am I looking for?"

"We're looking for anything that might be out of the ordinary. And for any medicines or syringes or anything like that," said Windflower.

Tizzard looked at him quizzically.

"Sanjay thinks that Prowse was poisoned," added Windflower.

"Poisoned?" said Tizzard, maybe a little too loud for Windflower's comfort.

"Quiet," said Windflower. "This can't get out until we can find out if it was accidental or deliberate. We're not there yet."

"My lips are sealed," said Tizzard, making the sign of a lock on his lips.

"Exactly," said Windflower.

"I'll get the key from the minister," said Tizzard, and he left the office.

Windflower reviewed the file again, but nothing else stood out. There was certainly nothing in there about Smithson and the minister. That was just creepy, thought Windflower. Elizabeth Frankford was still an attractive woman in her early fifties. But that was quite a gap for young Smithson, who might be twenty-seven or twenty-eight. Still creepy, he thought.

After looking at the file, he felt his stomach grumble and realized that it was past lunchtime. He went to the front and gave Betsy the Prowse file and drove the short distance home for lunch.

TWENTY-TWO

Sheila and Amelia Louise were out, probably at Sheila's meeting. Lady was happy to see him, though, and danced a few circles in the kitchen. She was rewarded with a treat and an escape to the backyard. Molly, on the other hand, offered no acknowledgement, but sat there until he gave her a treat as well. Then, no thank-you, only a silent glide away to eat her snack in peace.

Windflower rummaged around and found some cold cuts and added some lettuce and cheese to make a sandwich. He had to let a very wet Lady back in and then got to sit and eat his lunch in peace as well. He was just finishing up when his cell phone rang. It was Terry Robbins from the RCMP in St. John's.

"Good morning, boss," said Windflower. "Although I seem to have more than one of them these days."

"Welcome to the club," said Robbins. "How's Grand Bank?"

"Wet. Very wet. I think it's monsoon season."

"It's foggy here," said Robbins. "Quelle surprise."

"I'm glad you called," said Windflower. "You were on my list. I just wanted you to know that I'm still working with Langmead on the Morecombe case. I talked to him this morning."

"Good," said Robbins. "I had a call about the case this morning, too. From NCSI. They wanted to know who down here was snooping around on that file."

"They're fine people to talk about snoops," said Windflower. "I hope I didn't get you or your friend in trouble."

"No worries about that," said Robbins. "But I guess they do still have an open file on him. It was never completely closed."

"That's interesting," said Windflower. "I came across the name of someone who might have worked with him at Memorial University. Do you think NCSI might be interested?"

"Give me the name, and I'll pass it along," said Robbins.

"Charles Frankford," said Windflower. "He's a professor at MUN, and his wife is a minister in Grand Bank."

"Okay," said Robbins. "Are you coming back to St. John's anytime soon? Muriel wants her car back."

Windflower started to say that it wasn't Muriel's car, but of course, in her mind it absolutely was. "I was planning to come back for that training session on Thursday, but it's been postponed. You remember the girl that jumped in my van that night in St. John's?"

"Corrine or something?" asked Robbins.

"Cassie Fudge," said Windflower. "She's vanished."

"That can't be good," said Robbins. "I thought she was doing well."

"She was," said Windflower. "So, to answer your question, I'm not sure about going to St. John's right now. Can you ask Muriel for a few days grace?"

Robbins laughed. "I'll do my best."

After Robbins hung up, Windflower cleaned up his dishes, found a hermit cookie in the cookie jar and headed back to work. When he arrived, Betsy handed him a message to call Anne Marie Foote.

"Anne Marie how are you?" he asked when Foote answered his call.

"I'm okay," said Foote. "But I have to tell you that I'm worried sick about Cassie."

"What's the latest?" asked Windflower.

"We've got a report of her being dragged into a van downtown," said Foote. "The witness said they saw the van parked for hours near where she was staying."

"So they were waiting for her?" asked Windflower.

"Looks like it," said Foote. "Since last year, the gangs have moved around a lot, so we're really scrambling trying to find her. The other thing we're doing is contacting all the girls we met with last year to see if they can give us any more information. I was hoping you could reach out to Brittney Hodder. Our files say she's still in Grand Bank. Langmead said you were back there."

"For sure," said Windflower. "You know Brittney's father, the fire chief. I'll contact him today. If he can help, I'm sure he will. They were so grateful to have their girl back."

"Great," said Foote. "I knew we could count on you. Do you still want to do the workshop session if we reschedule?"

"Sure," said Windflower. "I was looking forward to it."

"Okay. I'll get back to you when we have another date," said Foote.

He called Chief Hodder's number and left a message. Not long after, the chief phoned him back.

"Sergeant, how are you? I heard you were coming back. Welcome home," said Chief Martin Hodder.

"Thanks, Chief," said Windflower, thinking that it was nice to receive such a warm welcome. Chief Hodder was the only full-time employee of the Grand Bank Volunteer Fire Department, but they did a good job of keeping the community safe and dousing the occasional blaze.

The last time that he and Windflower had been in contact was about his daughter, Brittney, who'd fallen in with the wrong crowd and went missing in St. John's. Foote and Windflower had found Brittney when there was a raid on the biker's clubhouse in St. John's. Unfortunately, they only got to her after a horrible car accident in which another girl died.

"How's Brittney doing these days?" he asked Hodder.

"She's doing grand," said Chief Hodder. "She's completely recovered from her injuries and is going to MUN next year, if we ever get out of this pandemic."

"That's great," said Windflower. "But there's another girl in trouble, and we're reaching out to some other families to see if they can help."

"Oh my God, that's awful," said Hodder. "What can we do?"

"The missing girl is Cassie Fudge," said Windflower. "Can you check with Brittney and see if she knows her or might have any information about where she might be?"

"I'll definitely do that when I get home," said Hodder. "We don't want any other family to go through what we went through."

"Thanks, Martin, talk soon," said Windflower.

TWENTY-THREE

Windflower spent some time going through the paperwork that Betsy had arranged for him in order to finalize his move back to Grand Bank. There was a lot. But one thing missing was anything about his vehicle. Come to think of it, he didn't see his old Jeep in the parking lot when he came in. He wandered around to the back of the building and peered out into the back lot but didn't see it there either. He went to see Betsy.

"Betsy, where's my Jeep?"

"Well, technically it wasn't your Jeep when you were reassigned," said Betsy. "It reverted back to the pool. And since Constable Tizzard didn't have a vehicle, it was assigned to him."

"So Tizzard has my Jeep?"

"Not anymore," said Betsy. "There was an accident."

"He wrecked my Jeep," said Windflower. "Unbelievable."

"Well, it is believable, sir," said Betsy. "I have pictures if you need to see them."

"Can I get a new Jeep?"

"That will take some time," said Betsy.

"But I've started the request process.

Here's the paperwork for you to sign." She handed him the forms.

"In the meantime, we have a cruiser at Wilson's garage getting tuned up for you. Because you have to give your car back. Muriel called me."

Windflower muttered to himself, which Betsy patiently ignored, signed the papers and handed them back.

"Thank you, Sergeant," said Betsy. "Enjoy the rest of your day."

Luckily for Windflower, there wasn't much left in this working day. He finished off his stack of paperwork, closed his computer and left for home. Next week he would begin to organize himself better and take a regular slot in the rotation, doing a few nights here and there. But he had decided to take it easier this week, and if he could, get home early every night.

Everybody was happy to see him. Stella wanted to tell him all about school, and Amelia Louise pretended she was at school too and rambled all in some gibberish once Stella started talking. He listened to them both and even spent an hour with them being served tea and what Stella called "trumpets." He pronounced them delicious. After that, he had another half an hour before supper according to Sheila, so he took Lady for a short walk in the still-pouring rain. Both of them got soaked, but neither minded, especially Windflower when he got home and smelled supper in the kitchen.

"Garlic bread," he said to Sheila. "The way to a man's heart."

"I have learned 'to bait the hook well, the fish will bite,'" said Sheila.

"Very good," said Windflower. "Garlic bread, macaroni and cheese and Shakespeare for supper. 'I bear a charmed life.'"

"Bear these plates out and get the girls to help set the table," said Sheila.

Windflower and his daughters set the table and sat while Sheila served them the garlic bread, which everyone ate first, and the steaming hot macaroni and cheese with some peas and carrots on the side.

After supper, Windflower and the girls cleaned up. Well, they made a great sinkful of soap bubbles and chased each other and Lady around the kitchen with handfuls of them. They made one attempt to involve Molly in their game, but she hissed them back to reality. After Windflower cleaned up that mess, too, he carried both of them upstairs for bath time. He ran the water while they ran after each other until finally Windflower caught them in turn and dropped them in the bathwater.

Sheila came up while they were splashing around.

"They seem happy," he said.

"Why wouldn't they be? They are safe and clean and well fed and well loved. Stella seems to be thriving at school, and Amelia Louise has me almost full-time and the daycare to socialize. It feels like these are the best days of our lives, too, doesn't it?"

"Yes," said Windflower. "When I forget about tomorrow or next week or where we'll be next year, I realize that I am perfectly happy."

"Me, too," said Sheila. "Don't screw this up."

"Moi?" said Windflower. "When did I ever screw things up?"

"Well," said Sheila.

"I think the girls need me," said Windflower, and he almost ran back into the bathroom. After towelling them off and helping them get their pyjamas on, it was story time. When they were finished, Windflower and Sheila went back downstairs. He took the dog for her evening walk while Sheila curled up with her book and a fresh pot of tea.

Windflower had put his rubber boots and rain slicker on for tonight's walk around Grand Bank. That was a good idea, since the eternal rain continued.

But he and Lady still had a pleasant stroll on the narrow streets, and he could peek into many of the windows along their route. The biggest thing by far in people's homes appeared to be their flat-screen TVs. In some cases, they took up the whole wall of the living room, and judging by the volume levels, the residents might need hearing aids as well.

But the houses that were occupied looked warm and welcoming to Windflower as they walked past them. Much friendlier than the dozens of homes that were vacant. That was one sign of the aging population of Grand Bank and many small towns in this province. The older folks had passed or moved into the senior's complex or with their children in St. John's or Mount Pearl. And there were few new families to take their place. That was a little sad, thought Windflower. But it was a reality and one that might face Sheila and Windflower before long as they pondered their future.

But not for tonight, thought Windflower as they passed the old B&B and headed for home. Tonight, he was just grateful for all he had, and he had a lot. He'd deal with anything else tomorrow.

TWENTY-FOUR

Tuesday morning woke grey and rainy, just like the past few days. Windflower got up with Sheila at the alarm and took Amelia Louise downstairs with him while she attempted to rouse Stella. He let Lady out and put on the coffee and four eggs to boil. While he was waiting for all that, he went to the living room, where Amelia Louise immediately made him part of her game as she pulled all of her dolls out of the toy box.

He was still sitting there surrounded by dolls when Sheila came down and brought him a cup of coffee. He had a few sips and then went back to the kitchen, where a soaked Lady was still outside.

"Sorry, girl," said Windflower as he let her in and dried her off. Lady seemed to forgive him immediately when he gave her a Milk Bone. Seeing that treats were on offer, Molly decided to rise from her bed to get her share. She stared at Windflower until he handed it over. "I'm not afraid of you," said Windflower.

"Who are you talking to?" asked Sheila.

Windflower pretended to ignore that question and asked his own. "Toast with the eggs?"

"Sure," said Sheila.

A few minutes later, a clean and smartly dressed Stella came down, and all four of them sat at the table for breakfast.

Not long after, Stella was getting on the bus and Sheila took Amelia Louise upstairs to get her ready for daycare.

Windflower took the opportunity to grab his rain slicker and his smudging kit and went outside. Lady, still wet from her previous adventure, didn't move from her bed as Windflower closed the door behind him. He stayed beneath the overhang and mixed and lit his smudge. This morning would be the quick version of his ritual, and he passed the smoke over his head and heart and his body. He gave a prayer of gratitude for all the good things in his life and went back inside.

Once he had showered and changed for work, he kissed Amelia Louise and made plans to come back and get Sheila at noon. He drove to the office and was pleased to see Smithson's car out front. He wanted to talk to him but didn't know how he was going to raise the issue of Reverend Elizabeth Frankford.

He found Smithson in the back room with a cup of coffee and a technical magazine.

"Morning, Sergeant," said Smithson. "Another rainy day."

"Good morning," said Windflower. "What are you reading?"

"It's an article about how to build your own robot," said Smithson. "With artificial intelligence, anything is possible now. Someday they might replace us."

Windflower poured himself a cup of coffee. "I wanted to talk to you about the late Reverend Prowse. You were the first on the scene at the manse?"

"I was the first one there after Beulah. She was pretty upset," said Smithson. "I got her out of there once Doctor Sanjay showed up. But I did interview her the next day. I did a report. Did you want me to get the file?"

"No," said Windflower. "I saw the file. Good report. I wanted to ask you about Gregory Dollimont."

"Him?" asked Smithson. "He showed up acting all high and mighty, said that nobody was to go into the manse. I went back to Corporal Lundquist, but he said to leave it alone. He said that Elizabeth, I mean Reverend Frankford, had made the request out of respect for Reverend Prowse. At the time, I didn't push it, because it looked like a heart attack or stroke, or maybe just an accident. Did I do something wrong?"

"You reported it up the chain of command," said Windflower. "A couple of more things on Beulah. Did she talk to you about Reverend Prowse, if he was prone to falling or anything? Did she say if he was on any medications?"

"That was part of the reason she was so upset," said Smithson. "She kept saying how healthy he was. Said he tried to walk two miles a day. I can remember seeing him out in all kinds of weather. And she didn't mention any medications or prescriptions. It wasn't an accident, was it?"

"Doctor Sanjay doesn't think so," said Windflower. "But until I talk to Reverend Woods in Marystown, this is definitely on the hush-hush. Tizzard knows, but that's it."

"Got it," said Smithson.

"As a matter of fact, Tizzard went over to the manse yesterday. Did you see him when you came in?"

"No, he was gone by the time I got here," said Smithson. "I guess he must have got the key from Eliz…Reverend Frankford."

"Is there anything else you want to tell me?" asked Windflower.

"No. What do you mean?" said Smithson, stammering a little and growing red in the face.

"If you ever want to talk, I'm here," said Windflower.

"Yeah, sure," said Smithson. "Can I go now?"

Windflower waved him out. As he was leaving, Betsy came in to say good morning and to tell him he had someone coming to see him. Actually, two people: the fire chief and Brittney Hodder.

Windflower had the office to himself for a while and got caught up on all the news and reports that had piled up in his in-basket. He had lowered that stack significantly when Betsy told him his visitors had arrived.

"Good morning, Sergeant. You remember Brittney," said Hodder.

"I do, nice to see both of you," said Windflower. Brittney Hodder looked a little nervous but gave him a slight smile and a glimpse of her braces.

"Brittney has something she wants to tell you," said Hodder. "Go ahead," he encouraged her.

The girl cleared her throat. "I'm no longer involved with any of them. But some of them keep contacting me. I didn't know the girl that's missing. Cassie, right?"

"That's right," said Windflower. "Cassie Fudge, from Corner Brook."

"Well, like I said, I don't know her. But someone else has been calling me," said Brittney. She paused and looked at her father. He nodded for her to go ahead.

"Mandy Pardy called me," said the girl. "She and I had been together for a while in St. John's, hanging around the same people. We connected because she was from Marystown and I'm from Grand

Bank. After I got home, I heard that she got out, too. But she never came back to this area. Then she called me, right out of the blue."

"What did she want?" asked Windflower.

"At first, nothing," said Brittney. "But then whenever she called, she was high. Really high. Manic, almost. I know what that sounds like."

"Meth," said Windflower.

"That's when I knew she was in trouble," said the girl. Now she was ignoring her father and talking directly to Windflower. "The last couple of times she called, it was loud in the background, and when I asked where she was, she said a party. She invited me to come."

"You didn't go," said Windflower.

"No," said Brittney. "I've been down that road before." She looked at her father again, and he took her hand. "Mandy offered me money to come back with them. There's no money worth it."

Windflower wanted to go and hug this girl. Instead, he asked her if she knew where Mandy Pardy was.

"I think she's still in Mount Pearl," said Brittney. "Here's her cell phone number."

TWENTY-FIVE

Windflower called Anne Marie Foote with the information he'd received from Brittney Hodder.

"That is great news," said Foote. "We probably still have an address for the Pardy girl in our files. We'll see if we can find her."

"If she's not gone, too," said Windflower.

"It's a lead," said Foote. "Better than what we have now. Thanks. I'll let you know if she or anything else turns up."

He called Sheila to see if she was ready. She was, so he rummaged around his briefcase to find the CD that Herb had given him. That would be a surprise for her. When he got home, Sheila had a surprise for him, too. She came out to the car carrying a picnic basket under her arm.

"What's in the basket?" he asked.

"You're a detective?" asked Sheila, laughing. "A few snacks and lunch. We have to eat."

"We do indeed," said Windflower as they drove out of Grand Bank and hit the highway towards Marystown. It was still raining, and a few fog patches lingered here and there, but nothing diminished their good spirits.

They listened to CBC on the radio and talked about their kids and life and politics as they moved past Grand Beach and Molliers.

Sheila got them some sliced apples and grapes from the basket, and when the radio faded out and they approached the emptiness of the barrens, Windflower took out the CD.

"What is this?" Sheila asked.

"It's Mendelssohn," said Windflower proudly. "Fanny Mendelssohn. String Quartet in E flat major."

"Herb Stoodley," said Sheila.

"Yes, it was his suggestion," said Windflower. "But he says I have great taste in classical music."

"That's because everything you know, you got from him," said Sheila.

"Shush," said Windflower and turned the music up. It was the perfect accompaniment to their drive. There were a couple of beautiful shorter sequences at the beginning, and the instruments kind of echoed back to them as they moved past the vista of rocks and small trees and empty lands. The music picked up in the middle in the Baroque style that was in great fashion during Mendelssohn's time and ended with a very moving and emotional third movement.

"Wow, that was so real, I could feel like she was almost here with us," said Sheila. "Thank you for that."

"You're welcome," said Windflower. "I'm glad you enjoyed it."

"Do we have time to stop for lunch?"

"I think so," said Windflower. "But where?"

"Take the Burin turnoff. Let's go down by the boardwalk," said Sheila.

Windflower happily agreed. Burin was one of his favourite places on Earth. When you drove into the area, it felt like you were entering a magical kingdom. Houses were hanging off the sides of cliffs, and everything overlooked the ocean. Even on a wet and foggy day, it had a mystical feel as they rounded one of the sharp curves and drove down to the area where the boardwalk was located.

In normal times this would be a bustling place, with a gallery and a mini-museum and a fabulous café that served homemade pies for dessert. But with the current situation, Windflower and Sheila found themselves alone at the edge of the water. He parked and they both got out to take a look. Not that they could see much. Driven back inside by the rain, Sheila took out their lunch and divvied it up between them.

There was hot salami and sliced Gouda and a fresh baguette, along with baby carrots and a small container of spicy olives. There was even a cupcake each for dessert.

"That was fabulous," said Windflower. "Thank you."

Sheila smiled and wrapped up the leftovers as they drove away. Windflower dropped Sheila at the mall and went to his meeting with the Reverend Elijah Woods. He drove up to the minister's house, a large three-storey affair that had clearly been modernized by the looks of the siding and new windows. He parked, walked to the door, and rang the bell.

He was met not by Woods, but by another man who he thought might be Gregory Dollimont. He assumed that was who it was because the other man didn't speak, simply ushered him in and indicated he should follow. They went upstairs to the second floor and Dollimont led him into Elijah Wood's office.

"Sergeant Windflower, thank you for coming," said Woods. Windflower noticed that the minister smiled when he said this, but he had no sense that the man was offering him any real welcome. That didn't give him any warm and fuzzy feelings about the minister.

"I hope you don't mind, but I've asked Gregory to join us," continued Woods.

"That's fine," said Windflower. "Thank you for seeing me today."

"As I said on the phone, this is a delicate matter," said Woods. "It needs to be treated with the utmost discretion."

Windflower nodded. They'd been through this already. "What is it exactly that you would like me and the RCMP to do?" he asked. "I met with Doctor Sanjay yesterday, and he believes that Reverend Prowse's death was not an accident. We are already moving towards a full investigation. I can keep this quiet for a little while. But people will start asking questions."

"We do not wish any preferential treatment," said Woods. "But we would like to know the results of your investigation before they are disseminated widely in the community. There are many other factors to consider."

"We can try to accommodate that request," said Windflower. "But in return I would ask that you not interfere or place any restrictions on our enquiries." When he said this, he looked directly at Gregory Dollimont, who scowled back at him.

"Certainly," said Woods. "Can I ask who you will be interviewing?"

"I thought I might start with your assistant," said Windflower, looking again at Dollimont.

"He is not my assistant," said Woods. "Simply a friend of the church. But you can ask him any questions you would like." Dollimont's scowl softened a little. More like a grimace, thought Windflower.

"What were you doing in Grand Bank the night of Reverend Prowse's death?" asked Windflower.

"I was visiting an old friend," said Dollimont.

"How did you find out about the death?"

"Everybody heard the commotion," said Dollimont. "Sirens and police cars. Grand Bank is a very small community, Sergeant."

"Constable Smithson says that you stopped him from investigating the scene," said Windflower. "Apparently you said that Reverend Frankford had requested that. Yet I don't think she was there that evening."

"Your constable must have misunderstood," said Dollimont. "I said I'm sure that Reverend Frankford would have wanted the manse to be undisturbed as possible.

You must remember that at the time we thought that there no foul play involved."

"Did you see anything unusual?" asked Windflower.

"I'm not sure what you mean," said Dollimont, a little too smugly for Windflower's liking.

"Any syringes or medications? Any prescription drugs?"

"I did not search the premises," said Dollimont. "I simply secured them. If anything was amiss, it would still be there today. Is that all, Sergeant? I do have another appointment."

"For now," said Windflower as Dollimont got up and left the room.

"I will interview Reverend Frankford next," said Windflower, and he, too, rose to leave.

"Then I suggest you do it quickly," said Woods. "She is being transferred this weekend to the west coast."

"That is rather sudden," said Windflower. "She hasn't been in Grand Bank that long."

"The church needs her out there," said Woods. "She will make the announcement at church on Sunday, so I hope you will keep it confidential until then. Thank you for your time, Sergeant, and good luck in your investigation."

TWENTY-SIX

W indflower walked out of the manse with his head spinning a little and certain of only one thing: he had to talk to Elizabeth Frankford before she left. She was at the centre of all of this, maybe even a murderer. But for now, he had a date with a friend and his lovely lady. He phoned Ron Quigley and Sheila and arranged to meet them both at the little coffee shop in the mall. Sheila was already sitting in one of the two tables when he arrived.

"How'd your meeting go?" asked Sheila.

"Tell me about your shopping," said Windflower. "It will be more entertaining than my meeting, that's for sure."

"I doubt it," said Sheila. "I got a new dress for Stella for church and some new pajamas for Amelia Louise. I desperately need a shopping trip."

"We can go to St. John's," said Windflower.

"Not St. John's," said Sheila. "I want real shopping. Montreal, Toronto. Maybe even New York."

"You can order online," said Windflower.

Sheila rolled her eyes in exasperation just as Ron Quigley was coming into the coffee shop.

"Saved by your friend," said Sheila.

"Ron, nice to see you," said Windflower.

Quigley went to Sheila and gave her a hug. "You look great," he said. "Maybe even younger."

Sheila looked at Windflower. "He never tells me that," she said.

Windflower started to protest when the other two started laughing. "I'll get the coffees," he said. He went to the counter and got three coffees and a package of date squares.

"I come bearing gifts," said Windflower as he laid the tray on the table.

"Something about beware of men bearing gifts," said Sheila.

"That was the Greeks," said Windflower. "Virgil," he added as he stuffed half a date square in his mouth.

"How did it go with Woods?" asked Quigley, snatching a square for himself.

"It was okay. I'll have to fill you in later," he said. "How's Bill Ford doing?"

"Nice deflection," said Sheila. "If you drop me at Sobey's, you can do your policeman thing."

"No, hang around for a minute anyway," said Quigley. "Bill Ford is well, but he's not going to be the new inspector."

"We already have an inspector," said Windflower.

"If everything holds the way it is now on the virus front, I'm going to Ottawa in the new year," said Quigley.

"That's great news," said Sheila. "We'll miss you, but I'd love to come to Ottawa. I was just saying how much I missed getting out for a shopping trip."

"Congrats, Ron," said Windflower. But he was visibly less enthused than Sheila. And she knew why.

He left Quigley to guard the remaining two date squares and drove Sheila to the supermarket.

"Will they ask you to apply?" asked Sheila.

"I'm assuming so," said Windflower.

"Are you going to?" asked Sheila.

"We can talk about it, but I'm not that interested. And I'm not sure I want to move to Marystown," said Windflower.

"But if you don't?" said Sheila. She left that dangling in the air.

"We'll cross that bridge when we come to it," said Windflower. "And whatever decision we make together will be the right one. 'It is not in the stars to hold our destiny but in ourselves.'" He kissed Sheila and went back to see Ron Quigley.

Quigley had saved him the last square. Windflower left it lying on the plate.

"You have my support, whatever decision you make," said Quigley.

"I know," said Windflower. "But at some point, it won't be in your hands."

"True. Let's take it one step at a time then," said Quigley. "Tell me about Woods."

"My gut tells me Woods is hiding something and that rat, Dollimont, is involved. Plus, he's transferring Frankford out."

"That's a surprise," said Quigley.

"It looks like they're trying to protect her. Or maybe he wants her out of the way," said Windflower.

"Well, she isn't without her flaws," said Quigley.

"You know about Smithson, too?" asked Windflower. "Why didn't you tell me?"

"I wanted you to find out about it on your own," said Quigley. "There's nothing illegal about it, for either of them. It just got too hot for Lundquist."

"Now, it appears it's too hot for her, too," said Windflower. "Or maybe it's something more sinister."

"You don't think she was involved in Prowse's death, do you?" asked Quigley.

"I don't know yet," said Windflower. "But I want to talk to her before she gets shipped out. That's for sure. I have a feeling that coming soon may be the winter of her discontent."

"If she's guilty, she'll let something slip," said Quigley. "'Suspicion always haunts the guilty mind.'"

His cell phone buzzed. It was Sheila. "I have to go," said Windflower.

"Okay, say goodbye to Sheila," said Quigley. "I will be over sometime soon to visit."

"That would be good. See you soon," said Windflower.

He picked up Sheila at Sobey's and helped her put her bags in the trunk.

TWENTY-SEVEN

Windflower was quiet on the drive home. Sheila sensed his need for a little solitude, so she said nothing until they were well out of Marystown.

"It was nice to see Ron," she said to break the ice.

"He's a great guy," said Windflower.

"Are you worried about having to move and all that stuff?" asked Sheila.

"It feels uncertain, but it will be okay because we'll be together," said Windflower. "No point worrying about tomorrow, let alone next year. I was actually thinking about my case."

"Maybe I can help you," said Sheila. "Talk to Detective Hillier, Sergeant."

Windflower laughed. "Something fishy is going on inside the church. What do you think of Elijah Woods?"

"Reverend Elijah Woods is a church politician," said Sheila. "There's not supposed to be a hierarchy inside the United Church, but he manages this part of the world for the Newfoundland Council. If there's an issue or a problem, he's always been the man to see."

"Did you have any dealings with him as mayor?" asked Windflower.

"Not much," said Sheila. "But the Church does own a bit of property around town and wasn't keeping it up.

He called me and basically asked me to overlook it. He said that's the way it had been in the past."

"What did you say?" asked Windflower.

"I told him to get someone to cut the grass or they'd be fined fifty dollars," said Sheila.

"What did he say to that?" asked Windflower.

"Nothing," said Sheila. "But the next day Gregory Dollimont was in my office telling me I would have a big problem on my hands if I went ahead with my threat. I told him it was a promise and got the clerk to write up the formal notice while he was still there. I don't trust Woods, and Dollimont is downright creepy."

"So I'll mark you down as undecided on them," said Windflower, laughing. "Thanks for the insight. It's useful."

"You should ask me for help more," said Sheila. "I think I would make a great detective."

"I think you would," said Windflower. "Are there any more snacks in that picnic basket?"

Sheila scrounged up the rest of the grapes and a small bag of pretzels. They nibbled their way across the barrens, and as they came over the hill going into Grand Bank, the rain slowed. When Windflower dropped Sheila at their house it had completely stopped, and they both sat admiring the rainbow that arched across the town.

"A good omen," said Windflower. "Maybe all that rain was worth it."

"The way I see it, 'If you want the rainbow, you gotta put up with the rain,'" said Sheila.

"That's good," said Windflower.

"Dolly Parton," said Sheila as she kissed him on the cheek. "See you for supper."

"You most certainly will," said Windflower. He waved goodbye as he drove back to the office.

Betsy had left for the day, but his messages were in his slot. He scanned them and called the first one, Eddie Tizzard.

"What's up?" he asked Tizzard.

"Well, no drugs or medications or anything," said Tizzard. "In fact, very little of anything in the bathroom. A toothbrush, soap and toilet paper. I'd say either Reverend Prowse was a very simple man or this place has been cleaned out."

"I was kind of afraid of that," said Windflower. "Did you do a print scan?"

"I did and have a couple of samples that came back clean," said Tizzard. "If I was to guess, I'd say one male and two females, judging by the size."

"Prowse and Beulah," said Windflower. "Maybe Reverend Frankford?"

"That would make sense," said Tizzard. "Did you want me to talk to her?"

"No, leave that for me," said Windflower. "Anything else?"

"I saved the best for last," said Tizzard. "I found a gun. An RCMP service weapon."

"Did you check the number?"

"Staff Sergeant Alison Morecombe," said Tizzard. "Isn't she dead?"

"She is indeed," said Windflower. "Killed in an incident in St. John's. Her service weapon was missing from the safe in her house. Any prints?"

"Morecombe's came back right away," said Tizzard. "And there's a partial set on the gun, but I didn't get anything back from our database. If it was in St. John's, they might have more at the RNC. They don't always share their stuff with the national database."

"Okay," said Windflower. "I have a message to call Langmead anyway. Good work, Constable."

"Thank you, boss. I'm just stopping in Garnish for an ice cream cone. Will you be there long?"

"I'm trying to get out soon," said Windflower. "We'll talk tomorrow."

He hung up and called Langmead.

"Thanks for calling me back," said Langmead. "I thought you'd want to know that we have a file on your man, Charles Frankford. Investigated following a disturbance at the university a couple of years ago. Another man wanted to press assault charges."

"Jerome Morecombe?" said Windflower.

"Correct," said Langmead. "We charged him, but the complainant never showed, and the case was dismissed."

"Very interesting," said Windflower. "We found Morecombe's gun, by the way. In a dead minister's house."

"Was he shot?" asked Langmead. "Isn't Frankford's wife the minister?"

"She is now, but not for long," said Windflower. "That truly is a long story. Are you going to pick up Frankford? I don't think he's around here."

"Apparently he has an apartment in town, up near the university," said Langmead. "One of my guys is heading up there now to get him."

"Listen, can you check a set of prints if I email them to you?" asked Windflower.

"Sure, send them over," said Langmead. "You have my email."

"Do you know if Foote has found Cassie yet?"

"I don't think so, but I don't see her as much," said Langmead. "If I do, I'll get her to call."

"Thanks. Have a good night, Carl," said Windflower. He had other messages, but they would have to wait. He searched the detachment database for the fingerprints that Tizzard had entered. He found the one that was marked Service Weapon and forwarded the file to Langmead. Then he closed his computer and drove home.

TWENTY-EIGHT

It looked like the rain was gone for good, and as he gazed out towards Saint-Pierre, there wasn't even a sign of fog. A remarkably fine evening for this time of the year, thought Windflower as he pulled into his driveway. So, too, did his dog and his children, since they ran out to meet him. He dragged the girls, with Lady close behind, back into the house, only to be shooed out again with instructions to take everyone for a walk.

Windflower didn't mind that at all. He got Lady's leash and the wagon and was about to leave when he remembered one more thing. He ran back into the house and grabbed half a loaf of bread from the bread bin. "Duck food," he said as he kissed Sheila on top of her head and ran back out again.

It was a wonderful walk down by the wharf with Lady happily trotting alongside the two girls giggling in the wagon. They waved hello to everyone they saw, and every time someone said hello back, they would burst into laughter. It was the best game ever, and they kept it up until they reached the side of the brook. Windflower kept a tight hold of Lady as the girls scampered out of the wagon to greet the parade of ducks that were swimming towards them.

They both squealed for bread. As fast as Windflower could tear it up, they threw it into the feeding frenzy in the water. A few seagulls tried to swoop in for a snack, but a vigilant Lady barked them away. The girls were still calling for bread and could have kept the feeding up for an hour, but Windflower had run out of supplies.

"Sorry, guys, next time," he said.

"Sorry, duckies," said Stella.

"Sorry, dwuckies," said Amelia Louise.

Windflower loaded them back in the wagon, walked a little farther down the brookside and then made their way home.

Sheila had made a chicken pot pie. When Windflower opened the front door, he just about swooned.

"Oh, my goodness," he said. "What's Mamma got cooking in the kitchen?"

Sheila laughed as everybody came into the kitchen, and the girls made exaggerated smelling movements to show how excited they were. If Lady could get any more excited, she would have died on the spot.

Windflower and the girls oohed and aahed as Sheila took the beautifully browned pie out of the oven. And then right behind that she took out another pie. She laid them both on the counter to cool.

"And apple pie for dessert," exclaimed Windflower.

By now the girls had started the "pie, pie, pie" chant and were marching around the kitchen and out into the living room. That gave Windflower and Sheila a chance to set the table and a few minutes later serve them up some pie and steamed broccoli.

"This is absolutely delicious," said Windflower. "How did you manage to pull this together so quickly?"

"I had them in the freezer," said Sheila. "'All things are ready, if our mind be so.'"

"Very nice," said Windflower. "I'm grateful to be a recipient of your preparedness."

"If you are really grateful you can clean up while I get the girls' bath ready," said Sheila.

Windflower cleaned up and even gave Lady a small piece of the chicken pot pie in her food bowl. When Molly decided to come try her luck, he gave her a couple of small pieces of chicken as well. Then he went upstairs to check on Sheila and the girls. They were all coming out of the bathroom, and Windflower picked up Amelia Louise and carried her to get her pajamas on. Then he asked her to pick out a book.

As usual, she brought back two. She chose *Goodnight Moon* and a book from the library he hadn't seen before. It was *The Circus Ship*, about a circus ship that runs aground off the coast of Maine in the United States. The animals all swim to shore and charm the locals. When the evil owner comes to collect the animals, the villagers help the animals to escape. Both Windflower and Amelia Louise loved the story, and he agreed to read it twice. Then they read *Goodnight Moon* together, and at the end they said goodnight to all the animals in the book, especially the little mouse. He turned off the light, kissed Amelia Louise, tucked her in and went downstairs.

Sheila was waiting for him with a pot of tea and the cribbage board.

"Come on," she said. "Let's play."

Windflower liked playing crib, and he loved Sheila. But together, it was not a good mix. He tried to pretend he was busy and had something else to do, but his fate was sealed. The reason he didn't like playing with Sheila was that no matter what happened, he lost. If she won, she was not a gracious winner. If she lost, she was not a gracious loser. Windflower was competitive, so he couldn't just let her win. So he offered to play one game, winner-take-all. Sheila agreed. When she lost the first game, she offered to play the best two out of three. When she lost the second game, she threw the cards on the floor. This was not going well, thought Windflower. Maybe time for a little diversion.

"I have a secret," he teased.

"I love secrets," said Sheila. "Tell me."

"You can't tell anyone, and when you find out, you have to act surprised," he said.

"I promise. Tell me," Sheila demanded.

"Elizabeth Frankford is getting transferred," said Windflower.

"That's what the special announcement is about," said Sheila. "All the church ladies and the people who help out like me are invited to a reception after church services on Sunday. Nobody knew what it was all about."

"Now you do," said Windflower. "Remember your promise."

"How did you find out?" she asked. "Oh yeah, you met with Elijah Woods. Did he say why?"

"Some convoluted answer about how her services were required on the west coast," said Windflower.

"Good job on the scoop," said Sheila. "I used to be better at it when I was mayor. I'm losing my touch."

"Oh, well," said Windflower. "'Some are born great, some achieve greatness and some have greatness thrust upon them.'"

"Take the dog for a walk and come to bed, O great one," said Sheila.

Windflower mumbled something about not getting any respect, which was completely ignored as she went upstairs. So he did as he was told: walked the dog, turned off the lights and went to bed.

He had just drifted off and was floating along when he realized that he was actually floating along. He checked his hands and confirmed it. He was dreaming. When he double-checked, he was not just floating, but flying. He tried to see if he could manoeuvre himself around, dipping a little, and then pulling back up.

That worked, so he did a great dive and plunged down, down, down until the ground got very close. Then he pulled himself back up.

This was fun, he thought. The most fun he'd had in a dream in a long time. Then, suddenly, he could no longer control himself and started tumbling over and over while falling ever faster. Just before he hit the ground, he woke up. It was a strange experience for Windflower. Usually, in his dreams there would be animals or people with messages or information for him.

Maybe he was having so much fun that he missed the meaning of his dream. Or maybe it was just a plain ordinary dream like everybody else has every second night.

He made a decision to talk to Uncle Frank about it tomorrow. And then, feeling a little tired from dreaming and flying and thinking about it all, he fell asleep. He didn't wake until he heard Stella talking to Amelia Louise.

TWENTY-NINE

Windflower let Sheila sleep while he took the girls downstairs. He gave them each half a banana and turned on the cartoons. It wasn't the best thing to have them watching TV, but it let him make his coffee and put some bacon on to fry while he scrambled the eggs. He let Lady out, and when the coffee was ready, he brought a cup to Sheila.

"Thank you so much," said Sheila. "I woke up to no children and the smell of bacon frying. And now I get a fresh cup of coffee. Am I dreaming?"

"Ah," said Windflower. "'When I waked, I cried to dream again.'"

"I'd settle for a few more hours sleep," said Sheila.

"By the way, where's Uncle Frank these days?" asked Windflower. "I never see him around."

"He's still in bed," said Sheila. "Usually gets up around noon, has lunch, and then he's gone. Comes back late. Like a teenage boy."

"Can you tell him I'd like to see him?" said Windflower.

"Have another dream?" asked Sheila.

"Yeah," said Windflower. "But nothing happens in this one."

"I'll tell him," said Sheila. "But something is always happening. We don't always see it."

Windflower went back downstairs and got the eggs and bacon ready. He called Sheila and the girls to the table. Lady and Molly came too, just in case. Both were rewarded by a snippet of bacon while Windflower and Amelia Louise were cleaning up. She was a great help for a while and then got bored and started chasing Molly around. The cat would tolerate a lot from the little girl, but when Lady tried to join the fun, Molly hissed at her and the dog slunk back to her bed in the corner. She knew when to get out at precisely the right moment, thought Windflower as Stella and Sheila came down.

Stella skipped to the school bus, and because it was such a fine day, everybody trooped along after her. They waved goodbye, and Windflower got himself ready for work. He was going to drive straight there but changed his mind. He went back and got his pipe, put it in the front seat and drove to the beach. He found his usual large rock, hidden from the road and anybody passing by, and took out his pipe. He put a little tobacco in and lit it, taking a few puffs and exhaling.

He felt calm and serene by the water. But nothing else. No mist, no fog, no sense of other people being present. No visitors. Nothing. He waited for a few more minutes. Only a few seagulls calling in the distance to break his quiet morning. He cleaned his pipe, packed it up and drove to work. Something else to talk to Uncle Frank about, he thought.

Betsy met him at the office with a pleasant greeting and more paperwork. "This is to transfer the service weapon back to St. John's," she said. "It needs your authorization."

Windflower signed the paper and handed it back to her.

"Thank you, Sergeant," said Betsy. "Such a shame about that poor woman. After all, she went through with her husband. Do they know what happened yet?"

"I don't think so," said Windflower. "The Constabulary is still working on it."

"Anything you need me to do today?" asked Betsy.

"Yes," said Windflower. "Can you call Reverend Frankford and see if I can see her today sometime?"

"I'll do that right away," said Betsy.

Windflower's cell phone rang right after Betsy left. It was Carl Langmead.

"He's gone," said Langmead. "Charles Frankford. His lady friend who was at the apartment said he had to go out of town on business. She didn't know when he was coming back."

"If he's left the province, it's easy enough to check," said Windflower.

"I don't think he was driving," said Langmead. "His car was in the driveway. Our guess is that he flew somewhere."

"Do you want me to get Smithson to check the airport?"

"That's what I was hoping you'd say," said Langmead. "We can do it here, but Smithson is a whiz at that stuff."

"No worries," said Windflower.

"I spoke to Foote, too," said Langmead. "She said to tell you that the Pardy girl was gone now, too. But they have a lead they're following. Apparently, the bikers, at least the Angel affiliates, have regrouped, and they're operating out of Paradise now."

"Paradise, what a great name for a place," said Windflower. "Although I'm assuming that the name might be a little misleading."

"Hang on there," said Langmead. "That's where I'm living right now. It became the place to go about ten years ago. It is one of the fastest-growing communities on the island. Has been for years."

"In any case, you seem to have attracted some bad neighbours," said Windflower. "But thanks for the update. I'll talk to Smithson."

When Langmead hung up, Windflower looked up, and there was Smithson.

"What do you want to talk to me about?" asked Smithson.

"I need you to find a passenger, Charles Frankford. We think he left sometime in the last day or so. Probably from St. John's airport," said Windflower.

"I can do that," said Smithson. "Right away." He walked away looking relieved, thought Windflower. He was thinking again about Smithson and the minister when Ron Quigley called.

"Good morning, Inspector," said Windflower. "How can I be of service today?"

"Well, it appears that you have perturbed Reverend Elijah Woods," said Quigley. "At least that's what Gregory Dollimont has to say."

"Isn't he an awful creature?" said Windflower, unable to restrain himself.

"That is one devil that can truly 'cite Scripture for his own purpose,'" said Quigley.

"I have never seen his face, but 'I think of hell-fire,'" said Windflower. "So, what did you tell him?"

"That the Royal Canadian Mounted Police is engaged in a confidential yet thorough investigation into the death of Reverend Prowse, as requested by his boss," said Quigley. "You are, right?"

"I am," said Windflower. "The search of the manse turned up little for our case. But we did find Alison Morecombe's service weapon there."

"How did that get there?" asked Quigley.

"That we don't know," said Windflower. "But we do know that Frankford's husband and Jerome Morecombe have a connection. And that they had some form of disagreement. Enough to result in assault charges against Charles Frankford."

"Are you talking to him?" asked Quigley.

"Once we find him," said Windflower. "Smithson is checking flights out of the province. But I will be talking to his spouse today. That should be interesting."

"Indeed," said Quigley. "You and Sheila talk about moving to Marystown on the way home?"

"Not really," said Windflower. "But we will, and I will get back to you soonish."

"That's good, because I got asked about you on my call with HQ this morning. They even wanted to know if you could come over early for a transition period before I leave," said Quigley.

"Patience, my friend. 'To climb steep hills requires a slow pace at first,'" said Windflower.

"'Time travels at different speeds for different people,'" Quigley responded. "Anyway, I have to go. 'Parting is such sweet sorrow.'"

THIRTY

Windflower was trying to think up another quick response, but Quigley was gone. When he looked up, there was Smithson again.

"Are you stalking me?" asked Windflower.

"No, Sergeant. I have the information you were looking for," said Smithson, holding a piece of paper in his hand.

"Go ahead," said Windflower.

"Charles Frankford on a one-way ticket to Ottawa on Monday night," said Smithson. "Business class."

"Can you find out if he's staying at a hotel in Ottawa?" asked Windflower.

"It'll take a little while, but yes, I can do that," said Smithson.

Smithson left to do his search, and Betsy came in to tell him that his appointment with Reverend Frankford would be at eleven thirty. Time for a little break, thought Windflower, and maybe a chat with Herb Stoodley.

He drove to the Mug-Up, and even better, Herb was just returning from a supply run at the supermarket. He unloaded his goods while Windflower had a coffee and then came to talk with him.

"Do you mind if we go for a little walk?" asked Windflower. "I love the café, but there's not much privacy."

"Sure," said Herb. "Let me tell Moira that I'll be back in a while."

Herb Stoodley and Windflower walked along the wharf and then back around to the other side where the fish plant was located. Everybody inside there was at work, and the few boats that were tied up to the pier were empty. The two men found a quiet place near the end and sat on the wooden bollards on the fish plant wharf.

"It must be serious," said Herb. "Everything okay at home?"

"It's not that," said Windflower. "Everything is near perfect at home. It's about work."

"Work's not everything," said Herb.

"Yes," said Windflower. "But 'he that is without money, means and content is without three good friends.'"

"True. Although a wise woman once said not to make money your only ambition. 'Don't make money your goal. Instead pursue the things you love doing and then do them so well that people can't take their eyes off of you.'"

"Marilyn Monroe?" asked Windflower.

"Maya Angelou," said Stoodley. "So, tell Uncle Herb what's going on. Trouble at work?"

"Not really at work," said Windflower. "More about where I will work, and maybe what I'm going to do."

"I take it Ron Quigley might be finally moving on," said Stoodley. "Well, you are his most likely successor. If you want it. Do you?"

"Probably not," said Windflower. "I don't think either of us really wants to move to Marystown. And being in St. John's has convinced me that I'm really not a desk guy. I need to be more on the go."

"And if you turn down the inspector job, they will relocate you?" asked Herb. "You've been here before and decided to turn it down. What's new now?"

"The pandemic has made everyone slow down and think about their lives. And some things just aren't as important to me anymore," said Windflower.

"Like being a police officer?" asked Herb.

"That's all I've done. My whole adult life," said Windflower.

"So what is really important to you? Right now, today?" asked Herb.

"Sheila, Stella and Amelia Louise," said Windflower. "And Lady, and I guess Molly the cat."

"They will always be with you, one way or another," said Herb. "But there's something deeper in there, Winston. You are more than an RCMP officer, more than a husband, more than a parent. You have gifts to offer the world."

"It's sometimes hard to see any of that," said Windflower. "All my time is already carved up into the roles that I have chosen. I don't want to give any of them up. But I need a little more room, a little more time, just to breathe."

"What you experience you become," said Herb.

"That's Richard Wagamese," said Windflower.

"I have been reading the book you gave me," said Herb. "You should read it some time. He is very wise."

"Thank you, Herb. So are you," said Windflower. "We better be getting back."

The two men walked along the wharf and back to the Mug-Up.

"I have something for you," said Herb. He went to his van and came back with a CD. "Here you go."

Windflower looked at the cover. He read the title out loud. *"Romance: The Piano Music of Clara Schumann.* Isata Kanneh-Mason. Interesting."

"I thought you might enjoy something smoother yet complex," said Herb. "Clara Schumann was a great composer and concert pianist. Her father, Friedrich Wieck, taught her to compose, and she wrote her most famous work, Piano Concerto in A Minor, at the age of fourteen. This album came out in 2019, the two hundredth anniversary of her birth. I think you'll enjoy it."

"Thank you, Herb," said Windflower. "I will definitely give it a listen." He waved goodbye to Herb and was getting into his car when he heard a familiar voice calling out to him.

"How's she going b'y?" yelled Doctor Sanjay.

Windflower walked to meet his friend and went to shake his hand. Then he remembered, we don't do that anymore, and it became an awkward wave. Sanjay didn't seem to mind.

"Okay, I've given you a few days to think about my offer. How about Friday night?" said Sanjay.

Windflower laughed. "It is a very kind offer, but I just got back, and I have my family responsibilities."

"Bring them, too," said Sanjay. "We don't have to do a big dinner. Come over after you have your supper, and we'll have snacks and dessert for the girls. Repa would love to have the company. I'm begging you. My Old Pulteney is begging you."

Windflower laughed again. "I will talk to Sheila. But no promises."

"Thank you, my friend," said Sanjay. "Repa will be so pleased. Don't worry. You will find the time. As Tagore would say. "'The butterfly counts not months but moments and has time enough.'"

Windflower smiled at Sanjay, got in his car and drove directly to the minister's house.

THIRTY-ONE

Reverend Elizabeth Frankford was cleaning up her garden at the front of her house when Windflower pulled up in the driveway.

"You are punctual, Sergeant," said the minister, who was wearing a large, wide-brimmed hat with tufts of brownish red hair poking out. "I was hoping you'd be late so that I could clean this up. Come inside and I'll get us a cold drink."

Windflower followed her into the house and into the kitchen, which had a glorious view of the ocean and Saint-Pierre in the distance.

"Great view," said Windflower as he accepted a glass of lemonade.

"Something else to miss," said Frankford. "I'm being transferred, you know."

"I did know that," said Windflower. "I spoke with Reverend Woods. I take it that it's not your choice."

"Our choices are always less than we believe," said the minister. "I guess I could refuse, but then I would have to leave this place anyway."

Windflower almost started talking about his own situation, which surprisingly was not much different, but decided not to.

He came to investigate, not commiserate. Besides, he wasn't sure yet about her involvement in Prowse's death. He pulled out his pen and notebook.

"Where were you on the night that Reverend Prowse died?" he asked.

"You don't waste time, do you, Sergeant?" said Frankford. "I was at a meeting with the Christmas bazaar committee. We had cake and tea after the meeting. Then I went to visit a friend in Fortune. I got a call from Gregory Dollimont and came right over. By that time, everyone but him had left."

Windflower looked carefully at Elizabeth Frankford as she was speaking. He was looking for signs of anxiety or nervousness, but she showed none of that. It didn't mean she wasn't lying, though. Just that she was comfortable with telling this part of her story. He also couldn't help but notice that since she'd taken off her hat and let her long red hair down, and that she was quite attractive, especially when she smiled. Which she was doing right now at Windflower.

He tried not to be distracted. "Did you ask Dollimont to keep people out of the manse after Reverend Prowse died?"

"Gregory Dollimont hardly spoke to me the whole time I was here," said Frankford. "I don't even remember what he said that night, but I most certainly did not give him any direction. Whatever he did, it was on his own, or from Reverend Woods."

"Was Reverend Prowse on any medication that you know of?" asked Windflower.

"No," said Frankford. "He was as healthy a man for his age that I've seen, and he didn't like medications or pills. Wouldn't even take an Aspirin for a headache. What's this about, Sergeant?"

"Reverend Prowse had his meals prepared here, didn't he?" asked Windflower, ignoring her question. "Who made them and delivered them next door?"

"My housekeeper, Jane Edwards," said Frankford, growing more agitated. "Do you think he was poisoned somehow? I ate the same food as Bob Prowse. What's going on?"

"We don't know yet," said Windflower. "But according to the toxicology reports, Reverend Prowse died from an insulin overdose."

Elizabeth Frankford's face turned white, and she sat down in a chair. This was a surprise and a great shock to her, or she was a great actor, thought Windflower. He pressed forward.

"Do you know anything about this?" When Frankford shook her head, he continued. "Do you know anyone who would have liked to harm Reverend Prowse?"

"No, no," said Frankford. "He was the kindest, gentlest man I know." She started to cry. Windflower wanted to console her, but that was not his job today. In fact, he was likely about to make the situation worse.

"I need to talk to you about something else this morning," he said, as gently as he could.

When she looked up, he paused and then said, "It's about your husband."

Almost instantly, the tears dried up and the colour came back into Elizabeth Frankford's face. "Charles?" she asked. "He couldn't have had anything to do with this. He wasn't even here."

"It's not about Reverend Prowse," said Windflower.

Now the woman started glowing red. "What kind of trouble is he in now? I'm not responsible for him. He only comes back around here when he wants to hide out for a while. So, tell me, Sergeant, what's the great Charles Morris Frankford done now?"

"When was he last here?" asked Windflower.

"Maybe a week ago," said Frankford. "He still has stuff here and shows up every so often. I let him because it's easier to keep up appearances. But you don't really care about that, do you?"

Windflower didn't, but he also couldn't say that, at least not yet. "Do you know Jerome Morecombe?"

"I know of him," said Frankford. "Charles got himself into a scrape with him when they were both at the university. But I never got into any of that with Charles. We have very separate lives, Sergeant."

"Do you know where he is now?" asked Windflower.

"I suspect he's at his cozy little digs in St. John's that the university still provides for him as Dean Emeritus or whatever they call him now," said Frankford. "But I'm guessing you knew about that, and he's not there. Correct?"

"He's not in St. John's," said Windflower. "He may be in Ottawa. Do you know who he might be in contact with there?"

"He has a brother who lives near Ottawa. Carp, I think. Do you want his number? I might have it," said Frankford. She went off to look for the number, and Windflower took a look around her house. He'd never been in here before. It was tastefully decorated, at least to his eye. Some nice old Newfoundland antique pieces in the living room and a beautiful oak-lined den with books from floor to ceiling.

"I will miss this place," said Frankford as she came out of her office with a paper that she handed to Windflower. "It's beautiful, isn't it?"

"It is," said Windflower. He put the paper in his notebook and put it in his pocket. "Thank you for your time. I only have one more question for you today. Did your husband have a gun?"

"Not that I'm aware of," said Frankford. "But then again, there's lots I don't know about Charles. He did talk one time about people being after him and that he needed protection. But I just thought he was being paranoid.

Who would care about what they're doing at a lab in Memorial University?"

"Thank you again for your time," said Windflower.

He drove by his house on the way back to work, hoping to say hello to Sheila and to catch Uncle Frank before he got out for the day. Sheila's car was gone, but he was in luck when he went inside; Uncle Frank was there. And he was taking the rest of the chicken pot pie out of the oven.

"Winston, nice to see you," said his uncle. "I was going to call you right after my lunch. Sheila's just gone to the supermarket. She said she'd only be a minute." His uncle sliced a big chunk off the pie and looked at Windflower. "You want the rest?" he asked, pointing to the smaller portion that was left on the pie plate.

"Don't mind if I do," said Windflower, put the pie on the plate and sat at the kitchen table with his uncle. The pie was too hot to eat yet, so Windflower started talking.

"I had a weird experience," he started. "Actually, two experiences. I had a dream, and while it was pleasant, nothing really happened. I mean, I flew for a while and then dropped, waking before I hit the ground. But no visitors or allies. Then, when I used the pipe this morning, nothing happened then, either."

"Nothing?" asked Uncle Frank, blowing on his pie to cool it and taking small bites to test it out.

"Well, I felt good, had a sense of peace and calm," said Windflower. "But no visions or anything."

"I think that's quite a lot," said his uncle, finally laying down his fork to wait for his pie to be ready to eat. "Sometimes the dreamworld lets us relax, takes us away from the cares of this world. When that happens, enjoy it."

"Okay," said Windflower. "But I was afraid that I was losing my connection. That I would be alone, I guess."

"We are never really alone," said Uncle Frank, digging into his pie. "Maybe Creator was giving you some time to sort things out on your own, without any other voices or distractions. Maybe she trusts you to make the right decision. The question is, do you trust yourself?"

That question hung in the air for a minute as Windflower and Uncle Frank finished off their chicken pot pie. The silence was broken by the door opening and the rush of little feet into the kitchen.

THIRTY-TWO

Windflower was a bit surprised when Amelia Louise ran straight to Uncle Frank and nearly jumped into his arms. But his disappointment was eased considerably when she quickly left his uncle and came to give him a great hug.

"Thank you, sweetie," said Windflower.

"Mila got necklace," she said proudly, moving as close as she could to show her dad her latest treasure.

"It's beautiful," said Windflower.

"We stopped at Riffs on the way back," said Sheila. "Always something interesting there for her for a couple of dollars. I see you finished off the pie."

"Just as good the second time around," said Windflower.

"I missed the first but totally enjoyed the second," said Uncle Frank. "Anyway, I gotta go. Richard Tizzard is taking me out on his boat today. Might be the last nice day for a while. He says we're coming into RDF season again. Rain, drizzle and fog."

Sheila finished putting away her groceries, and Windflower carried Amelia Louise out to say goodbye to Uncle Frank.

His uncle came and gave her a kiss on the cheek. "All of this doesn't mean you should stop looking for allies and asking for help," he said to Windflower. "The challenge of life is to remain open and teachable. Even for an old guy like me."

Windflower and Amelia Louise went back inside to see Sheila. "I saw Doc Sanjay today," he said.

"How is he?" asked Sheila.

"He looks great," said Windflower. "He invited us over for snacks and dessert on Friday night."

"And to sample his new Scotch, no doubt?" said Sheila.

"There may be a wee dram," said Windflower. "I think it'll be fun. Do you want to go see Doc and Repa?" he asked Amelia Louise.

"Doc, Doc, Doc," said Amelia Louise.

"Even recruiting the children against me," said Sheila with a sigh. "Sure, why not? We haven't seen them in forever. I'll call Repa."

"Perfect," said Windflower. "Now, I have to get back to work." He handed his daughter to Sheila and drove back to the office. Smithson's cruiser was parked out front.

"I'm just leaving," said Smithson. "But I wanted to let you know that Charles Frankford checked into the Hilton at the airport in Ottawa."

"Great," said Windflower.

"But he's checked out now," said Smithson.

"He has a brother in the area. Can you contact him and see if he knows where Frankford might be?" Windflower pulled out his notebook and gave Smithson the number. "Then you can go home."

After Smithson left, Windflower went through the notes from his meeting with Elizabeth Frankford. If she was to be believed, and Windflower didn't know that yet, it didn't appear that she was involved in whatever happened to the late Reverend Prowse. But she did raise a couple of red flags for the RCMP officer. High on that list was Gregory Dollimont and the role he played in securing, and perhaps tampering with, the scene of the crime.

The other thing that was beginning to more than bother him was the casual way that Elijah Woods was influencing, maybe even manipulating the whole process. What was his stake in all this? Someone wanted Bob Prowse out of the way, and now Elizabeth Frankford was being moved aside as well. That would leave the Grand Bank position wide open, but surely they, if it was a they, didn't have to kill an old, well-liked minister to do that.

She also mentioned the name of the housekeeper, Jane Edwards. Probably need to interview her, too. That was as far as he got with his review before Smithson came back in.

"It looks like he may be at his brother's," said Smithson. "Some kid, a teenager I think, answered and said his uncle wasn't there right now. He didn't know where he was. I didn't leave a message. Hopefully, the kid won't tell anybody we called."

"Do you have an address, or can you get it from the phone?" asked Windflower.

Smithson picked up his phone and after a few seconds replied, "It's on Craig Side Road in Carp. Near the Diefenbunker."

"What's the Diefenbunker?" asked Windflower.

"It's the coolest place ever," said Smithson. "I can't believe you've never been. We went on a school trip when we visited Ottawa, and I've been back twice since."

"Is it a museum or something?" asked Windflower.

"It's an underground bunker that was created as a nuclear bomb shelter where the federal government could operate in the event of a nuclear war. It was built during Prime Minister John Diefenbaker's term, and that's how it got its name. It has everything from communications equipment to a cafeteria and giant kitchen to a clinic and dentist's office. All totally preserved from the late 1950s," said Smithson.

This was the most excited he'd seen Smithson in a while. Windflower would have liked to encourage him to continue, but he'd seen Smithson go on and on before. He didn't have that kind of time.

"Carp is outside of Ottawa, right? Is it part of the city?" asked Windflower.

Smithson looked disappointed to not be able to talk more about the Diefenbunker but checked his phone. "Yes, it was part of the big amalgamation. Why?"

"That means it's covered by the Ottawa Police and not a local service or the Ontario Provincial Police," said Windflower.

"To track Frankford down," said Smithson. "Gotcha. Is there anything else?"

"No, thank you, Constable," said Windflower. "You are free to go."

After Smithson left, Windflower went back to his notes from the meeting this morning. He came across the housekeeper's name again: Jane Edwards. Betsy came in to drop off some mail and papers.

"Betsy, do you know Jane Edwards?"

"The housekeeper at the minister's house?" asked Betsy. Windflower nodded. "I know her a little. She's not from here. She's from Lawn. That's a Catholic community. But Jane is not. Her family is solidly United, and before that Methodist."

"How did she get the job as housekeeper?" Windflower asked.

"Well, Sergeant, I'm not much for gossip, as you know, but after old Marilyn Porter got let go, Jane Edwards just kind of turned up," said Betsy. "Some says that Marystown was behind it."

"Why was the old housekeeper let go?"

"They tried to blame the new minister," said Betsy. "But I know Marilyn well, and she told me that it wasn't her. She thinks that Gregory Dollimont was involved."

"Thanks, Betsy," said Windflower. Another reason to talk to Jane Edwards, he thought. He called Eddie Tizzard.

"Hey, boss, what's up?" asked Tizzard. "I'm just out at the construction site near the Garnish turnoff, helping with traffic control."

"When you come back, can you go and see Jane Edwards, the housekeeper at Reverend Frankford's?" asked Windflower. "I didn't see any reference to her being interviewed. Was she?"

"I don't think so," said Tizzard. "Anything particular I should ask about?"

"See if Reverend Prowse had any specific dietary requests and if she knew if he took any medication with his meals," said Windflower. "Have her run through what she did on the day he died, when she was over there, and when she last saw him."

"Will do," said Tizzard. "I'll get right on it after my midafternoon break at the Mug-Up, if that's okay with you."

"And a snack, too?" asked Windflower.

"Absolutely," said Tizzard. "Do you want me to bring you back a cupcake?"

"No, I'm good," said Windflower. "Let me know what you find out."

Windflower hung up with Tizzard and called Terry Robbins in St. John's. Muriel Sparkes picked up his line.

"Sergeant Windflower, so nice to hear your voice. We miss you already," said Muriel. "We would have had a party for you at the Legion if we knew you were going. But Betsy tells me you're happy to be home."

"I am happy to be in Grand Bank," said Windflower.

"And thank you for agreeing to send back my car," said Muriel. "You know what they're like at Headquarters about things like that. I'll make sure Sergeant Robbins calls you back as soon as he returns."

"Thank you, Muriel," said Windflower, happy that 'her' car was on the way back to St. John's.

THIRTY-THREE

He spent an hour processing the paper in his in-basket and filling out reports that Betsy had left him before leaving for the day. When he opened the front door to go to his car, a cool blast hit him, and fog was everywhere. That didn't take long, thought Windflower. The first few big, fat raindrops hit his windshield just before he reached his driveway.

Inside, Stella and Amelia Louise and Lady all seemed to be struggling over the same stuffed toy, and Sheila was trying to pull them apart, with little evidence of success. She looked at Windflower with pleading eyes. His response was to jump into the pile and join the game. Soon, everyone was rolling on the floor and first Stella, then Amelia Louise, and then both adults started laughing. Nobody knew what they were laughing about, but it was great fun.

Windflower got changed and was about to sit on the couch when Sheila again pleaded with him, this time to take Lady out for a walk. The girls thought this was a perfect idea and ran to get their boots and asked for their raincoats.

"Might as well go out," said Windflower. "Uncle Frank said this will be with us for a while."

Windflower got Lady's leash and led his little parade out into the fog and rain. The rain was fairly light, and it wasn't too cold yet. But it was still chilly enough to make the walk a short one, and besides, there weren't enough puddles to jump in yet. That was according to Stella, a sentiment that her sister heartily endorsed.

When they got back, Sheila had taken some pork chops out of the freezer. "I can thaw them in the microwave, if you'll grill them," she said.

"Perfect," said Windflower. He examined the pork chops. They were roughly an inch thick, ideal for the barbeque. When they were thawed, he rubbed olive oil on both sides of the chops and put them in a metal bowl. He added some black and cayenne pepper, sea salt and a heavy dash of his smoked paprika and rubbed the mixture all over the meat.

"This will only take about twenty minutes," he said to Sheila as he went to light the barbeque. When he came back in, Sheila was getting vegetables together and the fixings for a salad. The rain was coming down harder when he went back out to put the pork chops on, the grill sizzling and spitting at the same time. He seared the chops on each side for a couple of minutes and then reduced the heat.

He put the pork chops on the upper rack of the barbeque and closed the grill. He turned them once and ten minutes later brought the tray of cooked chops into the kitchen. Sheila and the girls had set the table, and Windflower cut up one of the pork chops for the girls while Sheila laid on the vegetables. Once they were served, he sat with Sheila to enjoy their supper.

"These are gorgeous," said Sheila. "Good job, Sergeant."

"Thank you," said Windflower. "I'm assuming they're from Warrens. They certainly have the best meat in Grand Bank."

After supper, Sheila suggested a board game and got out their Snakes and Ladders. Amelia Louise could play with a lot of help from her dad, who despite getting great rolls kept sliding back down again.

"Uh-oh," said Amelia Louise as he had to start over again. Stella didn't say anything but steadily climbed to the top and won the first and second games. Sheila won the third, and despite protests, she declared game time over. Windflower carried the girls upstairs and started their baths while they ran around his bedroom, naked and laughing. He managed to grab them one at a time and handed them to Sheila in the bathroom.

They were still laughing in the bath when Windflower's cell phone rang. He walked downstairs to take the call. It was Terry Robbins.

"Terry, thanks for calling me back," said Windflower.

"It's not too late, is it?" asked Robbins. "We had a training session on the new postpandemic protocols. It was brutal and long."

"No, it's good," said Windflower. "I have another favour, although this is directly related to Morecombe's gun. I need help in finding Charles Frankford."

"Is he in St. John's?" asked Robbins.

"He was," said Windflower. "But he's in Ottawa now, actually in Carp, just outside of town."

"The place where the Diefenbunker is?" asked Robbins.

"Does everybody but me know about that place?" asked Windflower.

"You don't know about the Diefenbunker?"

"Never mind," said Windflower. "I have an address for Frankford's brother. We're pretty sure he's staying there."

"So, what do you want me to do?"

"Can you talk to your brother, Scott?" said Windflower. "Can we get the Ottawa Police Service to pick up Charles Frankford? I can get a formal request from the RNC, if you need it."

"Charges?" asked Robbins.

"Not yet," said Windflower. "We do want to know how his prints got on Morecombe's gun and where he was on the night of the break-in and murder. That's enough to pick him up."

"I can do that," said Robbins. "I'll make the request from here and let you know what Terry says. If they need paperwork, I'll come back to you. Okay?"

"Thanks," said Windflower. "But if you need more, go to Langmead and let them do it. I'll give him a call to let him know."

After hanging up with Robbins, Windflower called Langmead and left him a message with the news that they might have found Charles Frankford in Ottawa. And that they were trying to get Ottawa police to pick him up. He hung up and started to walk upstairs. His phone pinged. It was Langmead replying with a happy face. Windflower smiled and went to help Sheila get the girls organized and into bed.

Both Sheila and Windflower were tired from the day and decided to turn in early. He took Lady for a quick and very wet spin around the block, dried her off and headed up to bed himself. Sheila already had the lights off, and he could hear her gentle nighttime breathing. He crawled in beside her and let that lull him to sleep.

Sometime during the night, he woke up in another dream.

This time he was flying again, and when he tried to dip a little below the clouds, he could see that he was above Grand Bank. He picked out some of the landmarks like the fish plant and the wharf area with the blinking red light on the lighthouse at the entrance to the harbour. He kept going down and landed on the beach, near the place where he'd sat before. He was enjoying the peacefulness of the scene within his dream when he heard what he first thought was a dog barking.

But when he listened more closely, he realized that it wasn't a dog; it was a seal. A large female seal, and she came out of the water to sit on a rock in the water near the shoreline. Then the seal spoke to him. It sounded a bit garbled, almost like an echo, and Windflower strained to hear what the animal was trying to say.

"What are you saying?" asked Windflower.

"Oh sorry," said the seal. "I was using my underwater voice. You can only understand human. Pity."

"It's all I got," said Windflower. Then, realizing that his time here might be brief, he decided to ask some questions. "Why are you here, and do you have any messages for me?"

"You don't waste time, do you?" barked the seal. "You know the drill. Why are you here? If you can answer that, we'll see."

Windflower thought fast. "I'm here because I need help from my allies."

"Not bad," said the seal. "A little humility doesn't hurt that much, does it?"

Great, thought Windflower. A sarcastic seal.

"I heard that," said the seal. "You forget that we can read your minds over here. You have no secrets. That's what makes it so much fun." And with that, the seal started to laugh, but it still sounded like barking, only much louder and more irritating.

"Okay, okay, I get it," said Windflower. "What are you supposed to tell me?"

"Believe it or not, I'm the best thing that ever happened to you," said the seal. "I bring you good news. My advice is very simple. Go with the flow." The seal stopped talking, turned over and started floating on her back. "Your road ahead looks unclear and uncertain. But I can see that it's almost smooth swimming once you get out of the way."

"How do I do that?" asked Windflower.

"Your expectations are too high. Simply do your best and let go of the outcome. It may turn out better than you dreamed," said the seal. Then she flipped over and dove. All Windflower saw was her tail and a giant splash that washed over him. When he woke, the seal was gone and he had the distinct taste of salt water in his mouth. That couldn't be, he thought. Then again, who knows?

He went to the bathroom and rinsed his mouth. He thought about his dream until his head started to hurt a little. Then he took the seal's advice and let it all go. When he did, he drifted back to sleep and didn't stir again until the morning.

THIRTY-FOUR

Windflower tried to allow himself to wake slowly, and he felt Sheila trying to do the same thing. That didn't last long. Two girls burst into their room a little while after he first woke with blankets draped over their shoulders and shouting something quite unintelligible but very loud. When he opened his eyes, he saw Stella standing there with her toy light sabre that she'd gotten for Christmas, pointing it at him. Amelia Louise didn't have a weapon, but she was brandishing a long, clothes-less doll that she pointed at him as well.

"You're our prissner," said Amelia Louise.

"Come with us," said Stella.

Windflower didn't feel like he had much of an option, so he wearily got out of bed and followed Stella as commanded. Amelia Louise kept her doll stuck in the small of his back in case he changed his mind. He could hear Sheila laughing behind him, but he kept a straight face and marched on into Amelia Louise's bedroom. There, Stella ordered him to the ground and the two girls stretched their blankets over his head and Amelia Louise's bed.

"Stay still, prissner," hissed Amelia Louise when Windflower started to move around.

Luckily, Sheila came to rescue him from his captors

shortly afterward, and he was able to go downstairs to put the coffee on. The girls followed him, intent on recapturing him, but they'd lost their blankets and interest in their game once he offered them a banana and some juice. He looked out the window, or tried to look out the window, but the fog had settled down on Grand Bank like an impenetrable cover. Nothing could get in and very little could get out, except for Lady, who had duties to perform in the backyard.

Sheila made oatmeal, and Windflower enjoyed the early morning familial scene while it lasted. He cleaned up while Sheila got Stella ready for school. Amelia Louise went with them when Sheila asked her to pick out her clothes for daycare that afternoon.

Windflower took advantage of this lull in the action to go outside and smudge.

At least the rain had stopped, he thought as Lady followed him back out. He lit his smudge mixture and watched as it hung in the damp air. No wind either, he thought. That was strange. There was almost always a wind around Grand Bank, usually from the cool Labrador current that stopped the jetstream in its tracks. But sometimes a mild breeze snuck through from the west that gave them those few muggy days each summer.

He brought some of the smoke back towards him and moved it all over his body, from his head to his toes. Then he settled in for a few moments of reflection to see if there was anything inside of him that wanted to come out. Today, there was. He could feel a jumble of emotions that he recognized as unfounded fears or anxiety. He let them sit there for a minute, and then as he had learned, he let them go. That felt nice, he thought, almost like a relief. He could also feel other things rising up in him, things that felt much better. The strongest one was a feeling that no matter what, he was going to be okay. He breathed in to hold on to that for as long as he could. And then he let go of that, too. He dumped the ashes from his smudge onto the ground and thanked Mother Earth for all his blessings. He said his usual prayers of gratitude and went back in to join his family.

Stella was all ready for school. Amelia Louise was all ready, too, even though she wasn't leaving until after lunch.

"She will likely change a couple of times before we go," said Sheila as she walked out to meet the school bus with Stella.

Amelia Louise stood in the window and watched her sister leave. "Mila go school," she said.

"Soon," said Windflower. "Soon." He waited until Sheila came back and then went upstairs to change for work. When he came down, Sheila and Amelia Louise were in the kitchen.

"Mila making cookies," she said proudly to her dad.

"Clearly, she's forgotten about the other thing," said Windflower as he kissed them both on his way out.

"Short-term memory," said Sheila. "Right now, it works in our favour. Have a great day."

"Enjoy your afternoon," he said. He drove through the fog and down towards the office. As he was coming into the parking lot, Smithson was pulling out with his lights and siren on. Windflower turned and followed him.

Smithson got to the highway and turned left, racing up the highway. Windflower sped up and followed close behind. Not far along the road, he saw the reason for the haste. The paramedics were already on the scene with their lights flashing. Smithson parked across the highway on the far side and jumped out. Windflower was close behind and did the same on the near side, both of them leaving their lights flashing. That would let traffic see them in the fog as they approached.

There was a car on its back in the ditch at the side of the road, and the paramedics were peering inside. Smithson ran towards them and Windflower followed.

"Looks like two people," said one of them to Smithson. "Not moving."

Windflower overheard that comment as he looked in the car. There were two people. He couldn't really see the driver, but the passenger looked familiar. He went closer, and even though her face was squished up against the exploded air bag, he could see it was Elizabeth Frankford.

"Can you get them out?" he asked the paramedics.

"Sorry, Sergeant," said one of them. "We can't seem to get the doors open."

As they were speaking, Martin Hodder showed up in the fire chief's vehicle. "The truck is on the way," he said, quickly inspecting the scene. "No gas leaking, that's a good thing. We've got the jaws of life coming."

A minute later, although it seemed like forever, the Grand Bank Volunteer Fire Department truck lumbered over the horizon, and when it arrived, Chief Hodder barked out orders. Soon, one of the firefighters was applying a battery-operated apparatus that opened the passenger side of the vehicle, almost like a can opener. The paramedics moved Elizabeth Frankford out as gently as possible and laid her on a stretcher on the ground. They examined her while the firefighter opened the driver's side door.

"She's alive, but her pulse is weak," said the lead paramedic.

The paramedics ran around to the other side and extricated the driver. They laid him on the ground on another stretcher. It was a man, and his face was mashed-up and bloody. It was hard to recognize him, but Smithson spoke up.

"I think that's Gregory Dollimont," said Smithson.

"I can't get a pulse," yelled the paramedic who was examining him. "Let's get him in the wagon, and I'll try CPR." They quickly loaded Dollimont's lifeless body onto a gurney as another ambulance arrived. The new crew of paramedics got Elizabeth Frankford into their vehicle. Soon all you could hear was the sound of sirens heading back towards the clinic in Grand Bank.

Windflower and Smithson took another look around the car. It was completely smashed in front, and they both knew what that meant. The large pool of blood on the highway confirmed it.

"It looks like the moose was injured," said Windflower. "And judging by the woods over there, they may not be too far away." He pointed to an area that had recently been trampled. "I'll secure the scene and call Betsy."

Smithson nodded and went to the back of his cruiser. He came back with a rifle and walked into the wooded area. Windflower called Betsy and got her to organize the highways people and a tow truck. He also asked her to ask Tizzard to come in early to help out. She told him he was already there, waiting for instructions. Bad news travels fast, thought Windflower.

"Ask him to come over right away," said Windflower.

THIRTY-FIVE

Windflower watched as Hodder and the volunteer firefighters sprayed a layer of fire-retardant foam around the overturned car. "Just in case," said Chief Hodder as he came over to Windflower.

The two men stood together silently in the fog as the firefighters packed up their truck and left the scene. A few moments later, they heard a single shot. Not long after, Smithson came out of the woods.

"She was beat up pretty good. I had to put her out of her misery," he said.

Windflower nodded. "Can you call Wildlife and get them to dispose of the body? Then start securing the scene. Highways and a tow truck are coming, and you can direct them when they get here. Tizzard is on his way, too. Can you write up the initial accident report, too?"

"That should be fairly easy," said Smithson.

"Get lots of pictures," said Windflower. "And when they get the car back to our yard, make sure to check it out."

Windflower followed Hodder to his vehicle. "People never seem to learn," said Hodder. "Even with the reduced speed limits you put in, they think they're invincible."

"Not to the moose," said Windflower. "How many accidents is that this year?"

"Seven, by my count. From here to Garnish alone," said Hodder. "So far, nobody's been killed. But that might change, by the looks of it."

"We'll find out soon enough," said Windflower. "I'm heading over to the clinic. How's Brittney doing?"

"She's really doing great," said Hodder. "We are so grateful to you and Constable Foote for your help with that. Brittney is, too. She's volunteered to do an awareness session down here, in Marystown."

"That is great," said Windflower. "I'm still hoping to get back to St. John's to do one with the RNC, maybe later in the fall."

"Okay, talk soon," said Hodder.

Windflower made a mental note to call Anne Marie Foote and waved goodbye to Smithson, who was standing next to his cruiser at the far end of the scene. He turned his car around and headed for the Grand Bank clinic. He passed Tizzard racing towards the scene and flashed his lights at him. Minutes after, he parked in the clinic parking lot.

Windflower put on his mask and half-nodded good morning to everyone as he raced to the triage area in emergency. As he was coming in, he saw a familiar face taking off her gloves and coming out of the emergency treatment area. Doctor Danette White had treated Windflower last year when he'd had an accident while inspecting an abandoned mine site. She came towards him.

"Good morning, Sergeant, how are you?" said Doctor White.

"Good morning, Doctor. I am well, and you?" replied Windflower.

"I'm guessing you're here about our recently arrived patients," she said. "I'm afraid the man was pronounced dead shortly after arrival. Do you know him?"

"Gregory Dollimont," said Windflower. "He works
with Reverend Elijah Woods in Marystown.
We can make that call, if you'd like."

"That would be good," said Doctor White. "The woman, Elizabeth Frankford, is still being examined. We've put her in an induced coma. Doctor Sceviour is with her now. She may or may not have something for you, if you want to wait around."

Windflower knew that with many accident victims it could take some time to reveal the extent of their injuries. That was if they survived. He decided not to wait.

"Can someone call the office if there's any developments?" he asked.

"We can do that. I'll put a note on her chart when I go back in," said the doctor.

"What do you think?" he asked before he left.

"It's always hard to tell until we know the extent of brain damage and internal injuries. We'll know more when the swelling goes down," said Doctor White.

Windflower left the emergency area and walked back to his car. He called Betsy.

"Oh my God," said Betsy when she heard the news about the accident. "That poor woman."

Windflower thought it was interesting that Betsy didn't have such a strong reaction to the sudden death of Gregory Dollimont. But maybe not surprising, he thought. He gave instructions to Betsy to call Elijah Woods in Marystown and for wording for a news release about the accident. They wouldn't give out the names yet, but it would be big news that a car-moose accident had claimed another life.

After hanging up with Betsy, he drove back towards the accident scene, where Smithson and Tizzard had the situation well in hand. The tow truck was just arriving, and he left them to supervise the removal of the vehicle and to stay and ensure that the highways crew cleaned up the area. He was pulling away when he saw the Wildlife truck coming from Marystown to look after the remains of the dead moose.

That's when it hit him that there were three victims this morning: Elizabeth Frankford, Gregory Dollimont, and the dead moose. Although the animal wasn't from his human family, he did believe that all animals were related and that they deserved respect and honour, even if we killed and ate some of them. And the moose had long been a friend and an ally of him and his people back home in Pink Lake.

He was thinking about this as he was driving back to work when his car, almost on its own, turned down the road to the L'Anse au Loup T. It was too damp and foggy to go for any kind of walk, and you couldn't really see anything anyway, but Windflower could feel the pull of the ocean and its calming influence come over him. He was just sitting there when he remembered the CD that Herb Stoodley had given him. He pulled it out of the glove compartment and put it into the player.

The music wafted over him with the piano and the violins accompanied by the music of the sea that was so close at hand. He listened to the first piece, the famous Clara Schumann Piano Concerto, and felt like he was being drawn back to the romantic era of the nineteenth century. It both calmed and relaxed him. As much as he would have liked to listen to the rest, he didn't have that kind of time today. He put the CD away and remembered why he'd stopped here in the first place.

He closed his eyes and prayed. First, for the well-being of Elizabeth Frankford. Not that she'd live or even recover. That was not up to him. He prayed that she would have the strength to go through whatever lay ahead of her. He also prayed for Gregory Dollimont, as much as he didn't like him. It wasn't his job to judge him, either. Finally, he prayed for the spirit of the moose.

In his culture, the moose was a symbol of endurance and survival, and to many families in his community, it was the main source of meat. It was also a close relative of Windflower's closest animal ally, the deer, so he felt the loss of the moose this morning as a loss in his own family. He prayed for the spirit of the moose and that it be given smooth passage to its next destination. When he was finished, he laid down a little tobacco for the moose. And just as he was starting to leave, he went back and did the same for Gregory Dollimont. "Not my place to judge," he muttered to himself. He got back in his car and drove to the detachment.

THIRTY-SIX

When Windflower arrived at the detachment, Betsy told him that the media were already calling. So, too, were Inspector Quigley and Reverend Elijah Woods. He took a quick look at the note Betsy had prepared for the media and initialled it. That would keep them satisfied for now but only increase their appetite for more information later. Serious accidents involving moose were not unusual, but deaths had been reduced somewhat. That had been true in this area ever since Windflower and the RCMP put speed restrictions in high-collision locations along the highway.

He called Ron Quigley.

"I saw the draft statement. I hear it's Gregory Dollimont," said Quigley. "How's Elizabeth Frankford?"

"You seem to know everything already," said Windflower. "We don't know yet on Frankford. But yes, the dead man is Gregory Dollimont."

"I just spoke with Elijah Woods," said Quigley. "He wants things to be handled as delicately as possible. He described Dollimont as a strong supporter of the church."

"What does that even mean?" asked Windflower.

"He asked that the body be turned over to his care as quickly as possible. And that the vehicle be towed directly to a location in Marystown," said Quigley. "I told him we would process the remains as quickly as we could but that there would be examination of the body, as in all motor vehicle fatalities. The car was ours until we inspect it."

"Good," said Windflower. "I'll talk to Doc Sanjay about an examination, and the car is being towed to our yard right now. Did he even ask about Elizabeth Frankford?"

"Not too much," said Quigley. "You find her husband yet?"

"We've got a lead in Ottawa," said Windflower. "I'm trying to get the locals up there to pick him up for us."

"Okay, keep me informed. Thanks," said Quigley.

When Windflower hung up with Quigley, Eddie Tizzard came into his office with a cup of coffee for himself and one for Windflower. He also had a small, round tin that he opened in front of Windflower.

"Can't be hungry," said Tizzard. "Raisin bran muffins. Carrie made them. My dad said if you had trouble going to the bathroom..."

Windflower took a muffin and stopped him. "TMI," he said. "But thanks for the muffin, and pass along my thanks to Carrie, too. How is she, and little Hughie?"

"They are great," said Tizzard, taking a muffin for himself. "If I had known how much fun it was being a dad, I would have done this long ago."

"You're very good at it," said Windflower. "I can tell just by watching you that you love being a father. But there will be some difficult times, especially when they're sick. You feel so helpless."

"I know," said Tizzard. "But I'm okay with that. Both of us are. Anyway, that was quite a crash this morning."

"Yeah," said Windflower. "One dead and another barely hanging on."

"And the poor moose," said Tizzard. "Smithson was a little broke up about having to shoot it."

"I'll talk to him," said Windflower. "Did you get a chance to talk to Jane Edwards?"

"I did," said Tizzard, taking another muffin and offering the tin to Windflower, who declined. "She seemed really anxious. Some women are naturally like that, and lots of people are afraid of the police, but she seemed more worried that whatever she told me would get back to somebody else."

"Who?" asked Windflower.

"Gregory Dollimont," said Tizzard. "She must have stopped me three times to ask me if I was going to tell him what she said."

"What did she say?" asked Windflower.

"Not that much, really," said Tizzard. "She said it was a normal day. She brought Prowse over his supper at five thirty. His usual time. Jiggs Dinner with salt meat, cabbage and pease pudding. Made me hungry just talking about it."

Tizzard went to grab another muffin, but Windflower pulled the tin towards him and snapped on the lid. "Focus," he said.

"She said Prowse was in good spirits, and she wished him a good night," said Tizzard. "That was the last time she saw him. She left shortly afterwards. Beulah would clean his dishes, and she would pick them up in the morning when she brought over breakfast."

"So, what didn't she want you to tell?"

"Maybe that Dollimont might be a diabetic," said Smithson, who came into the office from the backyard, where he had been going through the vehicle from the car crash. He held up a small black case and opened it. "Glucose meter, insulin pen, glucose tablets. Everything a person would need to get them safely back home in case of a diabetic emergency. Found it in the glove compartment."

"How do we know it was his?" asked Windflower.

"I guess we don't for sure," said Smithson. "But why would he have this in his car, if he wasn't?"

"Doc Sanjay should be able to confirm that when he does his examination," said Windflower. "Tizzard, can you call him with this info? Did Jane Edwards say anything else of interest?"

"That she cleaned up the house late that night," said Tizzard. "Dollimont called her and told her to come over. Then he told her to stay quiet about it."

"Did she see anything?" asked Windflower.

Tizzard shook his head. "Not that she would own up to, anyway. But I have a feeling that Dollimont may have gotten rid of any evidence."

"Let's bring her in for another interview," said Windflower. "Now that Dollimont has passed, she may feel freer to talk."

"I'm going home now, if that's okay," said Smithson. "I'll have the report on your desk tomorrow morning."

Windflower handed the muffin tin back to Tizzard. "Go and see if Betsy needs any help."

Tizzard grabbed the tin and left.

"Can you stay for a minute?" he said to Smithson. "Close the door."

Smithson closed the door and sat in front of Windflower.

"That was hard this morning, wasn't it?" asked Windflower.

"It's always hard to see death so up close," said Smithson. "But seeing that animal in distress and having to put her down was awful." He looked like he was going to cry.

"It's okay," said Windflower. "It's okay to not be okay sometimes. Why don't you go home and take a break? Play with the Internet or something. If you want to talk, I'm here."

Smithson blinked and smiled back at Windflower. "Thanks, Sarge. I'll see you tomorrow."

"Put all that stuff in evidence and ask Betsy to come in on your way out," said Windflower. Not long after Smithson left, Betsy came into his office.

"There's two new messages for you, besides the media," she said, waving a stack of yellow slips at him. "Reverend Woods and Scott Robbins from the Ottawa Police Service."

THIRTY-SEVEN

Windflower called Scott Robbins.

"Good morning, Sergeant," said Robbins. "My brother tells me you're back in Grand Bank. Is that good news?"

"It's great news," said Windflower. "Thanks for asking. I hope you have good news for me, too."

"Well, the good news is that we found Charles Frankford. He was at the address in Carp that you provided. He was a little indignant about being taken into custody but came along quietly. After we brought him back to the shop and did some initial processing, your guys showed up," said Robbins.

"Our guys?" asked Windflower.

"National Security Criminal Investigations," said Robbins. "Just showed up and claimed jurisdiction. Said it was a national security issue or something. I checked with my boss, and he said to go ahead and release him to their custody. So, he's gone."

"Gone where?" asked Windflower.

"Wherever the NCSI takes people," said Robbins. "Way above my pay grade. Sorry we couldn't have been more helpful."

"Thanks again for your help," said Windflower as he hung up. This was a new twist, he thought. But something that shouldn't be thought about on a relatively empty stomach. The muffin helped, but he needed more. And a break. He walked back out through the office. Betsy was on the phone and tried to flag him down, but he smiled, waved, and kept going.

He got in his car and thought about going for another drive, but instead he drove home and arrived just as Sheila was coming back from dropping Amelia Louise at the daycare.

"Can I buy you lunch?" he asked.

"You can indeed," said Sheila as she jumped in his vehicle. "I'm surprised to see you, with the big accident this morning."

"They will do fine without me for an hour or so," said Windflower. "I needed to get out."

"It must be awful to be a witness to death like that," said Sheila. "How do you deal with it?"

"I try to leave it at the office," said Windflower. "I learned that lesson the hard way when I worked on highway patrol in British Columbia. And I talk about it when I need to."

"Do you need to now?" asked Sheila.

"No," said Windflower. "Now I'd like to eat. With a beautiful lady."

Sheila smiled, and Windflower drove them to Fortune and stopped at the café on the main road next to the ferry terminal to Saint-Pierre.

"This is good?" he asked.

"Perfect," said Sheila.

The ferry was about to depart, and the café was nearly full of people waiting to go over to the little island off the coast of Newfoundland. Not many tourists these days, but at least the locals who lived there were free again to visit Newfoundland and do their shopping or check on their properties in Grand Bank. The French nationals had been barred from coming over during the pandemic, which limited traffic to essential goods and services. But now that things had cleared up, they were free again to move back and forth.

Those people all poured out of the café a few minutes later, leaving Sheila and Windflower with the place to themselves for lunch. He ordered the fried cod and scrunchions with mashed potatoes and gravy. She had the hot turkey sandwich with French fries.

"This was my favourite dining-out spot when I was little," said Sheila. She laughed. "It was also one of the few places to eat out in the area. There was the B&B, which was more of a hotel in those days, but that was reserved for visitors from out of town or the very rich, which we certainly were not. Our choices were to get chicken and chips at the takeout or come here. It was a special treat."

"It's a special treat to be with you," said Windflower.

Sheila laughed again. "Flattery will get you everywhere."

"That's my plan," said Windflower as their food arrived. He almost second-guessed himself when he saw Sheila's hot turkey sandwich and the rich brown gravy swimming over the bread and meat. But then he tasted his cod. It was perfect. Nearly as good as he could make at home and so fresh that it flaked off his fork. He ate it slowly, trying to savour each moment and letting the tastes linger, but still was finished before Sheila was halfway through.

He accepted her offer of a few of her extra French fries, and that tided him over until dessert. They shared a piece of ice cream cheesecake. It was creamy, smooth and delicious. It was only when they'd finished their cake and were enjoying their cup of tea that Windflower came back to the accident.

"I was thinking about what you said earlier. How hard it is," said Windflower. "Even though I'm used to it, doesn't make it any easier. I've just got better coping skills now.

But sudden death is always traumatic. Smithson was really upset this morning. Not only was he one of the first on the scene, he had to put down the injured moose afterward."

"Oh my God, that's awful," said Sheila. "Is he okay?"

"He will be," said Windflower. "But each time it happens, it hurts a little. And if we're not careful, it becomes cumulative."

"Is it like that for you?"

"No, I'm usually able to let them go," said Windflower. "My spiritual practices help with that. But every time it hurts, just the same. It's one of the reasons that I think I might leave the Force."

"That, and the fact that you might get shot any day when you go to work," said Sheila as the pair rose to leave the café. Windflower left a nice tip on the table and paid on the way out.

"I guess we should make a decision about Marystown," he said as they got back into his car.

"Let's talk on the weekend," said Sheila.

They didn't talk anymore as Windflower made the loop in Fortune, around the ferry terminal, which was very quiet now, and down past the old colourful fishing stages that lined the inner harbour. When they got back out on the highway, the fog lifted long enough for them to see the ferry almost make it to Saint-Pierre. But by the time he dropped off Sheila it had returned, and he could barely see her as she went into their house.

He waved anyway and drove back to work.

Betsy was nearly frantic when she saw him. "Reverend Woods called again, and Doctor Sanjay would like to speak with you. And somebody from the NCSI called. A fellow by the name of Albertson. He said you'd know what it was about. And there's these," she said, holding up a stack of yellow slips that Windflower figured must be from the media.

"I'll talk to Reverend Woods first," said Windflower. "If he's okay to release Gregory Dollimont's name, then let's bring the media in. Might as well do them all at once."

Betsy nodded, and Windflower called Elijah Woods.

"What's going on over there?" barked Woods when he got on the line with Windflower.

"I've been trying to reach you all morning."

"Sorry, Reverend," said Windflower. "It's been kind of busy. What would you like to know?"

"Do we know the cause of the accident? And where is Gregory Dollimont's body being held?"

Windflower noticed that he didn't ask about Elizabeth Frankford. He also decided to ask some questions of his own. "Is Dollimont a diabetic? And where were he and Elizabeth Frankford going?"

He could almost hear Woods 'harrumph' in the background but ignored it.

"Gregory Dollimont is not a diabetic, and they were coming to a meeting I called to discuss the transition," said Woods. "Where is his body?"

"His remains will be examined, and if there's nothing amiss, we can release the body to your care if you wish," said Windflower. "We believe that the accident was the result of a collision with a large moose. But our investigation is still incomplete. We do not have any information about Gregory Dollimont, his relations or next of kin. Can you assist with that?"

"He had no family, just the church," said Woods.

"Very well," said Windflower. "We will be releasing his name to the media. By the way, what was the transition plan you were talking about for the church in Grand Bank?"

All he heard back was a click as Elijah Woods hung up the phone.

THIRTY-EIGHT

Windflower walked out to see Betsy at the front. She put down her headset.

"Set up the media conference for about five o'clock," said Windflower. "Tizzard can help you get all the details on Gregory Dollimont." Eddie Tizzard was just coming around the corner with a plate of cheese and crackers.

"I'm having lunch," Tizzard protested.

"Help Betsy and then have your lunch," said Windflower. "I'll call Doctor Sanjay."

Betsy and Tizzard would get all the information together, and Betsy would notify the media. Despite the short notice, they'd all be there. This was big news around here, thought Windflower as he phoned the clinic and managed to get Doc Sanjay on the line.

"Winston, my friend, how's she going, b'y?" asked Sanjay.

"Busy," said Windflower, not having time for a lot of chit-chat. "Have you had a chance to take a look at Gregory Dollimont yet?"

"Yes, but only briefly," said the doctor, picking up Windflower's intensity. "He clearly suffered a major head trauma, and he's got lots of bruising, but all of that would be expected from the collision. I need to do a bit more probing, but unless there's something unexpected, this looks straightforward. Should I be looking for anything?"

"I'm really interested in whether or not Gregory Dollimont might be a diabetic," said Windflower.

"That might be difficult to say with certainty," said the doctor. "Blood sugar levels fluctuate after death. But I will do the test and also check for injection marks. I'll get back to you soon."

"Thanks, Doc." Windflower hung up the phone and waited until Betsy and Tizzard came back a little while later with a draft press release. Windflower read it quickly and noted the details on the deceased, Gregory Vincent Dollimont, fifty-six, Marystown. He initialled and signed it.

"I was going to wait until tomorrow to bring in Jane Edwards," said Tizzard. "Is that okay?"

"Fine," said Windflower. Betsy left to send the release to PR in Marystown for their final check, and then she would do up copies of the handout for the media. Tizzard went off, presumably to get a snack. Windflower called Albertson's number at NCSI in Ottawa.

"You called me," said Windflower when Albertson answered his call.

"Our guys picked up Charles Frankford," said Albertson. "They want to know why you were looking for him."

"Can I talk to him?" asked Windflower.

"Don't be cute," said Albertson. "You don't want my friends coming down on your head."

"Okay," said Windflower. "We wanted to talk to him about a gun we found at a house in Grand Bank. It was my old boss, Morecombe's weapon."

"That we didn't know," said Albertson. "I'll pass that along."

"Why did NCSI pick him up?" asked Windflower.

"Let's just say we need to keep him from talking right now," said Albertson. "I'll let you know if we need anything else."

He could see by looking out his window that the media were starting to arrive. Two TV trucks and both radio stations. It would be a big item on the evening broadcasts. He had time for one more call, so he phoned Carl Langmead.

"You're a busy man down there in Grand Bank," said Langmead.

"You know the story, Carl. We can have nothing for days, and then everything busts open all at once. The accident looks pretty straightforward. A car is no match for a moose."

"Tell me about it," said Langmead. "There may not be moose downtown, but everywhere else they keep showing up and people keep hitting them. We try and get them to slow down, especially in the fog…"

"I know," said Windflower. "I've got to run to do the media on this, but I wanted to let you know that we found Charles Frankford. But he's been snatched up by another agency. Part of the security apparatus."

"What? Why?"

Windflower paused. "I'm not supposed to tell anyone. I really shouldn't know about it myself. But a friend hooked me up with a guy who told me that Frankford and Jerome Morecombe were engaged in similar research. They picked Frankford up about that matter. Whatever it is."

"Any way of talking to Frankford?" asked Langmead.

"I doubt it," said Windflower. "But I passed along the fact that we wanted to talk to him about the gun we found. I don't think we'll hear back, unless they need me for something. Sorry."

"Not your fault," said Langmead. "We might have something from the canvass. A neighbour thinks she saw a van parked in the neighbourhood for a few days before the incident. I'm following up. I'll let you know if anything comes of it."

"Thanks," said Windflower, rushing to hang up, since Betsy was signalling him to come along to the media event.

Windflower walked out into the hallway and waited for the cameras to get into position to film him coming into the boardroom. He'd figured that one out a long time ago. If he didn't let them get that shot at the beginning, they'd want him to do it at the end. He walked to the makeshift podium and read the prepared statement. Afterward, he took questions.

Most of them were about what the RCMP was doing to protect drivers from the menace of the moose. Windflower answered several of them, until he'd had enough.

"Maybe, after all this time, we should learn to live with the moose," he said to one reporter who'd asked the same question for the third time. "We know what to do. Avoid driving at night if possible and reduce our speed in poor weather. It's not rocket science. Maybe people should smarten up."

As soon as those words came out of his mouth, he knew he was in trouble.

The reporter knew it, too. "Are you saying people around here are stupid?"

Windflower stumbled around, giving a long and rambling answer that satisfied no one, including himself. He stood there like a deer in the headlights, but there were no more questions as the reporters scrambled to grab their stuff and go file their stories. They had their headline.

Even Betsy knew there was something wrong. She told Windflower he did a great job, but the worry lines on her forehead gave her away. Tizzard just slunk past the reporters and into the lunchroom.

Windflower went back to his office and closed the door. It was relatively peaceful for a few minutes, and then Ron Quigley called.

Windflower tried to explain, but Quigley stopped him right away. "I just heard the clip. This is not good. And you can't explain it away. I'm asking my Comms guys to put together a written apology. Okay it and send it back right away."

Betsy came in to say goodnight as Windflower was waiting for the email from Marystown. She looked at him pityingly and smiled as she left. That only made him feel worse. A few minutes later, he opened his email and saw the apology. It was a straight-up grovel and plea for forgiveness. It probably wouldn't make any difference, but he typed "okay" and sent it back.

His phone rang again, and he cringed, thinking it was either Quigley or somebody from the media. Instead, it was Doctor Sanjay. Windflower was relieved.

"Hey, Doc," said Windflower. He must have sounded down, because the doctor picked up on his down.

"Hard day at the office?" he asked. "You know, 'Clouds come floating into my life, no longer to carry rain or usher storm, but to add color to my sunset sky.'"

Windflower laughed, despite himself. "I'm afraid I've created my own storm this time."

"That may be true," said Sanjay. "But no matter what you've done at work today, your daughters will greet you with great joy when you come home. And my Old Pulteney will welcome you tomorrow evening with unbridled passion."

"Thank you, my friend," said Windflower. "I am assuming you have news for me."

"I do indeed," said the doctor. "I did find needle marks on the late Gregory Dollimont's body. In many strange areas. In his feet and groin, for example."

"He may have had trouble finding a good vein," said Windflower. "Lots of diabetics have that problem."

"I do not believe he was a diabetic," said Sanjay.

"He was a drug addict," said Windflower. He whistled softly to himself.

"I will have to confirm with a tox report, but I am pretty sure that Gregory Dollimont was a long-term user of opioids," said Doctor Sanjay. "Some of the track marks are fairly recent."

"That is very interesting," said Windflower. "Thanks for the info. Keep me posted, and let me know if you find anything else."

"We will see you and your lovely family tomorrow night," said Sanjay.

THIRTY-NINE

It was a bit after seven when Windflower drove home. Even though the fog had lifted, his spirits had not. He was still beating himself up when he arrived at his house. But he couldn't stay there. His friend was right. Stella and Amelia Louise were waiting for him and had set up a surprise party for him in the living room. He looked at Sheila.

"Not my idea," she said. "This is all them. There's macaroni in the oven when you're done."

"I can smell that," said Windflower. "Garlic bread, too."

"Daddy," said Stella, a little impatiently. "Come on."

Amelia Louise joined in, and soon both were chanting, "Daddy, Daddy, Daddy."

Even Lady started to get into the act by barking and running around. Molly, on the other hand, was not impressed and went back to her bed in the kitchen. If she had hands, she would have put them over her ears.

"Okay, okay," said Windflower.

"Today is your Unbirthday," said Stella. "This is for you." She waved her arms towards the living room, where the girls had set up a tea party and what looked like lumps covered in Christmas wrapping paper.

"There pwesents," said Amelia Louise.

"I can see," said Windflower. He looked at Sheila.

"It's from Alice in Wonderland. They watched it again after supper," she said. "I did donate the wrapping paper."

"Daddy, come on," said Amelia Louise. "It's a pawty."

Windflower sat on the floor in the middle of the living room. Stella handed him a teacup and urged him to drink, which he did. Amelia Louise brought over his presents and dumped them in front of him. He unwrapped them one by one. There were dolls and balls and other toys from the girls' toy box. He was opening the last one when Sheila came in with a cupcake with a lit candle on top. All three of them sang "Unhappy Birthday" to Windflower and urged him to make a wish before he blew out the candle.

He closed his eyes and wished he would always remember this moment. He blew out the candle, and everyone cheered. The girls cheered again when Sheila brought them out their own cupcake. While they were eating, Windflower escaped to the kitchen and took a large scoop of the macaroni and cheese and a couple of slices of garlic bread out of the oven.

He and Sheila sat in the kitchen while he ate.

"I needed that tonight," he said.

"I saw the early news," said Sheila. "It's not that bad."

Windflower stopped eating and looked at her. "I've already signed my apology for calling the people of Grand Bank stupid."

"People forget about things quickly," said Sheila. "I learned that as mayor."

"Like someone else will say something even dumber?" asked Windflower.

"Forgive yourself and move on," said Sheila. "Enjoy the rest of your supper. I will look after the girls if you take Lady for a long walk. She's hardly been out all day."

Windflower savoured his macaroni and cheese and garlic bread as long as he could. Then he had his cupcake and grabbed Lady's leash. He could hear Amelia Louise and Stella squeal with delight as Sheila put them in the bath. He took a long deep breath, and as Sheila suggested, he let the rest of the day go and focused on enjoying his walk with Lady.

He and the collie wandered all over town from the wharf to past the fish plant and across the brook to the other side. He passed by Doctor Sanjay's house and then turned around to come back, taking his time as they walked along the other side of the brook, where a happy family was feeding the ducks. Lady would have liked to have a closer look, but Windflower kept her close so as not to interfere in the family's fun.

Then they walked through town and down towards the beach, where plenty of people were out and about, enjoying the pleasant evening. Maybe we'll get a few more nice days, thought Windflower. But those hopes were brief. As they rounded the turn for home, he could see the fog bank creeping its way back into the waters around Grand Bank.

He got home just in time to read Amelia Louise her story. She picked *What Are Stars?* It was a lift-the-flap book that she enjoyed playing with as Windflower read the words. It was a nice book because Amelia Louise was full of questions these days and had just discovered the magic of stars at night now that it was getting dark before she went to bed. Windflower enjoyed reading this book, too, as it explored the heavens and explained that the sun was our nearest star and what shooting stars really were. He even learned some things himself.

After story time, he kissed her goodnight and went back downstairs. He and Sheila watched TV for an hour, but when the news came on, he excused himself and let Lady out in the backyard. He couldn't bear watching himself and what the commentators had to say about his earlier remarks.

He reminded himself that he had decided to let that all go and watched Lady do her business. He tried to look up at the stars but couldn't even see the top of his house. When Lady came back, he let her in and went upstairs.

He brushed his teeth and got into bed. He thought about reading but didn't have the head for that tonight, so he simply lay there quietly and waited for Sheila. She came up shortly afterward and slid into bed beside him. She didn't say a word but moved closer to hold him. He fell asleep in that warm embrace and didn't stir until Friday morning.

Windflower opened his eyes and padded to the bathroom. A quick look out the window revealed more of what he saw last night: fog, and lots of it.

Everyone appeared to be still sleeping. He took advantage of the break in the action to go downstairs and put the coffee on. He picked up his smudging kit and tucked it under his arm. He grabbed his hoodie to go over his pajamas, and he and Lady went outside.

The morning was cool and very damp, but at least it wasn't raining. Windflower mixed his herbs in the bowl and lit it using his wooden matches. The smoke hung in the air a little and then started to drift off. He pulled some of it back towards him and smudged. Then he sat for a moment and let the scent of the sacred medicines cling to him and envelope him.

It brought him a feeling of peace and contentment. And then almost as quickly, a sense of gratitude for this life and all the gifts he had already received. It was overwhelming to the point he thought he would cry. Lady came back to see if he was okay. He offered his prayers of gratitude and asked for guidance to be a better man and a better person.

He was back inside, putting away his smudging kit, when it came to him. Be impeccable with your word. That was one of the four agreements from a book of the same name by Toltec master Don Miguel Ruiz.

A very simple teaching that could certainly lead to major self-improvement. Windflower had been gifted that book by his old friend, Bill Ford, a few years back. He had practiced the four agreements in his life for a year and got much better at a lot of things. Maybe it was time to go back to those teachings. Maybe talk to Bill Ford again, too, he thought.

He didn't have much more time to think, since he heard what sounded like a herd of cattle coming down the stairs.

"I thought you were a bunch of cows coming down," he said to Stella and Amelia Louise.

They thought that was the most hilarious thing ever, and soon both of them were mooing and rolling all over the kitchen floor. Luckily, Sheila came to save him, again. She took Stella to get dressed while Windflower and Amelia Louise went to the kitchen. Her helping consisted of eating half of the strawberries he cut up and chatting incessantly about nothing, but Windflower was still grateful for her company.

As a reward, she got half of the first waffle that Windflower shared with her. She was quick to point out that fact to her sister, who came down a few minutes later with her mom. Stella didn't seem to mind that at all, especially when Windflower plopped her half waffle on her plate.

"This is a special treat," said Sheila.

"It's a special day," said Windflower. He waited while everyone watched him to see what he would say next. "It's Friday," he announced.

The girls looked a little disappointed that he didn't have more to tell them about why this was a special day.

"And we're going to see Doc Sanjay and Repa tonight for treats," he added.

"Yay," said Stella.

"Yay," said Amelia Louise. And she started her "Doc, Doc, Doc" chant.

She was still chanting as Stella got on her bus, and for all Windflower knew, she might still be chanting as he walked into his office.

FORTY

Betsy hadn't arrived, and it was between shift changes, so Smithson was likely doing his rounds, and Tizzard hadn't come in yet. Windflower was happy to have the quiet office to himself. He made some coffee and enjoyed it while he could. He knew it wouldn't last. His first call was from Inspector Ron Quigley.

"You are a star on social media," said Quigley.

"Not in a good way, I take it," said Windflower.

"No, not too bad, actually," said Quigley. "Lots of people are trashing you, but many are congratulating you for your honesty, and they're talking about getting people to slow down."

"I still feel badly about it," said Windflower.

"Let it go, Sergeant," said Quigley. "The Reverend Elijah Woods has been beating on my door, demanding that Dollimont's body be released."

"He called me, too," said Windflower. "I told him that we had to examine the body first. He wasn't very happy with me, but I'm glad we did."

"Why is that?" asked Quigley.

"We thought he might be a diabetic, since he had an insulin kit in his car, which would have made things interesting as it was. But Doc Sanjay figures that Gregory Dollimont might have been an addict," said Windflower.

"Huh," said Quigley. "That certainly adds another factor to the equation."

"Exactly," said Windflower. "We still need to figure out how that matters. But I guarantee you it matters."

"Well, good luck with that," said Quigley. "By the way, Bill Ford is coming over your way today. He wondered if you might be free for lunch."

"Sure," said Windflower. "That would be great."

"Okay, I gotta go," said Quigley. "Remember, no one is listening until you make a mistake."

"That's good," said Windflower. "But you can't take it back once it comes out. Bill Ford told me about practicing restraint of pen and tongue. I think I need to practice that more often."

"It might save your marriage, if not your job," said Quigley. "Have a great day. Unless you have other plans."

That made Windflower smile. He was still smiling when Betsy came in to say good morning.

"You're in a good mood this morning," said Betsy.

"Life is good," said Windflower. "'I bear a charmed life.'"

"We all do around here," said Betsy. "Although I wish that blessed fog would blow away. Here are your messages. I took out the media ones. I was guessing you didn't want to talk to them."

"You would be correct," said Windflower as he ran through the slips. The one that caught his eye first was Doctor Sceviour. He called the clinic and waited for the doctor to be paged.

"Good morning, Sergeant," said the doctor. "I thought I would give you an update on Elizabeth Frankford. We tried to reach her husband but haven't been able to."

"He's unavailable at the moment," said Windflower. "How is your patient doing?"

"I think that eventually she may be okay," said Sceviour. "Her vital signs are stable, and she had an uneventful night. She's still in the induced coma now, and we'll know more once she wakes up. But I would say promising at this point. Unless there are complications."

That was covering all the bases, thought Windflower, but for now, that's what she was prepared to say. "Would you mind letting me know when she might be available to speak to me? We still have some questions about the accident."

"Surely," said Doctor Sceviour.

Smithson was the next one in his office. "Quiet morning out there today," said Smithson.

"Just the way we like it," said Windflower.

"I want to thank you for taking the time to talk to me," said Smithson. "About the moose and the accident. I phoned my brother last night and talked about it with him, too. I feel much better today."

"That's good," said Windflower. "Don't let that stuff build up inside of you."

"I also wanted you to know that nothing happened between me and the minister," said Smithson, turning as red as a beet. "I know people like to talk, but that's all me and Elizabeth did. She was more like a mother or an aunt to me. She listened to me. We had great chats about music and other stuff."

"Okay," said Windflower. "I believe you. But you have to remember that people will talk about you when you are not from their community. Especially if you are a police officer with authority over them. It's not fair, but you're held to a special standard when you put on that uniform."

Smithson nodded and left Windflower's office.

Windflower checked his messages again. There was one from Elijah Woods. He decided to ignore it, but he couldn't ignore Betsy when she called him over the intercom a couple of minutes later.

"Reverend Woods on Line one," said Betsy.

Having little option, Windflower said good morning to Elijah Woods.

"I am growing impatient," said Woods. "Will you release Gregory Dollimont so that the process of prayer and reflection for his soul can begin?"

"I think it will be very soon," said Windflower. "Did you know that he was an intravenous drug user?"

"He had a prescription," said Woods. "He had back problems and was in tremendous pain. Even with the medication, he still suffered tremendously. Have you no decency, Sergeant? Or respect for the dead?"

With that, the line went dead.

"That went well," Windflower said out loud to himself.

"What went well?" asked Eddie Tizzard, who had a package of croissants under his arm. "Wanna snack?"

"Not right now," said Windflower. "Aren't you bringing Jane Edwards in this morning?"

"I was, right after I...never mind," said Tizzard, laying the croissants on Windflower's desk. "I'll be back soon."

Windflower got himself a cup of coffee from the back and took one of Tizzard's croissants out of the package. He was enjoying his treat when his cell phone rang.

"Good morning, Sergeant Windflower," said Langmead. "How are you today? I guess you must have taken a bit of heat for yesterday. But around here, we're all pretty proud that somebody spoke up."

"Thanks, I think," said Windflower. "But that was so yesterday. I have lots more opportunity to screw up today. How can I help you?"

"Well, actually, I might be able to help both of us," said Langmead. "We've been going through prints from Morecombe's house and had no luck in our system. But when we plugged them into the Atlantic police network, we got a match. Gregory Dollimont. He's from down around your area. Are you familiar with him?"

"Dollimont?" said Windflower. "I do know him. Unfortunately, he's dead. Killed in the car accident yesterday. Did you say he had a record somewhere in the Atlantic?"

"Nova Scotia," said Langmead. "He was stopped on suspicion of being impaired, and they found a significant amount of controlled substances. He claimed personal use and got a conditional sentence plus two years probation."

"What did he have?" asked Windflower.

"Oxys, percs, codeine," said Langmead. "A drugstore was how the local cops described it. Too bad he's dead. I'd like to know what he was doing in Morecombe's house."

"Me, too," said Windflower as Tizzard walked past his door with an older lady who he assumed was Jane Edwards. "But I've got to go. Let me know if you find anything else. Thanks."

FORTY-ONE

He quickly finished his croissant, wiped the crumbs off his shirt to remove the evidence and went to the interview room where Tizzard was sitting with Jane Edwards

"Sergeant Windflower, this is Jane Edwards," said Tizzard as he turned on the tape recorder that was sitting on the table. "Don't worry about that," he said to the woman. "It's just a formality when we're in the office."

"Good morning, ma'am," said Windflower. "Would you like some coffee or a glass of water?"

Jane Edwards clutched her purse tightly and shook her head.

"Okay," said Windflower. "There's nothing to be nervous about. We just want to ask you a few more questions. I know you must be pretty upset with the news about Gregory Dollimont and the minister," he continued. "But we need to clear up a few things."

The woman didn't move a muscle. If anything, she grabbed her purse even tighter. Windflower knew it looked like she was impenetrable but that this was a point when a witness or a criminal might actually be quite vulnerable. If only he could find the key to open the door.

"I know you've talked to Constable Tizzard, but can you tell me what exactly you do at the manse?" asked Windflower.

Everybody liked talking about their job, and Jane Edwards was no exception.

"Well, sir, I cooks all the meals and keeps the house nice and tidy for the minister. I does the laundry and makes the beds, when the minister is there, I cleans her room and the kitchen and bathrooms. It's a lot of work, but I likes to keep a clean house. Everybody knows that about me," said Edwards.

"You also bring or used to bring Reverend Prowse his meals as well, is that right?" asked Windflower.

"Yes, sir, I did that for every meal. Reverend Bob was a wonderful man. I was very sorry to lose him," said the woman. She looked like she was going to cry.

"I think we all miss Reverend Bob," said Windflower. "You were one of the last people to see him alive. How did he seem to you?"

"He was his bright, charming self," said Edwards, now smiling as she talked about the dead minister. "He always called me Janey. He was so sweet."

Windflower had the opening he needed. Jane Edwards had let her guard down and was allowing her emotions to come out.

"On the night that Reverend Prowse died, you were called to the manse to help Gregory Dollimont. Did you see or notice anything unusual?" asked Windflower.

"Reverend Bob was dead in the bathtub, and there was water everywhere in the bathroom. Mister Dollimont was yelling at me to get it cleaned up fast. It was awful," said Edwards.

"Jane, is there anything you want to tell us about that night, or about Gregory Dollimont that you may not have mentioned before?" asked Windflower, as gently as he could. Like he was Jane's close personal friend.

The woman looked like a deer caught in the headlights. Before she could respond, Windflower prodded again.

"It's okay," said Windflower. "Gregory Dollimont is dead. He can't hurt you. There's nothing to be afraid of."

Jane Edwards looked around, as if she was thinking about making a run for it, but that didn't seem possible. With a great sigh and one very long breath that sounded like a whistle at the end, she started to speak.

She must have talked nonstop for fifteen minutes. She talked about that mean Mister Dollimont and how he was never nice to anybody. She said that he bossed and bullied the old minister and that if she didn't do what he wanted, he'd have her shipped back to Fortune. She had a sick husband at home, and they needed the money from this job. Then there was the drugs.

"I seen it with my own eyes," said Edwards. "Right after he did them, he'd be laying back in the chair like he was dead. I used to see the needles around everywhere. He told me to clean everything up and to keep my mouth shut."

"What did you see when you came over the night that Reverend Prowse died?" asked Windflower.

"Oh, my Lord, it was awful," said the woman. "They'd taken Reverend Bob out already, and it looked like the bathroom had been clean and tidied up. I guess Mister Dollimont did that. But downstairs there was drugs everywhere, and he was acting crazy, yelling at me. I just went about my business the best I could."

"Were you there when Reverend Frankford came home?" asked Windflower.

"I was getting ready to leave the manse when she came over," said Edwards. "Her and Mister Dollimont had an awful row."

"What were they fighting about?" asked Windflower.

"She had been in St. John's for something or other, and he was yelling at her about all kinds of things," said the woman. "Like he knew why her husband wasn't around and that she was a bad woman. He used a word that I can't say."

"That's okay," said Windflower. "Did Reverend Frankford say anything back?"

"She was trying to defend herself until it was like she gave up. Then she said something that will stick with me 'til the day I die. She said he finally killed him," said Edwards. "Reverend Bob."

At her last answer, Jane Edwards kind of crumbled, and Tizzard had to hold her up. She was still quietly sobbing when Windflower came back with Betsy.

"Okay, dearie," said Betsy. "Let's me and you go have a quiet cup of tea in the back."

"What do you think?" asked Windflower.

"Dollimont was a drug addict, and he may or may not have killed Prowse," said Tizzard. "She was certainly a lot more open now that Dollimont is dead."

"I agree," said Windflower. "There's somebody else who might be more cooperative as well now that he's dead."

"Elizabeth Frankford," said Tizzard.

"Exactly," said Windflower. "Now we have to wait until she wakes up. If she wakes up."

"While we're waiting, we might as well have a snack," said Tizzard, opening the croissants and stuffing half of one in his mouth. You?" He offered one to Windflower.

Windflower just shook his head and waved him out of his office. He spent a few minutes going through the rest of his messages, returning calls and mostly leaving messages. He was shuffling the papers in his in-basket when he saw Tizzard leading Jane Edwards down the hall and into his Jeep to drive her home. As he was watching, another RCMP vehicle pulled up, and Bill Ford stepped out.

Windflower grabbed his coat and met Ford in the hallway.

"Let's get out of here before somebody else is looking for me," said Windflower. He told Betsy that he was going out and would be back in an hour or so.

"Do you want to go to the Mug-Up?" asked Windflower.

"Where else?" replied Bill Ford.

FORTY-TWO

They found a parking spot close to the door. That was good, because Windflower noticed that Ford still had a slight limp and moved a little gingerly and slowly.

The two men found a table and waited for the waitress to come and take their order. Today, it wasn't Marie that served them, but a young girl instead.

"You're not Marie," said Windflower, jokingly.

"No, I'm Vanessa," said the girl. "I just came to help Nan and Pop as they're open full-time for dining now. Well, half-full, as you can see. My classes at the college are online, so I can do this and study too."

"Welcome, Vanessa," said Windflower. "I'd like a bowl of turkey soup and a grilled cheese sandwich, please."

"Same for me," said Ford. "And a cup of tea with fresh milk."

"I'll have tea, too, please, Vanessa," said Windflower. "What are you doing over here today, besides visiting me, which is very nice, by the way?" he asked Ford.

"I'm making the courtesy calls to the town councils. I saw Garnish on the way over, and I'll see Grand Bank next, and then Fortune before heading back," said Ford. "Plus, I get to see you. And I was hoping to see Frank, but nobody knows where he is."

"Uncle Frank is on his own path, that's for sure," said Windflower. "I've hardly seen him since I got back. How are you feeling these days?"

"I'm pretty creaky," said Ford. "I had a few issues with inflammation in my legs before the shooting, but everything is a bit worse now. And I'm certainly a lot slower."

"Are you going to stay working?" asked Windflower as their soup and sandwiches arrived. The soup was much too hot, so they nibbled on their sandwiches while they waited for it to cool.

"That's something I wanted to talk to you about," said Ford. "Now that Ron is leaving, I may leave, too. I can't see myself running after some young hot shot. But if you were to take the job, I might reconsider."

"That's interesting, and more than a little flattering," said Windflower. "But I haven't made my mind up on that yet. Me and Sheila will talk about it on the weekend."

Their soup had now cooled enough to eat, and the conversation grew quiet while they finished their soup. The turkey soup was fabulous, with big chunks of dark and white turkey meat and lots of vegetables in a savoury broth. Both men gave it thumbs up when Vanessa came to take their dishes away.

"I wanted to thank you for that book you gave me back a few years ago, *The Four Agreements*," said Windflower.

"It's a great little book," said Ford. "I've been reading little pieces of it as part of my daily readings for years now. It's simple but very powerful."

"I know," said Windflower. "I was reminded of that after I was certainly not impeccable with my words yesterday."

Bill Ford laughed. "If that's your biggest mistake, you've got little to worry about," he said. "I once set the detachment on fire in Corner Brook when I decided to have a late-night snack after being out drinking."

"But you don't do that anymore," said Windflower.

"And you won't either," said Ford.

They went to the cash and paid their bills, and Windflower drove them back to the detachment. When they arrived, Betsy told him he had a visitor. Bill Ford turned to go.

"No, he wants to see you, too," said Betsy.

Uncle Frank was sitting in Windflower's office with his feet up on the desk.

"I'm glad you finally decided to come back to work," said his uncle. "Nice to see you, Bill. How's it been going? I heard you got shot."

"It's going okay," said Ford. "If you want to come for a ride with me to Fortune and don't mind sitting in the car for a few minutes, I'll buy you a cup of coffee and a piece of pie."

"That's my kind of deal," said Uncle Frank. "I guess you're too busy to come along," he said to Windflower.

"That would be true," said Windflower. "But I would like to catch up with you. Maybe tomorrow morning for pea soup and por' cakes."

"That sounds grand," said Uncle Frank. "See ya later."

"We'll talk soon," said Bill Ford. "Nice to see you again."

"For sure," said Windflower, and he walked the two men out to the front door. Betsy was waiting for him when he came back to his office.

"Doctor Sceviour called," said Betsy. "She said Reverend Frankford was awake."

Windflower grabbed his coat and drove to the clinic. It was much quieter here on Friday afternoon, since most of the regulars had likely been there in the morning.

He put on his mask and asked for Doctor Sceviour at reception. She came out to see him a few minutes later.

"Sergeant, nice to see you," said the doctor. "Come with me."

Windflower did as he was told and followed Doctor Sceviour down the hallway to the Intensive Care Unit.

She pushed through the doors and went straight to Elizabeth Frankford's bed in the corner. Windflower had been in ICU many times before, but he was always surprised how loud and bright the place was. There were machines whirring and beeping and bright fluorescent lights everywhere.

Elizabeth Frankford was lying quietly amidst three machines with two intravenous tubes bringing fluids in and out of her body. One, for sure, was the painkiller, which she would certainly need after being smashed up in a car accident.

"Elizabeth," said Doctor Sceviour, gently but firmly. She held the other woman's hand until she opened her eyes. "Sergeant Windflower is here to ask you a few questions."

"Ten minutes, max," said the doctor as she let go of Elizabeth Frankford's hand and walked away. "I'll be back."

Windflower watched as Elizabeth Frankford struggled to come fully into this reality. She looked like she was trying to swim to the surface but being held down by the current.

"Elizabeth," he started. "Do you remember me? I talked with you at your house the other day. You have a beautiful garden."

He was attempting to help bring her into full consciousness as quickly as possible. For him and for her. He was rewarded for his mention of her garden with a slight smile at the corner of her mouth.

"Gregory Dollimont is dead. He unfortunately died in the accident," said Windflower. He paused and hoped that would sink in through her haze. "We know he was a drug addict. We think he may have had something to do with Reverend Prowse's death."

Elizabeth Frankford looked like she was trying to speak. But her mouth was dry and cracked. Windflower called the nurse over, and she gave Frankford a sliver of ice from a nearby plastic bucket. She sucked on the ice and stared at Windflower.

Windflower decided to press on.

"Do you know anything about Dollimont's involvement with Reverend
Prowse's death?"

The woman sucked even harder on the ice and struggled again to speak. This time she succeeded. But she only said one word before starting to cough. That brought the nurse back, and Windflower was strongly suggested to leave. He complied.

But the word that Elizabeth Frankford said haunted him all the way out of the clinic and all the way back to the office.

"Woods."

FORTY-THREE

He was still thinking about that word when Betsy came in a little while later to say goodnight and to wish him a good weekend. He stayed a few minutes longer and then packed up his stuff and headed home.

Chaos was in full swing at the Windflower-Hillier household, but after his day at work, he was happy to partake in some family fun. He took Lady and the girls for a walk around the block, and when he got back, he grilled some hot dogs that Sheila served with a plate of sliced vegetables. They knew they would get dessert at Doc Sanjay's house.

They bundled up the girls, a few toys, and a bouquet of flowers that Sheila had picked up for Repa and drove across the brook to the Sanjay house. At the entrance, they were greeted by Repa and Vijay Sanjay, and while Repa took Sheila and the girls to the kitchen to put the flowers in a vase, Windflower followed Doctor Sanjay into his den.

"Welcome, my friend," said Sanjay. "It has been much too long. Let us try the Old Pulteney, and then perhaps we can get in a quick game of chess before everyone comes back."

The doctor poured them each about an ounce of the Scotch and a glass of water from a nearby pitcher.

Windflower followed Sanjay's lead in sniffing the Scotch and then taking a small sip, followed by larger sips until the whiskey was gone. Then both men took a drink of water.

"Well, what do you think?" asked Sanjay.

"Excellent," said Windflower. "I can see why they call it maritime whiskey. It does have a hint of brine, almost like the air you taste around the ocean."

"Indeed," said the doctor. "There is also a special fruit undertone. Certainly citrus, but something peculiar as well. Like dried banana skins."

"You could be a professional taster," said Windflower.

"Shall we play?" asked Sanjay, pointing to the waiting chessboard.

The men managed to get through their first game with Doctor Sanjay handily beating Windflower in only a few moves. Windflower was doing much better in the second game when Sheila and Repa came in with the girls.

"We got tweets," said Amelia Louise proudly as she carried one small tray, and Stella behind her had another, larger tray. Repa helped the girls lay the trays on a side table.

"We have some onion bhajis and some beguni, and of course some vegetarian samosas," said Repa Sanjay. "Please, enjoy."

Windflower took a samosa and a couple of the bhajis, and a little of the cucumber dip that went with them. "What is the beguni?"

"It's a simple Bengali dish," said Repa. "Deep-fried eggplant slices. Take some chutney to dip them in as well."

"Delicious," said Windflower as he tried the beguni.

"You shouldn't have gone to all this trouble," said Sheila. "But it is very delicious."

They all enjoyed the snacks very much, and then Repa got the girls to help her bring the trays back into the kitchen. They came back a few minutes later with Repa carrying a large tea tray with a very aromatic blend coming from the teapot. The girls had their trays back, and Amelia proudly announced that she had dessert. Everybody got their own small earthenware pot.

"I remember this," said Windflower, tasting a spoonful of the dessert. "It's mista something. Baked yogurt."

"Very close, Sergeant," said Doctor Sanjay.

"It's called mishti doi," said Repa. "Another simple Bengali dish that we have at home with our own families. Just some sweetened yogurt with some spices and caramelized sugar and warm milk. You mix it, bake it and chill it."

She also poured the adults their tea.

"This is special Bengali chai tea," said Repa. "We call it doodh cha. It's a little lighter to enjoy at this time of day with our dessert."

"They say back home, 'To have doodh cha not when you need it, but when you feel like you've deserved it,'" said Vijay Sanjay.

The adults chatted for a bit with their tea while the girls played quietly. When they got louder, Sheila announced it was time to leave.

"So soon?" said Repa. "We love having you visit. Please come back again very soon."

"Yes," said the doctor. "These little girls are like our family. We have missed them and you, very much."

"We will be back soon. And we would love to have you come to see us. We will make you some Newfoundland food. Maybe a Jiggs Dinner," said Sheila.

"Salt meat and cabbage," said Vijay. "That would be very nice."

They said their goodbyes at the doorstep, and Windflower helped Sheila load the girls into the car. Vijay Sanjay called him back just before they left.

"I know that you have a lot on your mind these days," said Sanjay. "If you ever just want a quiet break, come and see me. I will always make time for you."

"Thank you, my friend," said Windflower.

"And remember," said Sanjay. "'Let your life lightly dance on the edges of time like dew on the tip of a leaf.'"

Windflower smiled and waved goodbye as he got in the passenger side.

"What was that about?" asked Sheila.

"He's my friend," said Windflower. "Besides you and the two monkeys in the back, 'I count myself in nothing else so happy, as in a soul remembering my good friends.'"

All they heard on the way back was two little girls pretending they were monkeys.

There was no way they were going to bed anytime soon, so Sheila put on a movie for them while Windflower took Lady for a walk. It was a cold, damp, miserable night, and even Lady was not disappointed when he cut about half off their regular route. The fog hadn't just settled in; it felt like it lived there now, thought Windflower, as he dried Lady off and went to see the end of the *Antz* movie the girls were transfixed by.

Even as they were nodding off, they both fought successfully to stay until the end. Then, Windflower and Sheila took one each and carried them upstairs. Minutes later, they were tucked in and falling asleep.

FORTY-FOUR

Sheila put on a pot of tea, and they relaxed in the living room. That was until Windflower's cell phone rang. "Sorry," he said and went to the kitchen to take the call. He glanced down at the caller ID. It was a 709 number, but not from around Grand Bank, where all the numbers began with 258. Must be St. John's, he thought.

He was right. It was Anne Marie Foote.

"Sergeant, sorry to bother you at night," said Foote. "But I need your help. Is this a good time, or can you call me back?"

"I can talk for a minute now," said Windflower.

"Thanks," said Foote. "We've found Cassie, or maybe she's found us. Brittney Hodder has been in contact with her and us. But Cassie won't talk to me or anybody at the RNC. She will only talk to you."

"Okay," said Windflower. "Do you have her number?"

"We have to relay the message back to her, and she'll call you," said Foote. "If it's okay with you, I'll give them your number."

"Sure," said Windflower. "But why won't she talk to you? I thought you were close."

"I don't know," said Foote. "But I'm really worried about her.

I'll pass the number on. Let me know if you hear anything."

Windflower closed his phone and went back into the living room.

"Everything okay?" asked Sheila.

"Yeah, a problem in St. John's with one of the girls we were working with," said Windflower.

"Why would they call you?" asked Sheila.

"One of the girls is missing again, and she will only talk to me," said Windflower.

"What's that about?" asked Sheila.

"I have no idea," said Windflower. "I can't predict the future."

"'It is not in the stars to hold our destiny but in ourselves,'" said Sheila.

"Are you talking about us now?"

"Very perceptive, Sergeant," said Sheila. "Let's talk about the elephant in the room. Marystown."

"That's the easy part," said Windflower. "I don't want the job and don't really want to move to Marystown. Do you?"

"Nope," said Sheila. "You're right. That was pretty easy. But that decision begets others, doesn't it?"

"Once I say no to the inspector job, they will transfer me out," said Windflower. "How do you feel about Flin Flon or Wawa?"

Sheila laughed. "I know about Wawa. That's where the giant goose is. And no, I'm not going to either of those places. Not willingly, anyway. What about Ottawa?"

"Now, that's a distinct possibility," said Windflower. "But it would be a desk job, and I think I've had my fill of working in an office."

"But Ottawa is so beautiful. The canal and Dow's Lake and the Parliament buildings," said Sheila.

"Let's go for a tourist trip, then," said Windflower. "But not to work."

"Your options are getting limited," said Sheila.

"'The choices we make dictate the lives we lead,'" said Windflower. "In this case more than ever. But let's take them one at a time. Say no to Marystown, and we'll see what unfolds."

"I say yes to you, whatever happens."

"And I to you, my fair lady," said Windflower. As he said that, the dog came out of the kitchen and sat in front of them.

"She has made her decision," said Sheila. "I'll see you upstairs. Oh, and Peter Fitzgerald called. He's coming tomorrow to pick up Stella early in the morning. I think they're going to St. Lawrence to that walking trail and then to Marystown. She was very excited."

"It's nice that her grandfather still wants to be part of her life," said Windflower as he got Lady's leash. "I was kind of surprised that he didn't try to adopt her."

"I've talked to him a few times now," said Sheila. "I don't think he thought he could manage it. He's on his own, and I think he's happy that Stella has found a safe place to live."

"Well, we've certainly been given a gift," said Windflower. "See you soon."

Lady led him outside and into a brisk walk around the neighbourhood. The fog made it hard to see much of anything, but that wasn't a problem in Grand Bank. This time Friday night most people were home, judging by the flickering TV screens in almost every window they passed. There were a few patrons at the pub across from the post office, but the band and the real party wouldn't start until much later.

As they turned for home, Windflower could feel the wind shift and rise up, even more than usual.

It was a mild breeze and maybe the harbinger of some other weather trouble brewing up from the south. He could check the weather later. For now, he had to get Lady dried off and get to bed, where Sheila was waiting for him.

Windflower fell asleep easily that night and was having what he would call a wonderful, grand sleep if he was telling his Uncle Frank about it, when he woke up. As usual, in a dream.

He looked around to get his bearings, finding his hands to centre himself. He took one long, deep breath and closed his eyes. When he opened them, there was a cat staring into his face. Not any cat. His cat. Molly.

When he got over his shock, he finally spoke. "Molly, what are you doing here? In my dream?"

Molly purred at first and then almost smiled at him. At least he thought it was a smile. "You're afraid of me, aren't you?"

"I'm not afraid of you," said Windflower. "I just don't understand you."

Molly stared at him, blinked and then started rolling around the floor. She was making some weird kind of noise that Windflower was certain was laughter. He had to get this dream under control.

"Thank you for coming to visit me, in my dream," said Windflower. "Do you have a message or something for me?"

Molly sat up straight. "They were right. You're not completely stupid. Could have fooled me, though."

Windflower didn't react but waited patiently for Molly to respond.

"You have a blind spot," said Molly. "Like that growing bare patch at the back of your head."

Windflower instinctively reached behind him to touch his head. "I'm not going bald," he started to say.

"Shush," said Molly. "Or, as usual, you'll miss the good part."

Windflower stayed perfectly still, despite a growing sense that he would like to give the cat a little tight squeeze… "I can see your thoughts over here," said Molly. "Well, I can see them over there, too, but never mind, let's get this over with."

"Yes," said Windflower, under his breath.

"I heard that, too," said Molly. "You need to go back in order to move forward."

"What does that mean?" asked Windflower. But as he was speaking, Molly was fading out of sight, and before he knew it, he was back in bed with Sheila. And wide awake.

Another puzzler, he thought. His next thought was he should talk to Uncle Frank about this time. And just before he went to sleep, he had one more thought. He and Molly would never be the same.

FORTY-FIVE

Windflower stirred and reached for Sheila, but she was gone. Then he opened his eyes and saw that it was light. He must have slept in. He heard noises from down below, including a strange male voice. He got dressed quickly and walked downstairs.

"There's coffee," said Sheila from the living room.

Windflower got his coffee, took a few sips and walked out to see both Stella and Amelia Louise sitting on a grey-haired man's lap.

"Mister Fitzgerald, this is my husband, Winston Windflower," said Sheila.

"I'd get up to greet you, but I'm kinda tied down," said Fitzgerald.

"Don't bother," said Windflower. "I know the feeling. Maybe one of you could give your daddy a hug and give this nice man a break."

Amelia Louise reluctantly got up and went to Windflower. She gave him a hug and then scampered back to Peter Fitzgerald.

"You're a very popular man," said Windflower.

"Where are you planning to go today?" asked Sheila. "Stella said you might be going on a hike."

"And to Walmart," said Stella.

"I was hoping the weather would clear, but it looks pretty damp out," said Fitzgerald. "But we'll have a nice drive and then maybe get ice cream."

"Ice cream, yay," said Stella.

"Yay," said Amelia Louise. Windflower didn't have the heart to tell her that she wasn't going. That would come as a great shock and disappointment to her. Better to deal with it when she found out rather than making two scenes.

"If you want, why don't you come back here for supper?" said Sheila. "It probably won't be very fancy, but you're welcome."

"Thanks, we just might do that," said Fitzgerald. "Come on, Stella, put your coat and boots on."

Stella went to get her boots and coat, and Amelia Louise followed closely behind. Both came back fully dressed and ready to go.

Amelia Louise was not happy to see her sister go off with her new best friend, and she made her feelings well known to her parents. After allowing her to express herself very loudly for a few minutes, Windflower bribed her with a blueberry muffin and the promise of a walk to feed the ducks. That appeased the little girl long enough to get the sobbing to stop and the household to resume some sense of normalcy.

True to his word, Windflower took Amelia Louise in her wagon and Lady on her leash and walked down to the brook to feed the ducks. It was foggy and cool, but of course, that really was perfect weather for ducks. Amelia Louise revelled in the fact that she had her daddy and all the ducks to herself, and she had a great time throwing handfuls of bread into the air and watching the ducks scramble for them.

She was still laughing when they walked along the wharf and then up past the Mug-Up café. There were already a few cars in the lot for a late breakfast or early order of pea soup and por' cakes. When they got home, Windflower and Amelia Louise went to rouse Uncle Frank so they could all go for their Saturday morning treat.

They all drove over together once Uncle Frank had been up for a while and had a cup of coffee to get him going. Despite the dismal weather, the Mug-Up was packed. Part of the reason for that was the café was still not allowed to operate at full capacity. But the Windflower crew still only had to wait for a few minutes for a large table to clear. They'd brought a juice pack and a few crackers for Amelia Louise, so that kept them going while they were waiting for their por' cakes and pea soup.

Vanessa was serving Windflower's table again today, and Moira Stoodley also came by to say hello.

"It must be nice to have Vanessa here to help out," said Sheila.

"She's been a godsend," said Moira. "We couldn't keep the other staff while the pandemic restrictions were on, since we only offered takeout. So they went on the benefits or got other jobs. Two of them went back with their families out of town. They will likely come back next summer, but for now we need the help."

"She's so pleasant, too," said Windflower.

Moira beamed and went to the kitchen to check on their order. She was soon back with their food and a special small plate for Amelia Louise with her own little metal pot of molasses. Windflower grabbed that before she could dump the whole thing on her por' cakes and poured a small circle she could dip her food into. She was just as happy with that and sang a little song to herself as she ate her food.

That gave the adults a chance to eat their own food and have a chat.

"How was your visit with Bill Ford?" asked Windflower.

"It was very nice," said his uncle. "I really like Bill. I like him better now that he's off the sauce."

Windflower and Sheila looked at each other. Uncle Frank had been known to take more than a drop in his day and was no stranger to trouble when he'd been drinking. But they stayed mum. No point rehashing bad memories. They were glad they did, because Uncle Frank surprised them with what he said next.

"I think I'm going back to Alberta," he announced.

"What?" said Sheila and Windflower, almost at once.

"I thought you were having a good time here," said Sheila.

"I am," said Uncle Frank. "But I'm getting older, and the damp air really gets to me. I love the place, and the people are the best. But the RDF is killing me. I think I'll go home for the winter. And if you'll have me and Creator allows, I'll come back in the summer to help out with the B&B."

"That would be perfect," said Sheila. "Do you need help making arrangements?"

"No," said Uncle Frank. "Richard Tizzard is going to help me get a ticket online."

"Well, whenever you're ready to go, I'll drive you to St. John's," said Windflower. "And I'd like a few minutes with you. Maybe later today, if that's okay?"

"Had another dream?" asked Sheila.

"Maybe," acknowledged Windflower.

"There's a cat in his dreams," said Uncle Frank.

Before Windflower could respond, Amelia Louise decided she was finished and dumped her drink and the rest of her molasses overboard and onto the floor. Everybody jumped, and she started to cry. And that was the end of their peaceful visit to the Mug-Up.

They managed to get Amelia Louise calmed down while Vanessa cleaned up and were soon back home again. Uncle Frank went to see Richard Tizzard about his trip to Alberta, with a promise to return later to talk to Windflower.

Sheila got out one of Amelia Louise's puzzles, and all three of them played with it on the floor in the living room until Windflower's cell phone rang.

FORTY-SIX

He excused himself and went to the kitchen to take the call.

"Windflower," he said, not bothering to check the number of the incoming call.

"It's me, Cassie," said the girl on the other end of the line. "You remember me?"

"Sure, I remember you," said Windflower. "How have you been doing?"

"Not so good," said Cassie. "I'm in trouble. I've got a serious problem."

"Tell me about it. Maybe I can help," said Windflower. "We can protect you."

"That's just it," said Cassie. "I don't know if you can."

"You might as well try," said Windflower. "What have you got to lose?"

"I dunno," said Cassie. "You probably won't want to get involved. You guys all stick together. I don't know why I'm even talking to you."

"I don't know what's going on, Cassie," said Windflower. "But I can promise you that whatever you tell me I will treat as confidential. Until you tell me it isn't. You trust Constable Foote and me, don't you?"

"I do," said Cassie. "But I can't talk to her about this. That's for sure."

Windflower was starting to get a very strange feeling about this situation. Whatever this young girl had going on, it just might have something to do with the RNC. That was why she couldn't talk to Anne Marie and why she wasn't sure about him. He decided to ask her straight-up.

"Does this have anything to do with the Constabulary?"

The girl stayed quiet for a moment. More than a moment. Then she spoke. Very softly. "Yes."

"Did someone inside there hurt you or threaten you in any way?" asked Windflower.

Cassie didn't say anything.

He tried another tack. "Are you afraid of anybody at that place?"

"Yes," said Cassie, again, very softly.

"Do you want to tell me who it is?" he asked. "I won't tell anybody, not even Anne Marie. And I won't do anything unless you let me."

"It's Frenchie," said Cassie. "You remember that night when I got in your van and you drove me to the cop shop?"

"Yes," said Windflower. "You were pretty scared that night, too."

"Frenchie was the cop I first met. At first, I thought he was just trying to be helpful. Then he started hitting on me. I told him to stop. But he said I was..." Cassie stopped talking, and Windflower could hear her crying on the phone.

"That's not right, Cassie," he said as gently as he could. "I'm sorry that happened to you. But if you want, I can help you. Do you want me to try?"

The girl continued crying but finally managed to speak. "Yes. I would like that."

"Okay, let me see what I can do," said Windflower. "If you can, don't worry about this. Can I call you at this number?"

"Yes," said Cassie, regaining her composure. "But I don't want Anne Marie to get in trouble. He said he would do that if I told anyone."

"She won't," said Windflower. "I promise you that. I'll call as soon as I know anything."

Windflower walked out to the living room, where the puzzle activity had degenerated into another crying, screaming, roll-around-on-the-floor tantrum by Amelia Louise. Sheila was looking on and trying to stay as calm as she could.

"I'd say it's nap time," she said.

Windflower picked up Amelia Louise and carried her upstairs. He let her work it out for a few more minutes and then handed over her stuffed rabbit, which she grabbed and hugged closely. He laid her in her bed and waited outside until her crying subsided and then went back downstairs, just as Uncle Frank was coming in the door.

"I got a ticket for Tuesday afternoon," said Uncle Frank. "Richard is a wizard on the computer. Got me a great deal, too."

"That's great," said Windflower. "I'll drive you in."

"The girls will miss you," said Sheila. "We will, too, but they are going to be heartbroken. Especially Amelia Louise. You're her only relative around here."

"I'll be back in the springtime," said Uncle Frank. "That won't be long at all."

"It's an eternity when you're a child," said Windflower. "Speaking of time, we should go out while the little one is down for her nap. Ready?"

"Let's go," said his uncle.

Windflower drove them down to the beach. They couldn't see anything with the fog, but it felt like a good place to have a chat.

"I love being by the ocean," said Windflower. "Even if I can't see it, I know that it's there. It's comforting."

"I know what you mean," said Uncle Frank. "It's one of the things I'll miss the most, after the people, of course.

The ocean reminds us of our place in the universe. How small and puny and unimportant we really are. Except inside our own heads. I'll miss having that connection."

Both men sat quietly and silently for a few minutes to allow the ocean and the calm to enter their presence. Then Windflower spoke.

"So, I wanted to talk to you about my dream," he said. He started describing the dream in detail. His uncle stopped him.

"What did the cat say to you in your dream?" asked his uncle. "I can see everything, but I can't hear what happens in your dreams."

"She said that I needed to go back in order to move forward," said Windflower.

"People talk about cats in dreams in many ways. Some say that cats represent our creativity and independent spirit, even our feminine sexuality. Others talk about cats symbolizing bad luck or deception. But I think that's our human projection," said Uncle Frank. "But it's your message. What do you think it means?"

"I take it literally," said Windflower. "I think I've missed something important. Maybe in my work or my family life. Maybe both. I'm going to have to figure that out. But how?"

"If you get the question right, the answer will come," said his uncle. "Pray and the question will come."

"It's that simple?" asked Windflower.

"Like all of my life," said Uncle Frank. "When we stick our oars in the water, things become difficult. We get off course. We can even capsize our canoe. Relax and let the current pull you along."

Windflower smiled. "I feel better," he said. "That was easy."

"It is and always will be," said his uncle. "When we let go of control. Now, I have a question for you. Why are you afraid of cats?"

"That's a very good question," said Windflower. "Why am I afraid of cats?"

"You know the answer," said Uncle Frank. "But I will say it out loud for you. It's because you are afraid of your feminine side. Afraid to let it out. Let the rest of the world see it. But here's another secret. We already do."

With that, his uncle started laughing and was still chuckling to himself when Windflower dropped him off at his friend's house on the way home.

FORTY-SEVEN

Windflower didn't go straight home. He pulled into the back parking lot of the clinic. He needed a few moments to process his discussion with Uncle Frank and his earlier call with Cassie. It was quiet today. The area around there had been well picked of blueberries, and few people would attempt that today in this weather. A great spot to sit and think for a few minutes.

Cassie came to mind first. Windflower wasn't often shocked or surprised about what a criminal would do. He'd just about seen it all. But he seldom saw a police officer take advantage of a situation like the one that the girl had described with French. True, there were some bad cops and certainly more than a few mean cops who used a bit more force than required. But nothing like this. To take advantage of someone in such a vulnerable situation…

He had to stop thinking about that. It upset him too much. But how to deal with it without bringing in Foote? That was an issue. He needed to talk to somebody. Finally, it came to him. He could call Langmead. He didn't have to give him all the details. But he could tell Windflower how they dealt with internal problems. Problems with one of their own.

He googled the RNC online. It had both a Public Complaints and a Professional Conduct section. Langmead might know who to talk to. He called and left a message.

Now, about his dream. He needed to go back, because he had missed something. Was it in his work or the rest of his life? It was easier to focus on his work. He had been trained to look for signs, clues. So, what was he missing in the primary case he was involved with? Again, it came to him. There was something suspicious about Elizabeth Frankford. It was even more than that. Almost everything about her was suspicious.

Mysterious might be a better word for it, thought Windflower. She appeared to be one thing and then turned out to be completely different. She was also a chameleon, changing to suit other people, or what she thought they wanted her to be. The more he thought about Elizabeth Frankford, the more he realized that he was missing something, maybe a lot of things about her. She also reminded him of one more thing: Molly, the cat.

That's what he was afraid of. It wasn't completely his feminine side, although he knew he had work to do in that area. He was afraid of being betrayed. When he couldn't see exactly what was being offered by a situation or a person, he pulled back instead of revealing himself. Just like Molly when he came too close sometimes. And maybe just like Elizabeth Frankford.

He was near the clinic, so he decided to go in and see if Reverend Frankford might be awake. He went into the building, put on his mask and walked right to the ICU unit. The duty nurse said that Doctor Sceviour was with Elizabeth Frankford but that she shouldn't be long if he wanted to wait. He took a chair near the door to the unit.

He waited for about twenty minutes and was about to leave when the doctor finally came out.

"Oh, Sergeant. I'm glad you here," said Doctor Sceviour. "She's not doing well. We've had to put her under again. It appears that her internal injuries are more significant, and one of her lungs collapsed. We've reinflated it, but the damage may be done. Are you sure there's no way to contact her husband?"

"I can try," said Windflower. "Is it that serious?"

"She may not make it through the night," said the doctor.

Windflower nodded and left the ICU. When he got outside, he called Albertson at NCSI.

"Don't ever call me," said Albertson. "Are you trying to get both of us fired? They monitor my calls."

"This is official police business," said Windflower. "Elizabeth Frankford may be dying. I need you to get that message to her husband."

"Oh," said Albertson. "They won't let him out. Even if she dies, they won't let him go to the funeral."

"I'm just doing my job," said Windflower. "You do yours."

He hung up before Albertson could say anything else and drove home.

Despite everything on his mind, having Lady and Amelia Louise come run to the door to greet him made up for everything.

Windflower allowed Amelia Louise and Lady to wrestle him to the ground while he attempted to talk to Sheila.

"I took out some salmon steaks for supper," said Sheila. "I can broil them if you don't want to barbeque."

"No, I'm good," said Windflower, managing to extricate himself from a tangle of dog and child and getting to his feet. "I can barbeque. If they'll ever let me go."

After a few minutes of playing with Amelia Louise, he managed to divert her by taking out her tea set and helped her set up a party for her dolls and Lady, who didn't know what the occasion was but was hoping for a treat anyway. She was not impressed when she found out they were imaginary.

Windflower escaped to the kitchen to get his rub for the salmon ready.

"Reverend Frankford is not doing well," he said to Sheila.

"Oh, no," said Sheila. "She wasn't my favourite pastor, but I am sorry to hear that."

"It doesn't look good at all," said Windflower. "She is a very interesting person. I'm not sure anybody around here, including me, really knew her."

"That's true," said Sheila. "We all got to see little pieces of her, but I don't think anybody saw the real person. It's hard to point to exactly why, but almost everyone seems to have their own reason for not liking her."

"Maybe she was holding a mirror up so that we could see our own faults?" said Windflower as he got all his ingredients together.

"Maybe," said Sheila. But that conversation ended when Sheila was summoned to the tea party in the living room.

Windflower spread the salmon steaks out on a baking sheet and mixed up his ingredients. It was a sweet and spicy rub with brown sugar, black pepper, sea salt, basil, garlic powder and smoked paprika. Plus a lemon that he would half zest and then use the other half to squeeze over the salmon while it cooked on the barbeque. He spread the mixture all over the salmon and laid it back in the fridge.

He took out some asparagus and put it in tin foil with garlic and butter, peeled and sliced some carrots with butter, ginger and a dollop of maple syrup in another tin foil packet. Both of those went in the fridge as well, just as Peter Fitzgerald's car pulled up in the driveway.

"We got dessert," yelled Stella as she and her grandfather, holding a large white cardboard box, came in the front door. Fitzgerald handed the box to Sheila, who put it in the fridge.

"What is it?" asked Windflower.

"What is it?" asked Amelia Louise.

"It's a secret," said Stella proudly, looking at her grandfather for approval. He smiled and nodded.

"We'll find out after dinner," he said.

Amelia Louise slumped, but her mood brightened considerably when Stella reached into the bag she was carrying and handed her little sister a new toy doll. It was Wonder Woman, and it came with a light up wand that captivated Amelia Louise. Stella had gotten one almost the same for herself, and after getting off the packaging, they both went upstairs to play with their new toys.

"You didn't have to do that," said Sheila. "I can pay you for Amelia Louise's doll."

"No, no," said Fitzgerald. "You do so much for Stella that I could never thank you enough. She has found a new family with you, and I am very grateful."

"Well, thank you," said Sheila. "Do you want a beer before supper?"

"I think I'll pass," said Fitzgerald. "I'm staying in Marystown tonight, and I don't want to take any chances with all the moose around. I hear somebody else died recently."

"It may be two," said Windflower. "One already, and one in the hospital that's struggling."

"It's pretty serious," said Fitzgerald. "I wish people would just slow down."

Windflower bit his tongue. He had no desire to get into that conversation again. "I think I'll put the barbeque on," he said instead. He walked outside and lit the barbeque, turning on the burners on the right side and leaving the left side cold.

The salmon with the brown sugar basting would burn on direct heat, so he would cook it by convection once the temperature inside the barbeque got hot enough.

He stayed outside for a moment while he waited for it to heat up. He looked in through the patio doors, expecting to see Lady waiting inside. Instead, there was Molly staring right at him.

FORTY-EIGHT

Windflower looked back at the cat, and they remained locked in a staring contest that seemed like it lasted forever. It was like they were both trying to read each other's minds. Windflower blinked first. He opened the door and let the cat out. She wandered around for a minute, checking things out, and then brushed past him when he opened the door to go get the salmon.

"That's a start," he said to Molly, who was long gone by now. But he also had a secret weapon to help him cement his new relationship with Molly: a full plate of salmon that he took off the counter. Molly reappeared and was clearly interested in what he was carrying. She tried to follow him out again, but he closed the door quickly. "Patience, my friend," said Windflower. "Good things come to those that wait," he mouthed. Molly stared even more intently, but he had grilling to do.

He placed the salmon on the cold side of the barbeque and let it cook. It would take a little bit longer this way, but once the heat warmed up the salmon and the spices and brown sugar baste, it smelled divine. Not long after, he was going back in with a plate of fully cooked and very aromatic salmon. The vegetables were perfect, too, and along with a large salad that Sheila had made, they had a wonderful supper with Peter and their children.

While Sheila was getting the dessert out of the fridge, Windflower took a nice chunk of the leftover salmon and put it in Molly's bowl. She didn't look at him but sat to enjoy her feast. When he glanced over a few minutes later, she was licking her paws and looking very pleased with herself. She saw Windflower looking at her and stared back. But Windflower felt it was different this time, maybe the beginnings of a new relationship? But no, she simply turned her back to him, curled up and went to sleep.

Everybody else was more excited by the cake that Sheila took out of the cardboard box. It had two princess figurines on top and was covered in chocolate icing and sparkles.

"It's a perfect cake for the girls," said Sheila. "Thank you, Peter."

"And for us too," said Windflower. "I'll have a big piece."

"Me, too," chorused the girls.

After cake and clean-up, they all retired to the living room, where the adults had tea and the girls played with their new dolls and the figurines from the cake. Peter Fitzgerald left soon afterwards to go back to his hotel in Marystown for the night. Windflower and Sheila put on a movie for everyone to watch. It was *Captain Marvel*, and while it was a little old for Amelia Louise, both girls loved it.

"It's nice to have a superhero movie with a female star," said Windflower.

"I was thinking the same thing," said Sheila.

It was fun and campy and not too serious, and all four of them enjoyed it. After the movie, Sheila took the girls to get ready for bed, and Windflower did dog duty with Lady. It was still foggy out, but the wind had died down and the air had grown warmer. It was a nice night for a walk around Grand Bank.

There were few souls out and about, and Windflower liked the feeling of being almost alone as he walked the narrow streets. It gave more room to breathe and to think. And as always, there was a lot kicking around up there. But when they got to the wharf, he stopped thinking for a moment about himself and thought about Elizabeth Frankford. He couldn't see much more than the blinking red light on the lighthouse with 'Grand Bank' written in large letters up its red and white sides into the mist.

He didn't have any tobacco with him, but he could offer a prayer for her body and spirit. That they both be strong enough for the next journey, wherever that might be. After praying, he let Lady tug him along, all the way home. He was just in time for story time. Tonight, it was his turn with Stella.

Stella had already picked her book, *The Paper Bag Princess*, and was lying in bed waiting for him.

"Did you have a nice day with your grandfather?" he asked. Stella nodded. "Do you ever think you'd like to live with him?"

Stella looked confused. "Why would I live with him? My family lives here."

Windflower gave her a hug and started reading. The story was a classical reversal of the princess and dragon scenario, and both Stella and Amelia Louise loved this book. After a dragon destroys her castle and all her fancy clothing, Princess Elizabeth is forced to wear a paper bag. She defeats the dragon, but when she comes back to her prince, he tells her she looks awful in her paper bag outfit. She dumps him and goes off to live on her own.

"The end," said Windflower, smiling to himself. When he looked up, Stella was fast asleep. He tucked her in, kissed her and went downstairs.

He and Sheila tried watching TV, but both were too tired. Windflower let Lady out for her final turn of the night and then turned off all the lights and went to bed. Sheila was having her bath, and he picked up his Richard Wagamese book from his nightstand. But as he started to read, he thought about Princess Elizabeth and then Elizabeth Frankford.

He had a strange sensation, an eerie feeling, like a cold wave washing over him. He had felt something like that once before in his life. He had been away at a camp with his grandfather the night his mother died. She had been sick for a long time and had urged him to go camping. But he felt that same cold breeze wash over him, like tonight. He knew Elizabeth Frankford had passed.

She must have had a hard life, he thought. Separated from her husband, away from her birth family and thrust into a community that was immediately suspicious of any outsider. She must have fought many demons, thought Windflower as he sent out as many positive feelings as he could towards her spirit.

He picked up the Wagamese book and opened it. The page he read was a conversation between Wagamese and an old woman elder in his community. The woman told Wagamese always to be a gentleman. He asked if that meant to be polite? She said no, to be gentle. "Act softly and kindly to others and yourself."

Windflower was smiling to himself as Sheila came to bed.

"You look like you've discovered the answer to world peace," said Sheila.

"Maybe I have," said Windflower. "Come closer and I'll tell you all about it."

FORTY-NINE

Windflower woke first and let Sheila sleep while he snuck downstairs to put the coffee on. He took a quick peek outside but couldn't see much as he let Lady out into the thick fog. The fog was an irritant, but it wasn't like the floods and tornados and hurricanes that they saw all the time on the news, thought Windflower. His second thought was that he was finally accepting the fog, and maybe he was one step closer to being a true Newfoundlander.

He let Lady in and got the first cup of coffee before he heard the girls chattering away upstairs. He went to retrieve them before they woke Sheila and brought them down with him. Instead of his usual Sunday morning treats, he made them each a slice of toast with peanut butter and half a banana on top. They were just as happy as if he had made them Pop Tarts.

He sat in the living room with them, watching cartoons and nursing his coffee until he heard Sheila. He brought her up a cup as she sat propped up in bed, reading her book.

"Good morning, beautiful. Here's your coffee."

"Thank you," said Sheila. "They're awfully quiet down there. What are you feeding them for breakfast? Cake?"

"Toast and peanut butter and bananas," said Windflower, feigning a little outrage.

"I am surprised," said Sheila. "Did you get any more information about Reverend Frankford?"

"I didn't even check my phone this morning," said Windflower. "But I'm not expecting good news. I'll go check, and then I'll make us a real breakfast."

"Sounds good," said Sheila. "I'll be down once I get this coffee in me."

Windflower went downstairs, where the girls were still absorbed in their shows. He picked up his phone and checked his messages. "You have four new messages," said the machine. They were from Doctor Sceviour, Langmead, Quigley and a surprise, Albertson.

The one from the doctor was no surprise. Elizabeth Frankford had passed last evening, and the doctor would like someone to confirm arrangements for the remains as soon as possible. Langmead, Quigley and Albertson could wait. He had to deal with the dead body first. Without having any next of kin other than her husband, who appeared to be unavailable, he called Elijah Woods. She was still a member of the clergy, or used to be until her unfortunate death.

He got the housekeeper, who told him that Woods was at church. It was Sunday morning, don't you know? Windflower left a message and went back to his regularly scheduled Sunday morning routine. Next up, breakfast.

Sheila came down and occupied the girls while he made scrambled eggs and fried bacon and bologna. He put frozen hash brown patties in the oven. Not as good as homemade, but the kids loved them. A large stack of homemade toast with fresh jam and a fresh pot of coffee, and they were all set.

"Breakfast is ready," he called, and the girls and Sheila came running.

After breakfast, Amelia Louise helped Windflower clean up while Stella went with her mom to get ready for church. That was the one place Amelia Louise didn't care to tag along with her sister.

"Mila no like church," she said to Windflower.

"Shush," he said as Sheila came downstairs with Stella.

"What are you two talking about?" asked Sheila.

"Nothing," said Windflower.

"Nutting," said Amelia Louise.

"We'll see you after church," said Sheila. "Are you going for a run in this?"

"Maybe more like a walk," said Windflower. "I thought we might go up to the trail. And I think I'll have to go into work this afternoon. I'd only be on the phone anyway."

"Okay," said Sheila. "They have a little craft fair at the high school. I might take the girls over there for a while. I think they have a children's area for them to play in."

"That would be nice," said Windflower. "Supper, tonight?"

"There's a pot roast thawing in the fridge," said Sheila. "I was going to ask Carrie and Eddie, if that's okay with you."

"Perfect," said Windflower. Sheila and Stella left for church soon after, and he and Amelia Louise got dressed for their walk. He put Amelia Louise into her car seat and buckled her in. He laid the carrier on the seat beside her, and once Lady had jumped in, they were ready to go. He was about to leave when something reminded him that he needed tobacco. He wasn't sure why, but went back in the house and retrieved a packet.

He drove to the clinic, where a hearse from Moriarty's Funeral Home was arriving at the back entrance. Might be to pick up Elizabeth Frankford, thought Windflower. That's why I need tobacco. He parked the car and got Amelia Louise and the dog out. He tried to put Amelia Louise in the carrier, but she wanted to walk. That wouldn't last long, but he let her have her way for now.

It simply meant that their walk was more of a sniff-and-stroll for his daughter and his dog. Neither could go more than a few steps without stopping to examine a flower or investigate a scent. Windflower took advantage of that slow pace to reflect a little on Elizabeth Frankford and to say a prayer for her spirit. When he was done, he laid down a little of his tobacco with another prayer, this time to Mother Earth to help guide Elizabeth on her journey.

Now Amelia Louise was tired.

"Uppy, daddy. Uppy," she said.

Windflower put her in the carrier and strapped her on his back. Now they could have a good, brisk walk up the trail. He could hear Amelia Louise singing as he strode up the winding trail until he reached the lookout at the peak. He stopped and laid Amelia Louise on the bench and got their snacks out, an apple and some water for them and a Milk Bone biscuit for Lady. After their snack, he put Amelia Louise on his back and headed back down. He was near the bottom when his cell phone rang.

It was Carl Langmead.

"Good morning, Carl," said Windflower.

"Morning," said Langmead. "How's the weather down your way?"

"Foggy," said Windflower. "But not too bad. Mild."

"Same here," said Langmead. "I wanted to let you know that we have more information from our witness. She said she saw a person near the van. A woman. Early fifties. Long, reddish hair."

"That sounds a bit like Elizabeth Frankford," said Windflower. "But what would she be doing around Morecombe's house?"

"Well, we'd like to talk to her," said Langmead.

"That won't be possible," said Windflower. "She succumbed to her injuries from the accident and passed last night. But let me do some digging around here, and I'll get back to you."

"Okay," said Langmead. "Feels like slogging through mud on this one. Every time we think we're getting somewhere, it goes nowhere."

"I hear you," said Windflower. "There's something else I need to talk to you about, though. Do you have a contact at the Professional Standards Section I can talk to? Discreetly."

"Do you want to tell me any more?" asked Langmead.

"I can't right now," said Windflower.

"Okay," said Langmead. "The best guy to talk to is Dan Williams. Do you want me to get him to call you?"

"That would be great," said Windflower. "Thanks."

After hanging up with Langmead, he picked up his pace. They were at the car in no time and back home as Sheila and Stella were arriving from church.

"How was your walk?" asked Sheila.

"It was good," said Windflower. "How was church?"

"It was very sad," said Sheila. "One of the lay ministers led the service, and at the end they had a special tribute for Reverend Frankford. We sang one of her favourite hymns."

"That does sound sad," said Windflower.

"There'll be a bigger memorial service later. Do you know where the remains will be resting?" asked Sheila.

"I don't know for sure," said Windflower. "But Moriarity's was picking up somebody at the clinic. I gave the information to Elijah Woods in Marystown."

"Don't talk about him," said Sheila. "The rumour is that money is missing from our church building fund. And that he's got something to do with it."

"Don't people blame Reverend Frankford?" asked Windflower.

"She's the one who reported it to the wardens," said Sheila. "Anyway, let's not talk any more about that. Let's have some lunch."

Lunch was simple, tomato soup with ham and cheese sandwiches, and afterward, Windflower took his leave and headed over to the office.

FIFTY

When he arrived, Smithson's cruiser was parked out front.

"Hey, boss," said Smithson. "I didn't expect to see you today."

"Lots of loose ends," said Windflower. "Did you hear that Elizabeth Frankford passed last night?"

"I did," said Smithson. "I talked to some of the people leaving church this morning. They were really sad."

"Can you find out what the arrangements are for her remains?" asked Windflower. "I saw the van from Moriarity's at the clinic earlier."

"Will do," said Smithson.

"I think Elizabeth Frankford was in St. John's recently, wasn't she? What kind of car does she drive?" asked Windflower.

"She has a Kia Soul," said Smithson. "But she also has an old van that she uses for errands and picking up stuff."

"I don't remember seeing a van at her house," said Windflower.

"She keeps it, I mean used to keep it, at the back of the manse," said Smithson.

"Get a picture of the van with the license plate and send it to Langmead at the RNC," said Windflower.

"Do you think she was involved in something in St. John's?" asked Smithson. "Elizabeth, I mean Reverend Frankford, wouldn't harm a soul."

"Do you know why she was going to St. John's?" asked Windflower.

Smithson started to turn red. "I think she was going to try to find her husband," he said. "He was not a nice man."

"This is a murder investigation now, Smithson. You need to tell me everything you know. Did she talk to you about this?"

Smithson turned even redder, if that was possible. He cleared his throat and started talking. "Her husband wasn't just unfaithful; he was violent sometimes, especially after a few drinks. She still loved him, but I think that's why Elizabeth couldn't stay with him. She also couldn't leave because of the church. Mostly it was Woods who told her that they'd drive her out of the province. Her husband had been kicked out of the university and was drinking even more. He was living in St. John's, and Elizabeth said she was going to talk to him. Try to talk some sense into him. That's all I know."

"Okay," said Windflower. "Thanks. Find out about her arrangements and get the picture of the van."

Smithson nodded and left.

Windflower picked up the phone and called Ron Quigley in Marystown. It rang a few times and Windflower left a message to call. Five minutes later Quigley phoned back.

"What's up?" asked Quigley.

"Elizabeth Frankford died last night," said Windflower. "Betsy's not here today, so can your guys in PR look after the media release?"

"Sure. Send them the details," said Quigley. "I'll tee it up. Too bad about the reverend. That's three people connected to the church dead in Grand Bank. Coincidence?"

"Well, two of them died in a car accident," said Windflower. "But I'm thinking that there might be a connection to the murder in St. John's, too."

"Morecombe? How does that fit in?"

"I don't know yet," said Windflower. "But Elizabeth Frankford may have been in St. John's when Morecombe died. So was her husband, likely. And Frankford's van may have been seen in the neighbourhood the night of the break-in. Just confirming that now."

"Very interesting," said Quigley. "What about her husband? Any sign of him?"

"I don't know if I told you or not, but he's in custody in Ottawa," said Windflower. "Our guys in NCSI picked him up and are holding him in Ottawa. I asked to talk to him, but nothing back yet."

"He's a national security threat?" asked Quigley.

"I don't know," said Windflower. "He and Morecombe's husband were in some dispute, and there was talk of the Chinese being involved. Way over my head."

"Mine, too," said Quigley. "What role do you think our friend Elijah Woods is playing in all this?"

"I'm trying to figure that out myself," said Windflower. "But he's certainly involved. Too bad Dollimont isn't around to squeeze."

"Speaking of being around, have you and Sheila talked about coming to Marystown?" asked Quigley.

Windflower paused, just to make sure his decision, their decision, still felt like the right one. It did. "I'm not going to apply," he said.

"Final answer, or do you need more time to think about it?"

"No, Ron. I'm sure," said Windflower. "It's not right for us."

"I understand completely," said Quigley. "I'll make a recommendation that you be allowed to stay in Grand Bank for the transition. That should give you a bit more time to figure out your next move. If you're going to make one."

"Thanks, Ron. That's great," said Windflower.

Windflower double-checked his instincts, and it still felt like the right decision. Plus, Quigley had just given him and Sheila a few more months to make a plan. Not a lot of time, but better than none. He was about to call Sheila to tell her about the conversation with Quigley when Smithson came back in.

"I've got the picture of the van," he said. "And you were right. Elizabeth is being waked at Moriarty's."

"Thanks," said Windflower. "Send the picture to Langmead, and when you're done can you get Reverend Frankford's details and email them to PR in Marystown? They will put out the release."

Smithson left to carry out his tasks and came back a few minutes later to tell Windflower that he was going out on his rounds.

"Be safe," said Windflower as he watched Smithson drive off to do his tour of town and then out onto the highway to resume his patrol. Windflower had done that thousands of times now. Almost always it was routine, ordinary, and very little happened. But stuff could happen, bad stuff, in an instant. Already in his time in Newfoundland, he'd seen both Eddie Tizzard and Bill Ford shot in the line of duty. Both survived, but each incident was terrifying in their own way for them, their fellow police officers and their families. And he'd seen murders and horrific car accidents and drug dealers and victims of human trafficking. Maybe he'd seen enough was his last thought before his cell phone rang.

"Windflower, it's Albertson. Frankford wants to talk to you."

"What does he want to talk to me about?" asked Windflower. "Is he coming back for his wife's funeral?"

"I don't know any of that. I'm only the messenger," said Albertson. "He will call you tomorrow morning at nine."

Windflower started to reply and then realized it wasn't a request. It was an order. Well, at least he could finally talk to Charles Frankford. He had a lot to ask him about. Like why his fingerprints were on the gun found in the manse in Grand Bank? What was his relationship with Jerome Morecombe, and did he have any contact with his old boss before she died? And what was his wife doing in St. John's the night of the break-in at Morecombe's house? Hopefully his chat tomorrow would provide some of those answers.

Then it hit him. Charles Frankford had asked to speak to him. What was he going to tell him? Windflower had so many questions, he was starting to get a headache. He went to the back, made himself a cup of coffee and spent an hour running through his notes and trying to make more sense out of what he'd learned so far. The big questions revolved around the Frankfords, the late Gregory Dollimont and Reverend Elijah Woods.

He was starting to understand Elizabeth Frankford better now. She was not the evil person that some made her out to be, or at least he didn't think so. More lonely and lost than anything else. Except for her visit to St. John's, where it looked like she was near the crime scene, if not much worse. Her husband might be able to help with that.

Gregory Dollimont was much easier to figure out, although Windflower would have loved to have another chance to interview him with what he knew now. Dollimont was a drug user, which made him dangerous, and he clearly liked exerting his power. Except he didn't have any power of his own. That came from only one source: Elijah Woods.

Then came Windflower's second major insight of the day. Elijah Woods was the connecter to all of this somehow. He was the person behind the scenes, the master puppeteer who controlled everybody. Woods was the person he'd overlooked in all this, the person he now had to go back over again. Windflower had nagging suspicions about Woods but couldn't quite figure out how to approach him and his haughty sense of self. He had insulated himself well. But that was when he had Dollimont to do his dirty work and to protect him. Maybe he'd be a little more vulnerable, a little more open now.

Then it came to him. Somebody very early on in Windflower's career as a police officer had given him a valuable piece of advice to use when it came to investigations: always follow the money. But how would he do that?

FIFTY-ONE

Windflower called Sheila and told her first about his conversation with Quigley.

"How does it feel?" she asked.

"It feels good," he said. "There's something else I wanted to talk to you about. You said something about missing money at the church and that Elijah Woods might be involved. Who could give me more information about that?"

"The parish finance officer, Ewart Rogers, could probably help you," said Sheila. "But I'm not sure it's a criminal investigation yet."

"I'm more interested in how Reverend Woods might be involved than the money," said Windflower. "Do you have Ewart's number?"

"I do. Let me get it," said Sheila. She came back a few seconds later with the number. "Supper is at five thirty."

"I'll be there," said Windflower. He'd picked up his office phone to call Rogers when his cell phone rang.

"Windflower."

"Dan Williams," said the voice on the other end of the line. "Carl Langmead said you wanted to talk to me about a professional standards matter."

"Thanks for calling," said Windflower. "I received a call from someone I trust about an RNC officer who may be behaving inappropriately. Are you the person to talk to?"

"I may be," said Williams. "Why don't you tell me about the issue?"

"I don't care about my name being used, but can the complainant be anonymous?" asked Windflower.

"We like to get any complaint on the record," said Williams. "Otherwise, it's hard to have it taken seriously by the RNC. Not to mention the difficulties this would cause with the union. But if you are vouching for the person, I'll see what I can do."

"I am," said Windflower. "The background is that I was involved with a human trafficking case last year."

"With Anne Marie Foote," said Williams. "I remember you now. We never met, but I saw you at the press conference with the chief."

"Yeah, that's me," said Windflower. "Anyway, I met several of the girls involved. It was one of them that contacted me."

"What did she say happened?" asked Williams.

"She says that she was harassed and interfered with sexually by an RNC officer," said Windflower. "She didn't tell me exactly what happened. Only that the officer threatened her if she didn't participate sexually with him."

"Do you want to give me the officer's name?" asked Williams.

Windflower paused to think about that question. "It was an officer named French. I think he works in logistics. I only met him once. It was on the night that I brought this girl in."

"Pretty serious allegations," said Williams. "The reason I asked for the officer's name is that we have had other complaints."

"About French?" asked Windflower.

"I'm not at liberty to talk about other complaints," said Williams.

"But I can tell you that they were anonymous as well."

"I see," said Windflower. "What do you need from me?"

"We'll need a statement from the complainant. She can give that to me or one of the other officers in this section. Or she can give it to you. We will need it signed," said Williams.

"I'm going to be in St. John's on Tuesday," said Windflower. "I'll talk to the girl and see what she wants to do. If she's willing to formalize the complaint and make a statement, I can do it then."

"Okay," said Williams. "Normally, I would move to have the officer in question put on leave, but I think that might cause more problems. For now, I'm just going to sit on it until I hear from you. But I want you to know that if this guy did this stuff, we'll go after him hard. There's no place in our service for cops like that."

"Thanks," said Windflower. "I'll call you when I know more."

After talking with Williams, he called Cassie. No answer, so he left a message. He called the finance person at the church instead.

A lady answered the phone.

"Can I speak to Ewart Rogers, please?" said Windflower. "Is he there?"

"Yes," said the lady. "May I ask who's calling, please?"

"It's Sergeant Windflower of the RCMP, ma'am." Windflower heard her yell to her husband.

"Ewart, the Mounties are on the line. You better come."

"Hello," said Ewart Rogers.

"Mister Rogers, it's Winston Windflower. Do you have a few minutes to talk about the church finances? I understand that there's been some problem."

"Well, we're not really at the point of engaging the police just yet," said Rogers. "And with the sudden passing of Reverend Frankford, the church council has decided to postpone any public discussion about our financial situation. Out of respect, you know."

"I understand completely," said Windflower. "I'm not formally investigating the financial aspects of church business. But it might help with another investigation if I had a clearer picture of what was happening on that end."

"I'm not really sure…" Rogers started to say.

"I'm investigating the death of Revered Prowse. We think someone deliberately hurt him," said Windflower.

"Reverend Bob?" said Rogers. "Who would hurt that poor man?"

"Can I come over and see you?" asked Windflower.

"Yes, sir. Come on over," said Rogers. "We're on Main Street, just down from the convenience store. The house with all the beach rocks in front."

That was easy, thought Windflower as he closed his office and drove over to see Ewart Rogers. The house was easy to find, too. There must be a hundred different coloured beach rocks lining the perimeter of a beautiful garden. It helped that they had a large Rogers sign on the front lawn as well.

Mrs. Rogers greeted Windflower and brought him into the living room, which she called the sitting room.

"Afternoon again, Sergeant," said Ewart Rogers. "'Tis a sad state of affairs around our little town these days," he said with a sigh.

"There are some troubles, but this is still a great place to live," said Windflower.

That brightened Ewart Rogers as his wife brought in a tray with tea and the obligatory cookie tray.

"Fresh or canned milk?" she asked as she handed Windflower a cup.

"Just like this, thank you," said Windflower. He also took a date square from the plate when she offered it. "Thank you," he said again.

"I'll leave you to it," said Mrs. Rogers as she went back to the kitchen.

"Have your tea, and then we'll go downstairs, and I'll show you the books," said Rogers. "Awful business about Reverend Bob and then the accident with our lovely Reverend Elizabeth." He reached for another square from the plate. He passed it towards Windflower, who politely declined.

"What kind of woman was Reverend Frankford?"

"The best kind," said Rogers. "She was pleasant and helpful and very spiritual. She was a pleasure to work with. I just don't think people liked somebody coming from outside of here being our preacher after Reverend Bob. Are you ready to come to my office?"

FIFTY-TWO

Windflower finished his tea and followed Rogers downstairs. The main part of the basement was a family room with two recliners and a large TV. There was also a laundry room and a storage area that may have been another bedroom at one point.

Rogers saw Windflower looking around. "That used to be Billy's room," he said. "He's been in Ontario for eight years now. Usually, him and his wife would be home with the grandkids, but not this year." He paused and looked at the pictures all around the spare room.

"Here's my office," he said as they walked into the last room. It was a fully operational office with computer, printer and a fax machine, along with three rows of filing cabinets. "I'm an accountant," said Rogers. "You have to keep everything."

"That's not a bad thing," said Windflower. "It's great if you have to go back and look something up."

"If it's financial, I can find it," said Rogers, running through one of the filing cabinets. "I just took over the church account last year, but I've been on the church council for years. We don't get all the details on the council, but as the accountant, I now have full access.

I'd been wondering for years why we couldn't seem to get into the black. Now, it's a little clearer."

He showed Windflower three files. One was marked Expenditures, one Property and another entitled Special Expenses. "Reverend Frankford actually tipped me off," he said to Windflower. "I had no idea these things were happening."

"What kind of things?"

"Monies being transferred from one account to another and mortgages being taken out against both the reverend's house and the manse, and those funds being moved into another set of accounts controlled outside the community," said Rogers.

"How much money are we talking about?"

"Tens of thousands that I can find," said Rogers. "Maybe as much as a hundred thousand dollars. All gone into a special building restoration account. Except there's no money in that account at the bank. It was all withdrawn and moved again to another account. In Marystown." He left that last word hanging in the air.

"Who's the signing officers on those other accounts?" asked Windflower.

"Reverend Elijah Woods and Gregory Dollimont," said Rogers.

"Maybe there's some explanation for all this. Have you talked to Reverend Woods?"

"He won't return my calls," said Rogers. "That's why I brought it to the church council."

"Would you mind if I asked Reverend Woods a few questions about this?" asked Windflower. "Informally, of course."

Rogers smiled for the first time all day. "That would be wonderful."

Windflower drove home with more questions than he started with, but also with some new ammunition to get the elusive Elijah Woods to finally speak openly with him. That made him happy. So, too, did a full home and that fabulous aroma of meat roasting in the oven when he opened the door.

Stella and Amelia Louise and Lady came running to meet him. He hugged all three of them and walked into the living room, where Sheila was sitting with Eddie and Carrie. Little baby Hughie was sleeping in his carrier, and Windflower went for a closer look.

"Thank God, he looks like you, Carrie," he said.

Everyone, including Tizzard, laughed at his joke.

"Come on, Uncle Eddie, we're having a tea party," said Stella. "Do you want to come, too, daddy?" she asked.

Amelia Louise didn't even bother asking. She grabbed Tizzard's arm and started pulling him. "Come on, unca."

"You go on upstairs and be quiet. You, too, Eddie," said Windflower.

Tizzard went off with the girls, and Sheila and Carrie took the baby to the kitchen with them.

"Why don't you get changed? Supper's almost ready," said Sheila.

Windflower went upstairs and had a nice hot shower. When he came out, he could hear the girls and Tizzard in Stella's room. They had Eddie in a corner with all the dolls placed around him, almost like a prison.

"Suppertime," said Windflower.

That was Tizzard's cue to break free, and he raced downstairs with the girls on his heels. Windflower came behind a little slower, and soon everyone was sitting at the table while Sheila served up their supper: beautiful slices of nicely browned roast beef with mashed potatoes, vegetables and a thick, hearty gravy. And the pièce de résistance, perfectly cooked Yorkshire puddings that were a great receptacle for more of Sheila's gravy.

After firsts, and then seconds and finally thirds for Tizzard, the girls were released from the table and little Hughie woke up. Tizzard and Windflower did clean-up duties while Sheila and Carrie went to the living room to look after the baby.

"Sheila told us you're not going to Marystown," said Tizzard. "I don't blame you. Marystown is a completely different experience than Grand Bank. It wouldn't be the same."

"We're both okay with not going to Marystown," said Windflower. "That would mean a commitment of two, maybe three years that I'm not sure I want to make. I'm actually not quite sure what to do next."

"They will offer you another posting," said Tizzard.

"I know," said Windflower. "I could probably take my pick of places. I'm not sure I want to go or even stay in the Force. It might be time for something completely different."

"Like being a private detective?" asked Tizzard.

Windflower almost asked if he was crazy when he looked over and saw Tizzard laughing. The reason he was laughing was because that had been his plan before he went to Las Vegas to get his PI certificate and ended up in jail. Windflower started laughing, too.

"What's so funny?" asked Sheila, who had come in from the living room. But by this time both men were laughing so hard, they couldn't respond.

"Room for dessert?" asked Sheila.

"I always have room for dessert," said Tizzard. "My dad says that if you don't have room for dessert, you should build a new house."

Sheila took a chocolate peanut butter cheesecake out of the fridge. That was Windflower's absolute favourite dessert in the world. He watched as Sheila cut the slices and without any apologies reached for the largest piece. The girls came back for dessert, and the room was filled with smiles and laughter. When Carrie came in with a rested and fed Hughie, the picture was complete.

Windflower ate his cheesecake as slowly as he could to savour the moment, and he smiled, too, at the scene around him. This is what's important, he thought. His second thought was that he could have this anywhere in the world he wanted. That, along with his favourite cheesecake, made him a very happy man indeed.

After dessert, Eddie and Carrie and the baby left for home. Carrie had to try to get Hughie settled for the night, and Tizzard needed to head into work for the overnight shift. Windflower and the girls walked them to the door, and after a round of hugs, the Tizzard family was gone. Windflower took Lady for a walk to break himself from the cheesecake haze he was floating along in.

The fog had lifted a bit, but it was still hovering near the edge of town, like a bandit who was waiting for the security guard to leave for the night. But it made their walk a little less damp and a lot more pleasant. Windflower went down by the wharf and sat on the edge watching the blinking lighthouse.

FIFTY-THREE

He and Lady were both startled when his cell phone rang.

"Windflower," he said.

"It's me. Cassie."

"Hey, Cassie, how are you?" asked Windflower.

"I'm okay," said Cassie. "You called."

"So, I talked to the Constabulary's internal investigating unit," said Windflower. "I didn't give them your name. But I did mention that French was involved."

"Oh no, he'll find out for sure," said Cassie.

"No, I don't think so," said Windflower. "Apparently there are other complaints."

"So why didn't they stop him before this?"

"Good question," said Windflower. "But not one we can do anything about right now. They will need a written complaint in order to move forward."

"No way," said Cassie. "I don't trust them at all. They always protect their own."

"This time it will be different," said Windflower. "I'm prepared to put my name and reputation on this as well. You can trust me."

Cassie was quiet as she thought about it. "I don't know," she said finally. "It feels like too much trouble, and it probably won't go anywhere anyway."

"That might be true. But you know that if we don't stop it here, it will go on and other girls will get hurt. Do you want that?" asked Windflower.

"No," said Cassie, a bit hesitantly.

"You've been brave before when you helped all those other girls and when you are part of the training program with Anne Marie. I need you to be brave again," said Windflower. "Will you do it? Will you make a statement?"

Cassie sighed. "Okay. I'll do it. But you have to check with Anne Marie first. If she says it's okay, I'll make the statement."

"Great," said Windflower. "I'll call her tomorrow morning, and then I'll be in St. John's on Tuesday. We can get together to help you write your statement. Okay?"

"Yeah," said Cassie.

Lady had wandered off while Windflower was on the phone, but she came back when he called her, and they continued their evening walk. As they turned the corner for home, the fog not only came back, but it also settled on their shoulders like an extra wet and heavy sweater. Both man and dog shivered involuntarily as they got back inside.

Windflower was in time to read Amelia Louise's story. That made him happy. He was even happier when she picked out *Goodnight Moon* and *Brown Bear, Brown Bear, What Do You See?* They read the bear story together, which was almost the most fun, ever. The book starts out with a picture of a big brown bear and the question: What Do You See? The next page has a colourful bird and the answer: I see a red bird looking at me. Amelia Louise would turn the next page and start almost reading along with Windflower. Sometimes, like tonight, he would make up different stories about other animals they might see, and Amelia Louise loved that game as well.

After they read the bear book twice, Windflower read *Goodnight Moon* and tucked Amelia Louise in for the night. He went downstairs with Sheila and had a cup of tea while they watched the news before they went to bed.

Windflower was tired, comfortable and relaxed when his head hit the pillow. He fell asleep easily. But that didn't last. He woke in a dream.

This time he was walking along a rural road in the country, but not anywhere that seemed familiar to him. It was a paved road with forests on both sides, and it was a hot summer day with the sun beating down on him as he walked along. It was eerily quiet as he walked, and he tried to remember to be observant of the things and animals around him. He didn't see or hear a living thing for a long time. In fact, he kept coming by dead creatures as he walked.

First, there was a small frog that had been squished by a passing car. Then, there was a dead mouse with flies and other insects beginning to hover around it. Next, he saw a beautiful orange and black butterfly lying by the side of the road. At first, he thought it was just resting, but as he got closer he could see it wasn't moving at all.

He was starting to get a little upset, but when he walked just a little farther, he could hear birds singing and water flowing.

There were jays and chickadees and all sorts of small birds, and then he heard some ducks and geese, and as he neared the water, which turned out to be a large, fast-flowing river, a heron flew directly overhead. When he looked down, he could see a campfire at the edge of the water and what looked like a person with a blanket over their head. He walked closer to the fire.

"Hello, Winston," said Auntie Marie, pulling the blanket down and wrapping it over her shoulders. "I love it over here, but I still miss sitting by the fire. I come over when I can. Come and sit with me. It's nice to have company."

"Auntie, I've missed you," said Windflower.

"I pop in sometimes to see how you're doing. Thank you for caring for Frank," said Auntie Marie. "Once again you are at a crossroads, I see."

"Big decisions ahead," said Windflower. "Where we'll live, where I'll work. If I'll work."

"All external things," said his aunt. "You may find temporary comfort or pleasure in a place or even an occupation. But you have a higher calling."

"What is that?" asked Windflower.

"To be a good and decent man, a good human being that cares for his friends and his family and community. Someone who respects Mother Earth and his ancestors. Someone who is grateful for the gifts that he has received and is willing to give them all away to someone who needs them," said Auntie Marie.

"I'm not there," said Windflower.

"No, but you are on your journey towards that life," said his aunt. "Now you have to decide who is going with you."

"You mean my family?" asked Windflower. "They're coming, for sure."

"Yes, but all your relations and your allies, too," said Auntie Marie. "You are letting some things go now so that you can make room for more."

"That's what the dead animals were on the road," he said. "Things I'm leaving behind."

"Very good, my boy," said his aunt. "The frog was a little boy who lost his way and was afraid to ask for help. The mouse was your fear that tries to hide out in the open, but everyone sees it. The butterfly was your last stage to becoming a man. A real man, kind and gentle."

"And the heron was my future," said Windflower. "Is my future."

As he was speaking, he could feel himself being lifted high into the sky by a giant heron. The heron carried him higher and higher until all things on the ground were only specks like grains of sand on the beach. Then the heron let him go, and he started to fall. Faster and faster, until he woke in his bed with a start. Sheila stirred behind him. "Only a dream," he whispered. She drifted back to sleep.

Sometimes after a dream he felt drained, exhausted. But tonight's dream left him feeling comfortable and relaxed.

Whatever decision he made about the future would be a good one, as long he had a good heart and good intentions. With that pleasant thought, he snuggled into Sheila and had one of his best sleeps ever.

FIFTY-FOUR

He woke to the sounds of the girls playing in Stella's bedroom and smuggled them downstairs without waking Sheila. He cut an apple in slices and set them up in front of the TV while he made coffee and scrambled some eggs. When the coffee was ready, he took a cup up to Sheila as her wake-up offering. She was very happy with it and him.

"I'll be right down," she said as Windflower went to finish making breakfast. He cut up a melon, made toast, and got the girls to help setting the table while he cooked the eggs. When Sheila came down, he served everybody up a helping and sat down to enjoy his breakfast with them.

"I like the service," said Sheila.

"We aim to please," said Windflower. "I thought I'd get things going, because I have to get into work early this morning."

"Big day?" asked Sheila.

"Elizabeth Frankford's husband is going to call me this morning. Wants to talk to me," said Windflower.

"I never met him," said Sheila. "Although he was much talked-about around town."

"I'll bet," said Windflower, finishing his eggs. "I'm going to get changed. But I'll clean up first."

"Don't worry about that," said Sheila. "Amelia Louise and I will do that after everybody's gone."

Amelia Louise looked up from her eggs and with a jam-stained face to smile and nod her agreement.

Windflower showered and changed into his clean uniform. He said goodbye to Sheila and kissed the girls on his way out the door. He wanted to leave early, not just to talk to Charles Frankford, but also to have time to smudge and do some meditation. It felt like today would be a very important day, and he wanted to be at his best. He'd remembered to bring his smudging kit with him, and it sat on the front seat of his cruiser as he drove down to the beach and parked.

It was foggy again this morning. Maybe even foggier than ever, thought Windflower as he tried to gaze out into the ocean. All he saw was an almost solid wall of fog. He found his favourite rock and unfurled his materials. There was only a slight breeze, which made it easy to light his mixture, and soon the smoke was rising in thin wisps from the bowl.

He made sure to capture some of the smoke as it started to drift off and passed it over his head and body and the soles of his feet. His memory of the dream and his visit with Auntie Marie was still vivid, and he wanted to be sure to get all the help he could from the universe to walk a good path today. He gave thanks for all his gifts, prayed for his family and ancestors and made a commitment to be extra grateful to his four-legged and flying and swimming and crawling allies. He closed with laying a little tobacco down for his aunt. She didn't really need it, but he knew she would be watching and would appreciate the gesture.

He still got into the office in time to say hello to Betsy and get a cup of coffee before his cell phone rang. It was Albertson.

"I've got Charles Frankford here," said Albertson. There was a pause, and then another man said hello.

"Hello," said Windflower. "It's Sergeant Windflower from the RCMP in Grand Bank. You said you wanted to talk to me."

"Yes, Sergeant," said Frankford. "Maybe I can clear a few things up for you. I know who killed that Morecombe woman in St. John's."

"Who was it?" asked Windflower. "And how do you know?"

"I was there," said Frankford. "So was my wife. That's really why I'm talking to you. I don't want you thinking that she had anything to do with it. We didn't get along well at the end, but I think it's the least I can do. Given the circumstances."

"So, you were in St. John's when Alison Morecombe died, and so was your wife. Who killed her?" asked Windflower.

"Let me tell you the story," said Frankford. "I was going to try to get some patent papers that Morecombe, Jerome Morecombe, had been hiding from me. I figured they were somewhere in his house. Elizabeth came along with me to help me get in, figuring she would let a woman in before me. But things went wrong. I never should have brought him along with me."

"Who?" asked Windflower.

"Greg Dollimont," said Frankford. "I brought him because I owed a lot of money, and I told him we'd all be rich if I could get that patent. But the patent wasn't there. We got the woman to open the safe. She went for the gun when we did, and Dollimont smashed her over the head. I just grabbed the gun, and me and Elizabeth took off. I don't know what happened after that."

"That's pretty convenient, blaming Dollimont after he's dead," said Windflower.

"Listen, Dollimont was only the henchman," said Frankford. "The guy that lent me the money and ordered him around was Elijah Woods."

"You borrowed money from Woods?" asked Windflower. "How much?"

"I needed cash for my, er, lifestyle," said Frankford. "The pension from the university is a pittance, and they only pay half of the apartment in St. John's. I lost all my savings in the court battle with Morecombe on the patent issues. I heard Woods was a money-lender."

"How much?" asked Windflower.

"Ten thousand the first time and then another fifteen later. All in cash from a safe in Woods's house," said Frankford. "I'll tell you something else. He probably killed that old minister, too. Elizabeth told me that the old guy talked to her about Woods. Said something fishy was going on with the money at the church. They were trying to scare her off, too. I bet that's why she was with Dollimont that morning."

"Why are you telling me all this?" asked Windflower.

"My life as I knew it is over," said Frankford. "The spooks here got me. The Chinese spooks want me, and I would really like to nail that slimeball Woods. I think he's responsible for Elizabeth's death."

Albertson came on the line. "That's it," he said. "No talking about anything in the national security interest. Call's over."

"Wait," said Windflower. "He's a witness in a murder investigation, the murder of an RCMP officer. He's still a suspect. We'll need to talk to him again. The local cops will want to talk to him for sure."

"Put in an official request," said Albertson. The cell phone line went dead.

Windflower sat in stunned silence for a moment until Betsy came through on the intercom. "Inspector Quigley on Line one."

FIFTY-FIVE

Windflower punched the button on his phone.

"Good morning to you, fair and gracious sergeant," said Quigley.

"Ah, Inspector. 'The morning steals upon the night, melting the darkness,'" said Windflower in response. "I just had a very interesting call with Charles Frankford."

"The reverend's husband?" asked Quigley. "So you found him?"

"The national security guys called me. But he wanted to talk to me," said Windflower. "He blamed Gregory Dollimont for a lot of stuff. Most of which is probably true."

"That's not the interesting part," said Quigley.

"No," said Windflower. "The interesting stuff is that he names Elijah Woods as a money-lender, maybe even a loan shark."

"That's not necessarily illegal," said Quigley. "If it's done completely informally."

"It is if you're lending someone else's money," said Windflower.

"What do you mean?" asked Quigley.

"There's money missing from the church in Grand Bank, and the accountant thinks Woods is involved.

And Frankford says he got the money directly from Woods, in cash, from a safe in his office," said Windflower.

Quigley whistled softly. "Do you have proof?"

"I have Charles Frankford's information, and the accountant at the church is digging into it," said Windflower.

"Maybe we should pay Woods a visit and talk to him about this?" said Quigley. "Can you come over today? I'm going to Ottawa on Tuesday for training. That's actually what I was calling you about. I'll be gone the rest of the week."

"I can come this afternoon. Why don't you make the appointment and let me know?" said Windflower. "Don't tell him I'm coming. It will be a surprise."

"I like that," said Quigley. "'We may surprise and take him at our pleasure.' I'll let you know about the time."

Quigley hung up, and Windflower smiled to himself at the thought of visiting Elijah Woods unannounced, especially with the information he had gathered. Then he thought about Cassie and her dealings with French, and his smile quickly faded. He called Dan Williams and left him a message that he would be getting a written complaint. Then he called Anne Marie Foote.

"That poor girl," said Foote. "No wonder she's scared. Can you tell me who it is?"

Windflower paused. It was a risk but one he was prepared to take. "It was French."

"That creep," said Foote. "You know he's always been a bit weird. He's hit on every female civilian and constable at the RNC."

"There may be other complaints, too," said Windflower. "The person at Professional Standards wouldn't confirm. But I got the sense he wasn't shocked at hearing French's name in connection with a complaint."

"No woman around here would be, that's for sure," said Foote. "I'm always surprised that they let these guys wear a badge. But the system seems to be designed to protect them. I know that there has been at least one internal complaint about French, but nothing happened. Anyway, good for Cassie for bringing this forward. How is she?"

"She seemed well on the phone," said Windflower. "The main reason she didn't come forward on this before was because she was trying to protect you."

"Protect me?" asked Foote. "From whom?"

"French told Cassie he would get you in trouble if she told anybody," said Windflower.

"That..." Foote started to say.

"Don't do or say anything about French," said Windflower. "Professional Standards will launch a formal investigation if Cassie will file a complaint, and she's willing if you say it's okay."

"It is super okay with me," said Foote. "I feel really badly for Cassie. We did bring her into all this."

"We did, but we also helped her get out of a very dangerous place," said Windflower. "And she's going to help a lot more girls along the way."

"Okay," said Foote. "What happens next?"

"I'm coming to St. John's tomorrow to see her and get her statement," said Windflower. "Then it's up to the RNC."

"Can you see if she'll meet me or talk to me after you see her?" asked Foote.

"I'll ask," said Windflower. "And I'll let you know when the complaint has been filed."

"Thanks very much," said Foote.

Betsy was waiting in his doorway just after he hung up with Foote.

"The meeting with Inspector Quigley and Reverend Woods is at two o'clock," said Betsy.

"Thank you," said Windflower. "Can you let him know I'll meet him at the minister's house?"

After Betsy left, he called Sheila to let her know he was going to Marystown.

"Great," said Sheila. "Can you see if the fish truck is in the parking lot near Shoppers?

If he is, can you get some scallops? Some shrimp, too, if he has any."

"I can do that. For sure," said Windflower.

"If you get back in time, I'll make a casserole for supper," said Sheila.

"I should be okay," said Windflower. "I'll call you with a progress report if I find the fish guy."

Windflower left the office and started his drive to Marystown. He stopped just before he hit the highway to find the CD that Herb had given him. He took a look at the cover again. *Romance: The Piano Music of Clara Schumann* by Isata Kanneh-Mason. He put it into the player, and the piano music filled him and his cruiser as they traversed the barren landscape outside of Grand Bank. He took the time to listen to the whole CD and was really pleased when other musicians joined Kanneh-Mason on various pieces throughout the recording.

There was an excellent cello soloist on one piece, and in another there was a delightful violinist who added another layer of listening pleasure as Windflower moved through the countryside. He didn't even notice how fast the time flew by, but that may have had something to do with the fact that he could barely see the sides of the highway until he began to near Marystown.

He was a few minutes early, so he stopped at Tim Hortons and got himself a coffee and a bagel for lunch. He was sitting in the window when a familiar face walked by. It was Bill Ford.

"Hey, Bill," Windflower called out, and the other man came to his table.

"I heard you may be over around here today," said Ford. "Let me get a coffee, and I'll be right with you."

The two men had a great chat sitting in the coffee shop until Windflower noticed the time on the clock on the wall. "I better get going," he said. "Your boss may be looking for me."

"Okay, see you soon," said Ford. "How's Frank doing?"

"I forgot to tell you," said Windflower. "He's decided to head back to Alberta for the winter."

"That's too bad," said Ford. "I was hoping to see him again."

"If you are here on Tuesday morning, we can stop by on the way to St. John's," said Windflower.

"That would be great," said Ford. "I should be here."

Windflower said goodbye to Bill Ford and left for his meeting. As he was driving out of the Tim Hortons, he could see that the red fish truck was just pulling into the parking lot across the way. Good news, thought Windflower. It was also good news to pull up in front of Elijah Woods's house and to see that Quigley's car wasn't there yet. He needed a few moments to compose himself and think about what he'd like to ask the minister. He was pondering that exact thought when Ron Quigley tapped on his window.

FIFTY-SIX

Windflower got out of his car and walked with Quigley to the entrance, where they were greeted by the housekeeper and shown into the parlour. Elijah Woods was sitting quietly, sipping a cup of tea. He rose and indicated both men should sit down beside him. If he was surprised to see Windflower at his meeting with Quigley, he didn't show it.

"Gentlemen, I'm glad you're here," began Woods. "The last few months have been quite difficult. I am hoping we can get back to more peaceful waters."

Quigley nodded to Windflower as a sign that he should begin.

"We still have some unresolved issues," said Windflower. "First of all, while our investigation is still incomplete, we can confirm that Reverend Prowse died of insulin poisoning and that it was deliberately administered."

"Those are strong allegations," said Woods.

"Not only that, but we also believe that Gregory Dollimont was the person who poisoned and murdered Revered Prowse," said Windflower.

"Really?" said Woods. "Now you want to drag a good man's name down with him, pouring dirt on his grave. That's shocking. I hope you have proof of this."

"We have proof," said Windflower. "We will provide that in the report you will receive. But we also wanted to talk to you about some other things."

"I'm a very busy man," snarled Woods.

"You'll want to hear this," said Quigley. "Trust me."

Woods scowled at Quigley but turned back to Windflower. "Go ahead, Sergeant. What great revelations have you discovered?"

"What do you know about the finances of the church in Grand Bank?" asked Windflower.

Woods was not expecting that line of questioning. He started to stammer about being a caretaker of all the flock, but Windflower stopped him.

"There is an investigation underway that shows you and your late friend, Gregory Dollimont, were custodians of some funds that appear to be missing. There are also suggestions that you were lending some of that money out to people at exorbitant interest rates. We call that loan-sharking," said Windflower.

"This is preposterous," said Woods. "How dare you come into a house of God and insult me and the church in this way."

"This is not a church or a sanctuary," said Quigley. "The information that Sergeant Windflower has obtained is credible, and he has sources to confirm it. What is your official response to these allegations?"

"Yes, Gregory Dollimont and I are, or he was when he was alive, guardians of the Building Fund in Grand Bank. We have served in that capacity for many parishes over the years. That's because we are honest and people trust us — trust me. Reverend Prowse in Grand Bank was the one who initially asked us to take on this role. But I can assure you that nothing untoward or amiss is happening with those funds," said Woods.

"That's not what the financial people in Grand Bank had to say," said Windflower. "We also have a witness who swears that he was in your office and that you loaned him thousands of dollars in cash from a safe in your office."

"Who was this so-called witness?" asked Woods.

Windflower ignored that question. "Do you keep large amounts of cash in a safe in your office? Do you make loans to people, and what interest do you charge them?"

"Listen, Inspector," said Woods, trying to bring Quigley to his side of the argument. "I have some cash in my safe for small emergencies. People sometimes come to me, and I dispense the money for the good and welfare of the community. There's no interest. Many times the money is never even paid back."

"So you won't mind letting us take a look at the inside of your safe?" said Quigley. "If you've nothing to hide." He let that comment hang there for a moment.

"That won't be possible," said Woods.

"In that case, we are going to have to ask you to come with us," said Quigley.

"Are you seriously arresting me?" asked Woods. "You can't do that. This is ridiculous. I want to call my lawyer." He started to rise and move toward the telephone on a nearby table.

Windflower stood between him and the telephone.

"You are not under arrest, yet," said Quigley. "Although if you attempt to interfere with our investigation in any way, we will have no hesitation in doing so. We want you to come with us for further questioning. You can call your attorney from the detachment."

Woods turned purple and looked like he was going to explode. "You will pay a price for this," he hissed. "I will not be treated this way."

"You can go with the sergeant to his cruiser, or I can put you in handcuffs to detain you," said Quigley.

Windflower put his hand under the minister's arm and guided him out of the room. The housekeeper watched in dismay as her employer was led by the RCMP officer out of the house and put in the back of his car. Quigley was following closely behind. He spoke to the housekeeper briefly and then joined Windflower, who was standing outside his vehicle.

"Well, now you've done it," said Windflower.

"You drive him back to the detachment and bring him up to my office. I'll call Bill Ford and let him know you're coming. Then I'm going to phone Judge Molloy to get a quick warrant to search his office and the safe," said Quigley.

"You need me for all that?" asked Windflower.

"Nah, we can handle it here. Look after Woods, and then you can go back to Grand Bank. I'll call you with any news," said Quigley.

Windflower drove a now stubbornly silent Woods back to the detachment and accompanied him up to Quigley's office, where Bill Ford was waiting.

"In here, please," said Ford, and he opened the door to his office, which was just outside Quigley's. "You can use the phone here if you'd like to make a call." Woods was picking up the phone when Ford and Windflower went outside.

"The boss thinks the warrant should be ready in a couple of hours," said Ford. "Does he really have bags of cash in a safe?"

"That's what a witness told me," said Windflower. "I sure hope he does, because if he doesn't, we're all in the soup."

"We'll find out soon," said Ford. "You staying around?"

"Nope," said Windflower. "I've got to see a man about some seafood, and then I'm going home. See you tomorrow."

He stopped by the red truck and waited until several people walked away with their orders. "Any scallops today?" he asked when it was his turn.

"Yes, b'y, I got a coupla bags left," said the man standing in the back. "And I got a few shrimps, too."

"I'll have one bag of each," said Windflower, paying the man and walking back to his car feeling pretty pleased with himself. He called Sheila with his good news.

"That's great," said Sheila. "Are you on your way back now?"

"Yes, ma'am," said Windflower.

"Perfect. We'll see you soon, then."

"Bye," said Windflower.

He drove slowly out of Marystown, still feeling good about his purchase and the afternoon when his cell phone rang. He pulled over to the side of the road to take the call. It was Ewart Rogers, the accountant from the church.

"I thought you might be interested to know what I found," said Rogers. "I got the records from the bank, and when I looked at the transfer documents, the signatures don't match. Well, some do. But one of them, dear old Reverend Bob, his name is signed differently on the main document that gives Reverend Woods and Gregory Dollimont signing authority over the funds. It's clearly not the same signature as on other documents."

"What are you saying, exactly?" asked Windflower.

"I'm saying that somebody else signed Reverend Bob's name on that document. And that's the one that allows Reverend Woods to have control over the monies. There's lots of other discrepancies, but that's a big red flag right there. I'm going to the finance committee tonight with a recommendation that we bring in the police to investigate. I wanted you to know that, too."

"Thank you for letting me know," said Windflower. "We'll be ready to move when you let us know." He thought about telling Rogers that the investigation had already begun, but that would be public knowledge soon enough.

FIFTY-SEVEN

After hanging up with Rogers, he called Ron Quigley.

"That's going to help, although I'm not sure we can get Woods for forgery," said Quigley. "But the fact that they are going to formally invite us in will let us dig deeper."

"Less grief from the higher-ups," said Windflower.

"I don't really care about that. I'll be gone in a couple of months anyway," said Quigley. "You?"

"Not really," said Windflower. "I'm more worried about getting this seafood back to Sheila so she can make my supper."

Quigley laughed. "Ah, 'appetite, a universal wolf,'" he said. "Enjoy the drive and your well-deserved meal."

"I do like to eat," said Windflower. "Have a good evening, my friend. 'I wish you all the joy you can wish.'"

Windflower drove slowly through the fog that persisted in heavy density until he came to the area near the outskirts of Grand Bank. Then, as he started to roll up and down the hills, he could see the fog slowly, but certainly, moving out into the Atlantic Ocean. Hopefully, that would be a sign of good weather to come, he thought, and early indications seemed to support that theory. By the time he reached his driveway, the fog had disappeared, and the sun was shining brightly.

He passed his delivery to Sheila, got changed quickly and was back out with two kids and a dog before the weather could change its mind. It looked like all of Grand Bank had the same idea, and Windflower and Lady and the wagon with the two little girls made multiple stops to say hello to their neighbours. They walked down to the wharf, where a full congregation of retirees had gathered and once again spent a few minutes visiting. He managed to extricate himself and moved on up past the B&B and then home, where Sheila was putting a dish in the oven.

"Twenty minutes to supper," she said.

"That was fast," said Windflower.

"It's not that hard," said Sheila. "Once I cleaned the shrimp and shredded the cheese, it was simple. The recipe I had called for haddock, but I substituted cod. I don't think we'll notice with all the heavy cream in there. If you'll chop up some broccoli, I'll make a small salad to go along with some rice and our casserole."

"Perfect," said Windflower, and he started getting the broccoli ready alongside Sheila while the girls played with Lady in the living room. Molly oversaw the festivities from her perch on top of the couch. She gave Windflower a bit of a stinkeye when he looked over at her.

"What's going on with Molly?" he asked.

"She's the same as always, at least to me," said Sheila. "Maybe it's your imagination."

Windflower started to protest and thought twice about it.

"How did your visit to Marystown go? Did you see Reverend Woods?" asked Sheila.

"We did," said Windflower. "From our perspective it went well. Not so much for him. I left him in RCMP custody."

"No way," said Sheila. "Under arrest?"

"Well, not exactly under arrest," said Windflower. "But in a heap of trouble. We think he was loan-sharking in addition to the missing money from Grand Bank."

"Wow, that is big news," said Sheila.

"Ewart Rogers is on the case, and it appears there is nothing worse than an accountant scorned. He found a possible case of forgery and is recommending that we be brought in for a formal investigation," said Windflower. "Here's your broccoli, ma'am."

Windflower went out to the living room to join in the fun with his dog and his daughters. He looked up at the couch for Molly, but she had disappeared. I wonder where she's gotten to? he thought. He didn't have long to think about that before Sheila called them all to supper.

She took a little of the casserole and put it aside to cool for the girls while she put some rice, steamed broccoli and salad on everyone's plate. Then she put a heaping scoop on Windflower's, and she watched with some amusement as he let the flavours and aromas of the seafood casserole wash up and over him. He blew on it to cool it but couldn't resist plucking out a plump scallop and tasting the edge of it.

"That is so good," said Windflower. "But very hot." He picked at his salad while he was waiting, and then when he could, he dug in and didn't come up for air until he passed his plate back to Sheila for seconds. "No more salad, thanks," he said.

"You're setting a bad example," said Sheila.

"Daddy's bad," said Amelia Louise, clearly enjoying the fact that her father and not herself was in trouble for a change.

Windflower said nothing until he finished his second helping. "Excellent job, Missus Hillier. You go put your feet up, and we'll clean up."

Windflower tried to get the girls to cooperate, but that soon degenerated into a mini skirmish. So he sat them down and gave them each a small bowl of sliced peaches while he finished up the dishes. When he was done, he asked them in a very loud voice, "What time is it?"

"Six o'clock," said Stella.

"Seben ocock," said Amelia Louise.

"Nope," said Windflower. "Mommy knows what time it is. Go ask her."

The girls ran to their mother. "What time is it?" they yelled.

"I believe it's ice cream time," said Sheila.

"You are absolutely correct," said Windflower. "Who wants ice cream?"

Both girls raised their arms high and held them like that all the way out the door.

"It's too nice an evening not to take advantage of it," said Windflower.

"Absolutely," said Sheila. "This might be our last outdoor ice cream of the year."

They were not alone in that thought. It seemed like half of the town was coming for ice cream this evening. The girls waited not too patiently in line for their turn to get into the dairy counter in a converted garage, but were instantly appeased when they got their small caramel sundaes with a little whipped cream and a maraschino cherry on top. Windflower got himself and Sheila small, dipped cones and they walked up to the park, where they sat to enjoy their treats.

They waved hello to the many people who passed by, and just as the sun was starting to go down and it got much cooler, they headed for home.

"We may never get them down tonight," said Sheila. "But it was still a great idea and totally worth it."

Sheila was right. It was an hour past their normal bedtime before there was any hope of getting their daughters to settle down and go to bed. But finally they succumbed, and Windflower and Sheila had a few minutes of respite before they also called it a day.

Windflower let Lady out in the back and gazed up at the stars. At least he could see them tonight now that the fog had finally gone on vacation. Lady wandered around the backyard and found the appropriate location for her evening activity and then came back to the door that Windflower held open for her. He had just finished filling her bowl and Molly's, although the cat was still nowhere to be seen, when his cell phone rang.

"Good evening, Sergeant. I didn't get you up, did I?" asked Ron Quigley.

"Nope, just letting the dog back in," said Windflower. "Big night tonight, ice cream after supper."

"Good night for it," said Quigley. "I thought I'd give you an update on Woods and the situation over here. I'm off to Ottawa first thing in the morning."

"Is he still there?" asked Windflower.

"No, we had to let him go," said Quigley. "We're not quite ready to charge him. But we did get the warrant and an agreement from Woods to stay away from his house until we complete the search."

"Did you find the safe?" asked Windflower.

"We did," said Quigley. "But Reverend Woods would not extend his cooperation by giving us the combination, so we've had to call in a professional. Bill Ford is over there now waiting for him."

"Okay, I'll check in with Bill in the morning," said Windflower. "I'm coming through on my way to St. John's with Uncle Frank."

"Good," said Quigley. "Bill can look after things here, but I'd like you to be the lead on the investigation."

"Sure, I can do that," said Windflower. "You know, it feels like Woods may be at the end of his reign of terror. But he's a slippery old fool, isn't he?"

"He hasn't survived all this time without being super crafty," said Quigley. "But sooner or later they all screw up. Usually, they grow cocky or overconfident. Woods had good reason to think he could just do what he wanted."

"Except, 'lawless are they that make their wills their law,'" said Windflower.

"Exactly," said Quigley. "He forgot one big thing in all his lies and conniving. 'No legacy is as rich as honesty.'"

"Goodnight, Ron," said Windflower. "Have a good trip."

FIFTY-EIGHT

Windflower went up to bed and was soon drifting off into a soft and pleasant sleep. Then he woke up. Molly was sitting on the bed, looking directly at him.

"Are you just going to lie there?" asked the cat.

"Shush," said Windflower. "You'll wake up Sheila."

"She can't hear me," said Molly. "Only you. It's a dream, remember."

"Let's go downstairs anyway," said Windflower, and he got out of bed and was followed downstairs by the cat. He was kind of surprised when Lady didn't rise out of her bed to greet him.

"She can't hear either," said Molly. "Loyal and lovable, but not that bright. Not her fault, just her species."

"Thank you for coming to visit me again," said Windflower. "I'd be happy to hear your message."

"You'd be happier to be back in your warm bed," said Molly. "But at least you're polite. Not all of your species are. I'll give you that."

Windflower wanted to say something but bit his tongue. He also tried restraining his thoughts. But he wasn't fast enough.

"I don't really care what you think about me," said Molly. "I know I'm the superior being."

Windflower simply nodded. He had to admit that was true.

"Good, we're in agreement," said Molly. "So, here's the deal. You have gone back and found some of the pieces you have been missing. Purely by luck, but you got some of them."

"Thank you," said Windflower, feeling both proud and surprised by this compliment from a talking cat in his dream.

"Don't get too cocky," said the cat. "When you are panning for gold, you are bound to get a few nuggets if you look in the right area. But there's still a whole other piece that you haven't found yet. Because you aren't even in the right pool."

"What do you mean?" asked Windflower.

"Figure it out," said Molly, and she started to slink away.

"Wait, where should I be looking?"

"It's not where, but who," said Molly. "And you can thank me with another piece of salmon, whenever you like." The cat then went to her bed in the kitchen, curled up, and went to sleep. Windflower's eyes got heavy, and he fell asleep too. When he woke up, the morning light was just creeping through his bedroom window.

Sheila stirred beside him and went to the girls. Windflower lay there for a moment, thinking about his dream and wondering if it really happened. If it did, what did it mean? But not too much time for that now. He could hear Sheila talking to the girls, and he went to rouse Uncle Frank for their trip to St. John's.

He got dressed and walked downstairs to help Sheila, but she had everything well in hand. He let Lady out back and looked around for Molly, but no sight of her. He was almost glad of that. He didn't think he could take a talking cat first thing in the morning.

Breakfast was simple: cold cereal and toast with fruit bowls, and a couple of cups of strong coffee for the adults.

Windflower looked after Amelia Louise while Uncle Frank finished packing. Once he was ready, he hit the road, and Uncle Frank snored his way to Marystown while Windflower kept an eye out for moose.

In Marystown, they picked up more coffee, including one for Bill Ford, and headed over to the RCMP offices.

"Can you wait here for a minute?" Windflower asked Uncle Frank as he left him in the waiting area outside Ron Quigley's office. "I need to speak to Bill about some police business."

Uncle Frank was happy to sip his coffee and chat with Quigley's admin assistant and secretary while Windflower went inside Bill Ford's office and closed the door. He handed the other man his coffee and sat across from him.

"We found piles of cash in the safe and a series of promissory notes, including one from Charles Frankford," said Ford. "There were a few other names on papers in there that we're following up on, too."

"Anything about how much interest he charged people?" asked Windflower.

"Nothing," said Ford. "So far, none of the people named will talk about it either."

"Well, that's too bad," said Windflower.

"Can you talk to Frankford?" asked Ford.

"Not easily," said Windflower. "The NCSI guys have him. But I'll give it a shot. Unless we get somebody to talk to us about the process, it may be difficult to get Woods on loan-sharking. I'm sure he'll say that he was just helping members of the community. Anything else?"

"One of our guys found insulin, syringes, pens, testers in Woods's bathroom," said Ford.

"So, Woods is a diabetic?" asked Windflower.

"Looks like it," said Ford.

"That's very interesting," said Windflower. "Especially since Reverend Prowse was killed by insulin poisoning.

I'm not sure how we connect him back to that, but he's definitely connected."

"Our guys are still over there this morning. I'll let you know if there's anything else," said Ford.

"Great. Thanks, Bill," said Windflower. "Can I use your phone to call my guy at NCSI?"

"Go right ahead," said Ford. "I'll visit with Frank before he goes."

Windflower found Albertson's number and punched it in. He figured it would be better to call from another number than his cell phone. He was right.

"Albertson," said the person on the other end of the line.

"It's Windflower. I need to talk to Frankford again."

"Forget it," said Albertson. "And don't call me again."

"Wait," said Windflower as he felt Albertson starting to hang up. But it was too late.

Time to call in the cavalry, thought Windflower. He phoned Ron Quigley.

Quigley answered on the first ring.

"Where are you?" asked Windflower.

"I'm at the airport, ready to take off for Ottawa," said Quigley.

"Great," said Windflower. "I need you to do something when you get there. Ford found the money in the safe, along with some promissory notes. But no reference to interest, and nobody down here will talk. I think they're afraid of Woods. We need to talk to Charles Frankford."

"What do you want me to do?" asked Quigley. "Isn't he with the national security people?"

"Yes," said Windflower. "That's why I need you to make the request, formally if you have to. Without Frankford, we're not getting Woods on this stuff. We might be able to get him on the overall finances, but that's going to be hard to prove and will take a lot more time."

Windflower could hear Quigley thinking.

"Who was the guy you were dealing with?" asked Quigley.

"Albertson," said Windflower. "But he won't talk to me."

"But he might talk to me, or my new boss," said Quigley. "Give me his number. 'Having nothing, nothing can he lose.'"

"Boldness be your friend," said Windflower.

"I'll call if I have anything," said Quigley.

"Thanks," said Windflower. He hung up with Quigley and went back out to the main office. All of the admin staff and Bill Ford were sitting in a circle, listening to Uncle Frank tell a story. Windflower just caught the tail end of it and the loud round of laughter that ensued.

"Oh, my ride is here," said Uncle Frank when he saw Windflower. He said goodbye to the admin staff, and he and Bill Ford followed him out to their car.

Uncle Frank and Bill Ford started to shake hands, and then both laughed and did some kind of weird elbow bump.

"I'll miss you," said Ford.

"See you next summer," said Uncle Frank. "When we can hug again like civilized people."

FIFTY-NINE

Uncle Frank was quiet again as they drove out of Marystown, and when Windflower peeked over at him, he noticed he had drifted off. Windflower enjoyed the countryside and emptiness of the barrens and felt calm and peaceful. That changed abruptly when Uncle Frank woke up and started fiddling with the dials on the car radio.

"What are you looking for?" asked Windflower.

"I'm trying to find *Open Line*," said Uncle Frank. "I never miss it when it's on."

"And when you're out of bed," said Windflower.

Uncle Frank pretended not to hear that remark and finally found what he was looking for. A caller was going on about all politicians being crooked and that he wasn't going to vote in the next election because it only encouraged them. The host was making a valiant attempt to defend voting and democracy, but the caller was having none of that.

"No, b'y, Paddy," said the caller. "Dere all the same, b'y. Everyone of them got der hand in my pocket, and they're getting a bit too close for comfort, if you knows what I mean."

"Don't go there, Captain," said the host.

But the caller ran right through that stop sign, and the host cut him off.

"I gave him fair warning. Now he's banned for a week. Remember, we can have a civilized debate without being crude or obnoxious. Who's next? I think we have Mary from the Goulds."

Uncle Frank turned down the radio. "I love Paddy, but Mary drives me crazy. I can't take her."

"You know all these people?" asked Windflower. His uncle ignored him and turned the radio up to see if Mary was gone, but she was still droning on. "See what I mean? She goes on and on," said Uncle Frank.

Then it dawned on Windflower. "Do you call in to that program?"

Uncle Frank looked like a deer in the headlights. "Why don't we listen to CBC?" he said and switched the dial quickly. He went back to being quiet when the news came on, and before long Windflower could hear him snoring.

Once again, Windflower didn't mind the silence and solitude. That shifted a bit when they came to the curves before Swift Current and the traffic picked up. He pulled into the gas pump at Goobies a short while later. They didn't stay long, just enough to fill up their tank and grab a snack for the road.

It was busy on the highway from Goobies to St. John's. It always was. Lots of people lived in small communities all along the highway and drove into the city to work every day, and there was a never-ending round of construction that paused traffic more than once on their way. But soon Mount Pearl, the smaller sister city to St. John's, came into view as Windflower moved into an even busier stretch of highway.

Luckily, they weren't headed downtown and could circle around the city and go almost directly to the airport. Windflower stopped in front of the terminal and let Uncle Frank out. He parked his cruiser at the end of the departures area and joined his uncle inside. Frank was already moving through the check-in, and Windflower helped him load his bag onto the scale. They still had a few minutes, so they stopped for another coffee at the food court just outside the security area.

Uncle Frank sipped his coffee and looked around. "I'm not much for St. John's," he said. "Cities are really not my place."

Windflower nodded in agreement.

"But I'm going to really miss Grand Bank. A big part of it is my friends. I will really miss them," said Uncle Frank. "But I will also miss being close to the ocean. It has a calming influence on my spirit."

"I know what you mean," said Windflower. "It's funny how people like us, who never grew up near the ocean, can feel so attracted to it. But I have the same feeling, the same attachment. We will miss you too, Uncle."

"The hardest thing about leaving is the girls," said Uncle Frank. "I mean, I love you and Sheila, but they are so close to my heart that it hurts to be away from them. They are great teachers, Winston. Watch and learn."

"I know," said Windflower. "We think we are the ones leading them, and we are in the ways of the world. But they teach us how to be truly alive."

This time his uncle nodded. The security announcement for Uncle Frank's flight came over the loudspeakers. Windflower walked with his uncle to the security entrance. They stopped and hugged each other wordlessly for at least a minute. It was like neither man wanted to let go. Finally, Windflower released his uncle and watched as he rode the escalator to the top and disappeared.

That was harder than he had imagined, thought Windflower as he dabbed at the corner of his eye. It was tough to let your closest living relative move away, and he knew that everyone back home would be feeling the same way.

As much as his uncle could be an irritant sometimes, he also brought great energy and enthusiasm to everything he did. That was why the girls loved him. He was the real deal.

He was still thinking about Uncle Frank when his cell phone rang. It was Carl Langmead.

"Carl, how are you?" asked Windflower.

"I'm well, but stuff has hit the fan over here," said Langmead.

"What do you mean?" asked Windflower.

"I'm calling to give you a heads up," said Langmead. "French is on the warpath, and the union is involved. My friend at Professional Standards suggested you might want to know about it."

"Thanks," said Windflower. "What have you heard about all this?"

"Just that there's a complaint against French from somebody outside the RNC. He's demanding to see the complaint, and he's got the union backing him up. Dan Williams said that it would be a good time to get any complaint that you may know about into him."

"Got it," said Windflower.

"Between you and me, we all know French is a problem," said Langmead. "But he's managed to wriggle off the hook a few times now."

"I'm in St. John's right now, and you can let your friend know I'm dealing with it," said Windflower. "Thanks again."

After hanging up with Langmead, he called Cassie's number. No answer, so he left a message. Then, despite the fact that he and Uncle Frank had snacked their way from Grand Bank to St. John's, he felt his tummy grumble. He knew what would fix that: fish and chips. And Windflower knew exactly the place to get it.

He drove across town to the area known by the locals as the Higher Levels. It was the part of St. John's that was almost straight up from the harbour. When the city was first permanently settled after many years of temporary fishing parties that only stayed the summer, this became the place where ordinary people could build a home. It was still pretty much a working-class neighbourhood, although gentrification was creeping in.

In the middle of the Higher Levels were a number of small shops and restaurants and more than a few that specialized in fish and chips. Leo's was Windflower's favourite. He had been introduced to the small diner-like restaurant by Ron Quigley, who grew up in this area of St. John's. He told Windflower about being a kid and watching fishermen deliver their catch of the morning to the back door of Leo's, which rightly claimed the freshest fish in town.

Windflower wasn't too hungry, so he ordered a small, one-piece fish and chips, St. John's style. That meant the fish and chips came covered in dressing and gravy. The dressing by itself was kind of dry, but with the gravy on top it was delicious. When his order came, Windflower took a moment to admire the golden-brown French fries and the large piece of deep-fried cod with the gravy and dressing. If he had been a millennial, he would have taken a picture. But he was Windflower, so he dug in.

He was halfway through his lunch when Cassie called him back.

"People are telling me that he knows," was the first thing she said.

Windflower thought about asking which people but didn't figure that would help. "He was bound to find out sooner or later. What's important is to make sure he doesn't get away with it." he could almost hear Cassie thinking about that.

"We don't control his reaction, but if you file the formal complaint, they will act," he continued.

"Is Anne Marie okay?" asked Cassie.

"She'll be fine. She wants to get French as much as anybody," said Windflower. "So, where will we meet?"

Once again, Cassie paused. "There's a small coffee shop right next to the War Memorial. I can be there in fifteen minutes," she said.

"See you then," said Windflower. He ate a few more bites, paid for his food and drove downtown. He found a parking spot on Duckworth Street and took his mini-recorder and his pen and notepad and walked to the café.

SIXTY

The café was quiet, with only one other customer playing on their phone. Cassie was sitting in the corner. Windflower got them both a coffee and sat down across from her.

"You ready?" he asked. She nodded. He turned on his recorder and let her speak for almost thirty minutes. At the end, he asked her if that was all, and she nodded again. He passed over his notepad and got her to sign her name, signifying that this was her statement of complaint. He signed as witness.

"I'm really sorry this happened," he said.

"Me too," said the girl. "I was just starting to think I was pulling out of that old life, and all of a sudden I'm right back in." She looked like she was going to cry. Windflower handed her the few napkins he had picked up at the counter. She started crying quietly into her hands.

"Don't let him do this to you," he said. "You have come so far, and you have so much good you can still do. So many other girls need you."

"But I'm not that strong," said Cassie. "See how easy it was to pull me back?"

"That's not true," said Windflower. "As soon as you could, you reached out for help. That's all you have to do now. I will help you. So will Anne Marie. And I'm not supposed to say this, but after French gets the boot, you can sue him and the whole RNC."

Cassie's eyes grew wide. "Or maybe I could get them to really fund the program that Anne Marie started."

"That's an even better idea," said Windflower. "Now, I've got to get this complaint in and get back home. Can I give you a ride somewhere?"

"No thanks," said Cassie. "The last time I got a ride with you, I ended up in the police station."

Windflower laughed. He stood, and they looked awkwardly at each other until Cassie grabbed her knapsack and walked out of the café in front of him.

"Don't forget to call Anne Marie," said Windflower. "She's expecting to hear from you."

"I will," said Cassie. "Thank you for believing me."

"No, thank you," said Windflower.

He waved goodbye to Cassie as she walked away, and as soon as he got to his car, he phoned Dan Williams at the RNC.

"I hope you've got good news for me," said Williams.

"I have a taped statement and her signature," said Windflower. "Can I drop it off?"

"Call me when you get here, and I'll meet you at the front," said Williams.

Windflower drove up the steep hill from downtown and was at the RNC Headquarters shortly after. He called Williams from his car and walked to the front entrance.

He was standing near the door when Williams came out of the elevator.

"Dan Williams," he said, offering his hand but then pulling it back. "I always forget."

"No worries. Winston Windflower. Here's your statement," said Windflower as he handed over the recorder.

"Excellent," said Williams. "Do you have a few minutes?"

"Sure," said Windflower.

"Let's grab one of these interview rooms," said Williams. He found the first empty one and laid the tape recorder on the table. He turned it on and listened.

"Okay," he said when it played to the end. "We have enough. I'll go the chief, and we'll get French pulled off the job today. The investigation will take some time, but this feels pretty solid. I'll let you know how it goes."

"We'll need to make sure that the girl is protected," said Windflower.

"We'll make it clear to French and his union rep that any contact with the complainant will bring immediate criminal charges," said Williams. "I'll also get Constable Foote to help in that regard."

"She'll be more than happy," said Windflower. "We're done?"

"Thank you, Sergeant," said Williams.

He left the Constabulary building with a special spring in his step and was still smiling when he hit the overpass that signified the beginning of life outside St. John's. For the people of the city, the townies, as they were called, this was near the end of the civilized world. For everyone else in the province, this was the beginning of paradise. And aptly enough, one of the first places outside of town was called Paradise.

That made Windflower smile, too. He was happy to be out of the city and heading back to Grand Bank. He put on his CD and listened to it again to get himself in an even better mood. By the time he hit Goobies, he was feeling great. He stopped and got himself a cup of tea and an apple flip and sat for a moment to enjoy it. He had just finished his snack and turned onto the highway down towards Grand Bank when his cell phone rang. He pulled over to answer it.

"Winston are you on your way back?" asked Bill Ford.

"I'm coming," said Windflower. "I just left Goobies."

"You better stop in to see us along the way," said Ford. "Woods and his lawyer are freaking out. Mostly Woods.

The lawyer is demanding we allow Woods back into his house, and I don't see how we can stop him."

"Ask the lawyer to come over to meet me," said Windflower. "I should be there in an hour and a half. That should give your guys a chance to finish off the search."

"Perfect," said Ford. "See you soon."

Windflower hung up with Ford and started to drive again but didn't get far before his phone rang again. He stopped and said hello.

"They just arrested French," said Carl Langmead. "He wasn't happy about being formally charged and tried to have a go at Foote. That did not go well, and now he's behind bars."

"Wow, that didn't take long," said Windflower. "Thanks for letting me know."

"Thank you, Winston," said Langmead. "I know our force is a little backward, but we're trying to weed out the bad apples. You just helped all of us."

"Just doing my job," said Windflower.

"Anyway, thanks," said Langmead as he hung up.

That gave Windflower another lift as he went back on the highway and drove through the curvy turns around Swift Current before moving into the barrens on the way to Marystown. He went in and out of radio service as he travelled and finally turned the radio off to enjoy the relative silence and the emptiness all around him.

SIXTY-ONE

By the time he hit the traffic coming out of Marystown, he was relaxed and back in a great mood. That helped when he saw the red-faced lawyer sitting outside Bill Ford's office.

"Gerard Templeton," said the lawyer. "You must be Sergeant Windflower."

"I am," said Windflower.

The lawyer started almost yelling at Windflower about his client and his rights and how what they were doing was illegal. Windflower just stood there and took the barrage until Ford's door opened.

"Give us a minute," Ford said to the lawyer. Templeton started to protest, but Ford pulled Windflower inside and closed the door.

"Look at what we found," said Ford, pointing to three cardboard boxes on the floor in his office. Windflower went closer and pulled back the flaps on one of the boxes. Inside were magazines and books and tapes. He picked up one of the magazines and almost threw it down in disgust.

"They're awful," said Ford. "We haven't gone through them all, but this is one of the largest collections of child pornography I've ever seen. It was in a locked room in the basement of the house. It was the last area our guys searched."

"Oh my God," said Windflower. "He's a pedophile?"

"Well, a collector of child pornography at the very least," said Ford. "We've seized three computers from the house as well. I was thinking that maybe Smithson could have a look and see if he's engaged in any online activity as well."

"Absolutely," said Windflower. "I'll send him over. This certainly changes the complexion of the investigation. Now we know why he was so anxious to get us out of his house."

"Let's start with possession of child pornography," said Ford. "We can process that while we're waiting for the financial information. What do you think? It's your investigation."

"Okay. That sounds like a plan. Let's charge him right away," said Windflower. "Good work," he said to Ford as he stood to leave. He opened the door, and the lawyer jumped to his feet and started screaming at Windflower.

"Easy," said Windflower. "We've completed our search. But your client won't be going back home right away. In fact, you can make arrangements for him to be brought in to be charged, or we'll send a car over to handcuff him and take care of it ourselves. How would you like to proceed?"

The lawyer started yelling and stammering again, but Ford motioned for him to come into his office. Once he saw what Ford had as evidence, he grew much quieter. Windflower waved goodbye to Ford and went back to his car to drive to Grand Bank.

Another stunning development in a case full of them, thought Windflower as he drove out of Marystown. And another great reason to dislike Elijah Woods. He was still mulling all of this over as he drove the last half hour home. When he got to Grand Bank, he zipped right by the detachment and went straight home.

"I was wondering when you'd get back," said Sheila. "You could have called."

"It was quite the day," said Windflower. "I'm not even sure I remember everything that happened. But I'm happy to take all of these creatures out from under your feet in exchange for some of whatever's cooking in that pot."

Sheila smiled as Windflower gathered up the girls and the wagon and got Lady's leash. He looked around for Molly, but still no sign of her. He thought about asking Sheila but didn't want to answer any questions about why he was concerned about the cat. He walked outside instead, and then remembering, he went back in and grabbed a half a loaf of bread.

They walked down to the brook and were greeted immediately by a flotilla of ducks and an aerial bombardment from the seagulls. The girls squealed and threw the bread everywhere, and Lady had to be held back from getting herself and a passel of ducks in big trouble. When the bread was gone, they meandered down near the wharf and then headed for home. He had just opened the door when his cell phone rang.

"Mission accomplished," said Quigley. "Charles Frankford will be available for a telephone or online interview at your convenience. Call Albertson to set it up."

"That's great," said Windflower. "But there's been some developments. Have you talked to Bill Ford?"

"No, what's up?" asked Quigley.

Windflower stepped back outside and told Quigley what had been discovered in Wood's house.

"To quote Eddie Tizzard, 'Holy jumpins,'" said Quigley. "I didn't see that coming. That is going to shake a lot of people around town. Is he in custody?"

"Bill was working through that with his lawyer," said Windflower. "But it does change the complexion of our case against him. I'll still keep moving on the money side, but this is a shocker, that's for sure."

"Sometimes it does feel like 'hell is empty and all the devils are here,'" said Quigley.

"I know," said Windflower. "So many people trusted him, too. I guess 'trust dies but mistrust blossoms.'"

"That's impressive, Winston. Sophocles? You've really upped your game. I'll call Bill," said Quigley. With that, Quigley was gone and Windflower went back inside where Sheila was organizing everyone for supper.

"Just in time," he announced and sat at the table.

Sheila laughed and poured up two small bowls. Windflower sniffed the aroma of herbs in the kitchen and then the unmistakable scent of moose stew. His mouth watered as Sheila passed around a basket of bread and put some salad on a side plate for the girls. He waited none too patiently until his turn came.

He paused for a moment and allowed himself to take in all the smells and dipped his fork in to spear a thick chunk of moose meat. Moose had long been a part of the diet back home in Pink Lake, and when a hunter returned home with a successful kill, there was a celebration and a community feast that almost always featured moose stew. Moose meat was actually better for humans than beef because it was very lean. But Windflower didn't really care about that. He loved the wild, gamey taste that reminded him of many pleasant days as a youth and young man.

As per usual, he didn't say a lot until he had drained his first bowl.

"Thank you, Sheila. I think that was the best moose stew ever," he said as he passed over his bowl for a refill. He took a little more time with this helping, savouring the meat but also the carrots and turnip and potatoes swimming in that aromatic broth. When he was finally done, he stood and walked to Sheila and gave her a great hug and kissed her on the forehead.

"Maybe we should have stew more often," said Sheila.

Windflower helped Sheila clean up, and while she gave the girls their bath, he took Lady for one quick walk.

When he came back, Amelia Louise was waiting for him in her bedroom, and she had about a dozen books laid out on her bed.

"Pick one," he said.

Amelia Louise thought it was a multiple-choice question and laid three in his lap. They were *Goodnight Moon* and two library books that Windflower hadn't seen before.

"Did you go the library with Mommy today?" he asked.

Amelia Louise nodded vigorously. "Lieberry," she said.

The first was *A Good Day for a Hat*, a happy and funny book about a bear who has to keep changing its hat as the weather keeps changing. Windflower thought the bear would have a hard time keeping up with the changes here in Grand Bank, and Amelia Louise laughed at the antics of the happy bear. It has a great ending when the bear gets to his destination and finds out that his friends have a surprise birthday party for him. Of course, Windflower had to sing "Happy Birthday" to the bear with his daughter.

The second was called *Black Bird Yellow Sun*, about a black bird who flies around exploring the world and all the colours it finds along the way. Amelia Louise loved following the bird and its friend, a little worm, as they saw the beautiful yellows, greens and pinks before finally stopping at a bright blue moon. That led perfectly to *Goodnight Moon*. By the time they had said goodnight to everybody in the book, Amelia Louise's eyes were closing. Windflower kissed her and went downstairs to see Sheila.

SIXTY-TWO

Sheila had made a pot of tea. She poured him a cup.

"What's going on?" she asked.

"What do you mean?"

"You are not exactly hiding the fact that something is bothering you," said Sheila. "You go through the motions, but you might as well be on another planet because you're not really here."

"Sorry," said Windflower. "I'm still trying to process what happened and what I heard and saw today. It appears that Elijah Woods is not just a crook, but also has a liking for child pornography."

"Wow," said Sheila. "I guess you never really know people. I knew Dollimont was a creep, and if you told me that he was a child molester, I'd believe it. But Woods? That is a real surprise."

"Yeah," said Windflower. "It makes you wonder what other secrets are buried around here."

"Lots, I bet," said Sheila. "I didn't tell you this, but when I was first elected mayor, I had a number of notable citizens approach me with suggestions that I shouldn't look too closely at some of the previous dealings of the town council."

"You didn't follow that advice," said Windflower.

"Heck, no," said Sheila. "I had an even bigger group telling me to dig deeper and pointing out where to look. But this is different than the petty thievery that goes on in municipal politics. What'll happen next?"

"He'll be arrested and charged and then have his day in court," said Windflower.

"The court of public opinion will make its judgement more quickly than the justice system," said Sheila.

"'Justice always whirls in equal measure,'" said Windflower. "In the courtroom and out."

Sheila sighed and came closer to him. "I'm sorry you have to be exposed to so many bad things."

"You know what, I think I've seen enough," said Windflower.

"Does that mean what I think it does?"

"Let's get some sleep, and we can make a decision on the weekend, but I'm pretty close. We may be bankrupt and, in the poorhouse, but we'll still have each other and our sanity."

"We'll be okay," said Sheila. "Besides, they say 'love is merely a madness,' and yet we seemed to have worked that one out."

"I love you," said Windflower, hugging her closer. "I'll let Lady out back."

"See you upstairs," said Sheila.

The kitchen was dark when Windflower went in to get Lady. The collie jumped up immediately and came to him. But he could see a pair of glowing eyes in the corner. Not a movement. Not a blink. Certainly not a smile from Molly. Windflower thought some very bad thoughts and then checked himself. What if she could read him? So he smiled his best smile and nodded towards the cat, hoping his newfound good intentions would save him. He wasn't sure, but he could certainly feel those green eyes burning a hole in his back as he let Lady out and then almost as quickly brought her back in.

He patted Lady on the head and smiled another goodwill gesture at Molly before heading to bed, still wondering if that cat was the same one in his dreams. He didn't wonder long after he got into bed and Sheila pulled him closer. He had one of his best sleeps ever and woke in the morning to the beautiful sounds of his daughters playing in Stella's room.

The morning was always an interesting time at the Windflower household. He had come to embrace the push and pull and sometimes tears of the a.m. routine. This morning, Amelia Louise had once again made the decision she was going to school. After breakfast, she raced upstairs and got dressed and was waiting at the door with her knapsack when the school bus came for Stella.

Windflower had to hold her, kicking and screaming, until it was safe for Stella to run to the bus. Afterward, Amelia Louise went to the living room and curled up in a ball. When Windflower came to comfort her, she gave him a look that he was sure was designed to convey some version of "I will never forgive you for this."

She would, but not this morning, thought Windflower as he kissed her on the top of her head and said goodbye to Sheila.

"I'll call you," he said.

"That would be nice," said Sheila.

Windflower drove quickly to work. He had a lot to do this morning. The detachment was empty, and that gave him a few minutes to get organized.

He called Albertson in Ottawa. It was early there, but that wasn't really his problem.

A groggy Albertson answered the phone. "I was going to call you. Just not in the middle of the night."

"Good morning to you, too," said Windflower. "I want to talk to Frankford. When can you set that up?"

"I can do it later today," said Albertson. "But I want to tell you something first."

"Go ahead," said Windflower.

"The reason we're keeping Frankford is because he has another matter outstanding, and we need to keep him here for

national security issues," said Albertson.

"I know, the Chinese want him," said Windflower.

"Not the Chinese," said Albertson. "The Ontario Provincial Police. They have an ongoing investigation into Charles Frankford on possession of child pornography and a report that he tried to lure a young boy."

"What? He's a child molester?" asked Windflower. "Why didn't you tell me this before? Why are you covering it up?"

"We're not hiding it," said Albertson. "The OPP knows what we're doing, and he's enrolled in a diversion program."

"And you still need him for the national security issue?" asked Windflower. Albertson started to answer, and Windflower stopped him. "Never mind. What time can I talk to him?"

"Can I call at noon, your time?" asked Albertson.

"You have my number," said Windflower, and he hung up.

SIXTY-THREE

Another connection between Frankford and Woods. This one worse than the first, thought Windflower. He was still thinking about that when Bill Ford called.

"Good morning, Winston," said Ford. "I'm calling to tell you that Woods will be coming in after lunch. He and his lawyer asked for the morning so that he could clear up a few things. I could have played hardball, but that's not my job. I'm going to put out a press release soon announcing his arrest. The media will look after spreading the information."

"I have another piece of news," said Windflower. "The national security guys who are holding Charles Frankford told me that he was in the same game as Woods."

"So it wasn't just about money," said Ford.

"Looks like that," said Windflower.

"Are you sending Smithson over to look at the computers?" asked Ford.

As they were speaking, Smithson's cruiser pulled into the RCMP parking lot.

"I'll speak to him in a few moments and see if he can go over this morning," said Windflower.

"Great," said Ford. "Talk later."

Windflower walked to the back and poured himself a fresh cup of coffee. Smithson came in moments later.

"Morning, boss," said Smithson. "Everything go okay in St. John's?"

"Everything is good," said Windflower. "I need you to go over to Marystown. Can you go this morning? Bill Ford needs help looking at a computer."

Smithson eyes almost glowed at the thought of working on a computer. "Sure thing," he said.

"It's not that kind of work," said Windflower. He explained the situation about Woods and what they had found in his house.

"Oh," said Smithson, his spirits visibly sagging.

"Yeah, I know," said Windflower. "We all have the same reaction. Thanks for doing this."

"Part of the job," said Smithson. "I'll finish my paperwork and head over."

Something about that last comment struck Windflower like a lightning bolt. That's it, he thought. There are too many parts of the job that I just don't want in my life or in my head anymore. He left the office and walked to the Mug-Up. He needed the air and the space to breathe. By the time he got to the café, he felt a little better. His mood got even better when Herb Stoodley came over to his table with two cups of coffee and sat across from him.

"Good morning, Sergeant. Looks like you could use a little company this morning," said Stoodley.

"Thanks, Herb," said Windflower. "Having an existential crisis, I think."

"Pretty fancy diagnosis," said Stoodley. "Maybe you're just down. Your job will do that to you."

"That's exactly the point," said Windflower. "I'm tired of having this job, this work, bring me down."

"Anything particular got you down?" asked Stoodley. "You can tell Uncle Herb. My lips are sealed."

Windflower sighed. "It's Elijah Woods and everything going on with that right now. Plus, a cop in St. John's hit on one of the girls that we were helping get herself and others off the street."

"That bad cop will get weeded out. They always do," said Stoodley. "And it is too bad with Woods. All that money."

"It's worse than that," said Windflower. "It looks like he was a pedophile, too," he added, whispering.

"You found some evidence of that?" said Stoodley. "Okay, now I get it. I think that was one of the worst things I had to deal with as well. How can men, especially those in positions of respect in the community, do those things?"

"Exactly," said Windflower. "I think I'm going to leave."

"Well, I don't blame you," said Stoodley. "You've given a lot to us, to this community and to people all over the peninsula. What will you do next?"

"That's the million-dollar question," said Windflower.

"'It is not in the stars to hold our destiny but in ourselves,'" said Stoodley. "You'll figure it out."

"That quote keeps coming up," said Windflower. "Maybe I should pay more attention to it." He stood to leave and then turned back to Stoodley. "The other one that comes to mind is 'We know what we are, but know not what we may be.' Thanks for listening and for the coffee."

Windflower walked back to the detachment, still feeling dread, but certainly lighter than when he set out. He hoped that was enough to get him through what was almost certainly going to be a difficult day.

Betsy was there when he arrived, and she passed him a handful of messages, most of them from the media.

"They're calling about Reverend Woods," she said. "Is it true that he stole money from the church?"

"I believe so," said Windflower, not bothering to add the other charges that were coming. "But that will all come out in court."

"I can't believe that people we trusted could be so…" Betsy struggled to find the word. "Dishonest," she finally said.

"I know," said Windflower. "It's pretty disappointing." He handed most of the slips back to Betsy. "I won't be commenting on any of this," he said as he walked back into his office. The one message he hung on to was from Anne Marie Foote.

"Hi Sergeant, thanks for calling me back," said Foote. "I guess you heard about French."

"I heard you handled the situation very well," said Windflower.

"It was all I could do not to clock him," said Foote. "Luckily, there were other officers around to help restrain me."

"I hear he's under lock and key," said Windflower.

"And getting a mental health assessment at the Waterford, which is probably a good idea, too," said Foote. "In any case, he's off the job and very unlikely to come back. I want to thank you for that."

"No worries," said Windflower. "Have you talked to Cassie?"

"She called me," said Foote. "I'm seeing her this morning. I think she's going to come back into the program. I am hoping you will come back, too."

"We'll see," said Windflower, not wanting to make a commitment that he might not be able to carry out. "Things are up in the air around here with my boss leaving and everything."

"The offer stands," said Foote. "I enjoyed working with you, and Cassie just gushes about you."

"Stop," said Windflower. "You're making my head swell. But thank you. It has been a pleasure working with you, and if it's possible, I'd certainly like to do it again."

SIXTY-FOUR

After hanging up with Foote, it made him think about the good things that came along with the job. And there were lots of them. Many people in this community and every other one he'd worked in showed him respect and kindness, not in a small part because of his uniform and his role. He got to put some bad guys in jail and make the town safer for the residents. He was able to help out in emergencies like the flood they had one year and the many winter storms that closed off Grand Bank from the outside world. He was part of a team that people called when they were in trouble.

His cell phone ringing jolted him out of that reflection.

"I've got Frankford right here," said Albertson.

"You haven't told me everything," said Windflower. "So why don't you fix that before I have to get you pulled out of there and back in court down here."

"The finance stuff is true," said Frankford. "I was kind of hoping that would be enough to get Woods out of my hair."

"I'll need a statement from you," said Windflower. "Dates, times, monies paid out, interest charged."

"No problem," said Frankford. "On the other stuff...I'm getting help for that."

"Great," said Windflower, more than a little sarcastically. "How were you and Woods connected in this?"

"We shared stuff," said Frankford. "The problem we had was that Jerome Morecombe found out about it somehow, and he managed to hack into my computer and stole some files. He tried to use them against us. But then he got sick and died. We thought it was over. But his wife found some of it and she called me. My wife took the call, and that was a problem."

"I'll bet," said Windflower. "That why you all went to Morecombe's house?"

"I just wanted to get the files back," said Frankford. "But Dollimont had other plans. He killed that woman. I didn't have anything to do with it."

"What about Reverend Prowse?" asked Windflower.

"That was about the money," said Frankford. "And nothing to do with me."

"I know," said Windflower. "Dollimont again."

"That's the truth," said Frankford.

"I guess a judge will have to sort all this out," said Windflower. "But we'll need another statement from you on all of this. Let me talk to Albertson." When the other man came on the line, Windflower gave him directions about how he wanted the statement and the areas to be covered. "You got that?"

"Got it," said Albertson.

When he hung up, Betsy was standing in his doorway.

"You need to call Sergeant Ford," she said. "Something's happened to Reverend Woods."

Bill Ford, who must have been waiting for the call, answered immediately. "Templeton called me," said Ford. "The housekeeper found Woods dead in his house. Paramedics are on their way over there now. The lawyer said he was lying on the floor in his bathroom with a needle in his arm."

Windflower paused before saying anything. "Insulin poisoning, likely," he finally said. "The examiner can tell us for sure, but that would be my guess. He would know exactly how much to use. But I guess that doesn't really matter now, does it?"

"I guess not," said Ford. "It would have been better to have him face the judge and his community, but that's not to be."

"He has another judge to face," said Windflower. "He can't avoid that fate."

He hung up with Ford and sat in his office by himself for a few minutes. He needed to breathe his way through all of this. Betsy came in soon after.

"Oh my God," she said. "Isn't this awful? Reverend Woods was a crook and a pervert, too. It's all a bit much to take. Now he's gone. Did he kill himself, Sergeant?"

"It looks like that, Betsy," said Windflower. "I guess he couldn't bear to own up to what he did. Or maybe he wasn't prepared to have his own sins on public display."

Betsy thought about that for a moment. "I heard this quote one time, and it always stuck with me," she said. "'However wickedness outstrips men, it has no wings to fly from God.'"

"That's true, Betsy, very true," said Windflower. "I think I'm going to take the afternoon off," he announced. "Any media calls you can send to Bill Ford, and if anybody else needs me I'll be in tomorrow morning."

"That's a very good plan, Sergeant," said Betsy.

A few minutes later, Windflower was walking along the beach up towards the Cape. He climbed the narrow path to the top and sat on a rock overlooking Grand Bank. He didn't have his smudging gear or pipe, not even any tobacco. But he could still pray. He offered prayers first for the people who had died over this last period of time, all of them needlessly. Reverend Bob Prowse, whose crime seemed to be being the one honest man in a house of thieves. Reverend Elizabeth Frankford, who suffered much from the actions of others, and Alison Morecombe, who discovered a secret that ultimately proved lethal.

He had to pause and think about the newly dead Elijah Woods. He could not bear to use the term reverend when it came to Woods. He could also not yet begin to pray for him. But he could pray for his victims, like the young people that had formally or informally come into his orbit. And all the parishioners who had trusted him and looked up to him and relied on his guidance to deal with the real problems in their lives. That was who he felt sorry for. Not Elijah Woods.

When he was finished his prayers, he walked slowly back to his car and drove home. Sheila was surprised and happy to see him. "I heard what happened," she said. "I'm glad you came home."

"Me, too," said Windflower. "Me, too."

SIXTY-FIVE

It was Saturday night, and Eddie Tizzard, Carrie and the baby, and Richard Tizzard had come over for dinner. Windflower was barbequing steaks, and everybody was enjoying their time together.

Windflower caught Sheila's eye and winked. She nodded back.

"So, I have an announcement," he said. "Sheila and I have talked, and I want you to be the first to know that I am resigning from the Force at the end of the year. It's time for something new."

"What's that going to be?" asked Eddie Tizzard.

"'All the world's a stage, and all the men and women merely players: they have their exits and their entrances.' This is my exit," said Windflower. "We'll see what the next act is going to be."

The End

About the Author

Mike Martin was born in St. John's, NL on the east coast of Canada and now lives and works in Ottawa, Ontario. He is a long-time freelance writer and his articles and essays have appeared in newspapers, magazines and online across Canada as well as in the United States and New Zealand.

He is the author of the award-winning Sgt. Windflower Mystery series set in beautiful Grand Bank. There are now 11 books in this light mystery series with the publication of *Buried Secrets*. *A Tangled Web* was shortlisted in 2017 for the best light mystery of the year, and *Darkest Before the Dawn* won the 2019 Bony Blithe Light Mystery Award. Mike has also published *Christmas in Newfoundland: Memories and Mysteries*, a Sgt. Windflower Book of Christmas past and present.

Mike is Past Chair of the Board of Crime Writers of Canada, a national organization promoting Canadian crime and mystery writers and a member of the Newfoundland Writing Guild and Ottawa Independent Writers.

You can follow the Sgt. Windflower Mysteries on Facebook.

https://www.facebook.com/TheWalkerOnTheCapeReviews AndMore/